Remember Me

Lynda Renham

Re-published in 2023 by Bloodhound Books.

www.bloodhoundbooks.com

Print ISBN: 978-1-5040-8330-0

Chapter One

She stands on the doorstep. She's shivering. She isn't wearing a coat and I can see the outline of her breasts through her thin blouse. She sees me looking and pulls her cardigan around her.

'Hello,' she says. 'It's freezing isn't it?'

Her lips quiver with the cold. She looks shy and apologetic. Some hair has escaped her loose ponytail and she brushes it back. She looks at me through rain-splattered glasses.

'I'm Sharni,' she says. 'We've just moved in to number 24, next door.'

She points and my eyes follow her direction to a removal van. The house had been empty for a few months and Chris and I had wondered who might move in.

'I'm Clare,' I say. 'It's nice to meet you.'

She seems nervous and embarrassed.

'I'm sorry to be a pain, already,' she smiles. 'But I've been sent some flowers and I can't seem to find a vase anywhere. There are just so many boxes and ...'

'Oh, of course, come in,' I say opening the door wider.

She closes it quickly behind her but not before a flurry of

autumn leaves has blown in with her. Their rustic brown matches the colour of her hair.

'It's lovely and warm in here,' she comments.

'Do you not have heating?'

'Oh yes, but with the door open all the time it's impossible to stay warm.'

She looks vaguely familiar and I try to recall where I have seen her before.

'I'll get you a vase,' I say, leading her into the lounge. 'Would you like a coffee?'

She turns away and rubs her glasses on the sleeve of her cardigan.

'I'm steamed up,' she laughs. 'A coffee would be great.'

Small gold hoops dangle from her earlobes and I notice ink smudges on her hands. Newspaper print I imagine. I remember Chris and I were covered in it when we moved in.

'If we ever move again, remind me not to use newspaper,' he'd complained.

I search under the sink for a vase. My hand encounters dirty dusters and old bottles of cleaning liquid, but no vase. A mousetrap slams shut on my finger and I fight back a cry. I hear Sharni talking to Ben. Her voice is warm and soft. Ben gurgles happily. I try another cupboard without success and finally reach for the hand-painted vase on the top shelf of the Welsh dresser. Chris had bought it for me on our honeymoon. I hesitate for a second. It's not like she'll have it for long. She'll probably give it back as soon as she's unpacked.

The kettle clicks and I make the coffee.

'Oh, that's lovely,' she says on seeing the vase. She's on the floor helping Ben colour in his rabbit pictures.

'My husband bought it for me when we were honeymooning in Ireland.'

'If you're sure?' she asks. 'I'll bring it back tomorrow. It's just I don't want the flowers to die.'

'That's fine,' I say, pushing my lesson plans off the coffee table and placing a mug in front of her.

'He's adorable,' she says, looking at Ben.

'He is,' I agree.

She strokes the top of his head, her hand lingering.

'You have a lovely home,' she says, glancing around.

'Thank you.'

'I'm keen to get ideas. I want our house to look really nice. You've done a great job here.'

She fingers the art décor lamp on the side table and I smile. Ben begins to get irritable and I bend down to him.

'Do you mind if I ask where you bought this?'

'John Lewis, if I remember. They have lovely things there.'

Ben lets out a burp and we both laugh.

'How old is he?' she asks.

'Almost two,' I say.

He struggles from my arms and wobbles towards Sharni like a newborn fawn.

'He's just discovered his legs,' I laugh.

She catches him as he tumbles towards her.

'Do you have children?' I ask.

Her face clouds over. It occurs to me that maybe I shouldn't have asked. She then smiles and I wonder if I imagined it.

'No,' she says flatly.

I struggle to think of something to say.

'Are you in interior design?' she asks.

I laugh.

'Me? No, I wouldn't know where to start. I'm a teacher, well, only part-time now that we have Ben.'

'But this room is gorgeous, you have excellent taste. I'll have to pick your brains when I start decorating ours.'

'It'll be nice to have neighbours of our own age,' I say.

Her eyes shine. She places her mug on the table and leans towards me.

'I've got a great idea, why don't you and your husband come over Saturday evening for house-warming drinks. We can get to know each other better.'

'But you'll be up to your eyes won't you?' I say, surprised at the invite.

'We'll need a break. Do say you'll come.'

'I'll need to check with Chris, my husband, but I'm sure it will be okay.'

'Great,' she smiles, getting up from the couch. 'Shall we say about eight? If you can't get a sitter then bring the toddler with you.'

I open my mouth to speak and then change my mind. I had hoped we could take Ben with us. I hate leaving him with sitters but I imagine she wants an adult evening.

'Thanks,' I say hugging Ben close. 'Enjoy your flowers.'

'Flowers?' she questions.

'The ones you needed the vase for.'

'Oh yes. My mum sent them. Thanks Clare. See you on Saturday.'

'I see someone's moving in,' says Helen, nodding towards the removal van.

I follow her gaze.

'Yes. I met her this morning. She seems nice.'

We watch as a white sofa is carried into the house. I shiver as the cold air cuts through me.

'Do you want a coffee?' I ask, stepping back into the warm.

'No, I just popped around for the lesson plans. I've got a pile of marking to get through.'

She closes the door and waits for me to get the plans.

'They've invited us for drinks on Saturday,' I say. I don't know why I'm telling Helen. Maybe I'm hoping she'll make me feel better about not wanting to go.

'God, they'd have barely settled in.'

'I know. I'm thinking we should maybe say no.'

'That's daft. Of course you should go. I'm sure you can get a sitter,' smiles Helen. 'You're always saying how Chris moans because you don't go out much.'

I force a smile. It's very short notice to ask Kathryn to babysit and I really don't trust anyone else. It's all right for Helen. Not having children she couldn't possibly understand. I know she thinks I'm overanxious and maybe she's right. It's not that I wouldn't like to go out for the evening but it's not much fun if I'm worrying about Ben all the time.

'I'll speak to Chris,' I say.

'How's Ben?' she asks, peeking around the door to wave at him.

'He's great. I love the days I'm home.'

She hugs me and opens the front door.

'We need to do a trip to Ikea,' she says, her face lighting up.

'Great.'

'We'll get a date at school tomorrow. Better fly.'

I watch as a black Audi pulls up outside the house next door. A smartly dressed man emerges from it. He pulls a suitcase from the boot and wheels it to the house. I brush some leaves from the step and close the front door.

One year earlier

She sat in her usual chair in the therapist's room, her hands clasped together, her shoulders hunched.

'Do you want to talk about the birth?' Leah asked, handing her a mug of coffee.

No, I don't want to talk about the birth, she thought. The rain splashed at the windows and her eyesight blurred.

'I don't really remember much,' she said. It didn't sound like her voice. It was too far away. 'I know it was raining. I remember hailstones hitting the windows. I was excited that it was happening.'

She squeezed her hands tightly, the nails sharp and painful in her palms.

'I remember thinking it doesn't matter about the pain. It would all be worth it, and it was.'

'It's a good memory?'

She nodded.

'But I wanted three. I always wanted three. I'd planned that we'd have the second a year later. That way they could grow up together ...'

Her throat seemed to close up and she struggled to breathe.

'Do you need a glass of water?' Leah asked kindly.

She shook her head. All she seemed to do here was drink endless amounts of water.

'I still can't accept it. I do try. I remember the pain, it went on for hours. I would have liked a natural birth but I was relieved when I was taken to the operating theatre. Everyone said I should be grateful to have a baby but I only felt disappointment and anger. It was my mother who told me that I couldn't have any more'.

'Are you still angry with the doctors for taking away your womb?'

She shrugged. Her hand trembled and she carefully placed the mug of coffee on to the table next to a solitary box of tissues. She found herself wondering how often Leah replaces the box. Every day? Every few hours?

'You need to get past this if we're to move on. You have to accept.'

It's easy for her to say, she thought angrily.

'Do you have a family?' she asked.

'It's not about me,' said Leah

'I have to go,' she said suddenly, standing up.

Leah didn't seem surprised.

At least she'd stayed longer than last time.

Chapter Two

'You look incredible,' says Chris.

'You don't think it's too much? I could wear my jeans.'

'You look great. I like you in that dress. Although I don't know why we're bothering if they can't even return our vase.'

'They've probably had a lot on their plate,' I say, excusing Sharni.

'It's been five days. The flowers will be dead by now, surely.'

'I expect they are busy people and just haven't got around to returning it. I remember being overwhelmed when we moved in here.'

'Why are you making excuses for them?'

'I'm not.'

I smile at his reflection in the mirror. He's wearing a crisp white shirt and a pair of underpants. I laugh at the absurdity. He smells of Aqua De Parma.

'You smell nice,' I say.

He kisses my neck and his hand slides down to cup my breast. I shiver under his touch.

'I've just changed,' I say.

'You can just un-change then,' he whispers huskily into my ear.

'Kathryn will be here any minute. Besides, Ben ...'

'Is happily playing in his pen.'

What if Kathryn knocks and we're both naked or worse still Chris has a tell-tale bulge. What will she think?

'Chris ...' I begin.

The dress slides from my shoulders and I shudder.

'Christ Clare, you're so sexy,' he moans.

The doorbell chimes, making me jump.

'Shit,' groans Chris.

'I did warn you,' I smile. 'She's always early.'

He zips up the dress, kisses me and hurries to the bathroom. The scent of the Aqua De Parma clings to my dress and I find it comforting.

'I'm a bit early,' says Kathryn, giving me an admiring glance. 'That's a gorgeous dress Mrs Ryan.'

'It's new,' I say, sounding like a child with a new toy. 'I'll get Ben from the bedroom.'

I can't help wondering if Kathryn compares our home to the houses of her other clients, not that I know any of her clients. Chris and I have only lived in Kensington for eighteen months. I don't really know anyone apart from the staff at the school, and I really only know Helen well.

'You know where everything is?' I say. 'And how the TV works?'

'Yes, I remember,' she smiles.

I'm sounding overanxious again.

'I'm going to finish getting ready.'

I brush past Chris on the stairs.

'We have to go in ten minutes if we want to be fashionably late,' he says, tapping me on the bum.

I look at myself in the mirror and begin to doubt what I've

done with my hair. I thought curls would look good but my hair is too fine and it looks flat. There's no time to spray some dry shampoo into it, and nowhere near enough time to clip it up. I stroke some lipstick across my lips and dab with a tissue. I've put too much blusher on. With shaking hands I dab at my cheeks too.

'Clare,' Chris calls. 'Are you ready? We should go.'

I step into my heels and take one last look in the mirror. I remember that I have no perfume on and quickly spray some Jo Malone Grapefruit on to my throat. Damn it, now it will be too fresh. I grab Ben and hurry down the stairs.

Chris fidgets at the front door.

'I don't know what I've done with my handbag,' I say looking around.

'It's here Mrs Ryan,' Kathryn calls.

I check that the bottle of diazepam is in there and let out a small sigh of relief.

'You won't need those,' Chris says softly.

I pretend not to hear him.

'You have our number,' I say to Kathryn. 'Don't hesitate to phone no matter what. Ben's beaker is in the kitchen. I've left some juice out for him.'

Chris sighs.

'No worries Mrs Ryan. You both have a good time.'

'Clare,' Chris says taking my arm.

I nod and shrug into my coat. I give Ben one last look and follow Chris out of the house.

Chapter Three

'You're wearing Grapefruit,' sniffs Sharni. 'I love Jo Malone.'

'It's one of my few luxuries,' I say and then realise it sounds like I can't afford it. The truth is I can't. My salary as a part-time teacher doesn't pay that much and although Chris works hard and takes every bit of overtime he can, we don't have much left over once the mortgage and bills are paid. The Jo Malone perfume was a special treat for my birthday last year and I'm making it last.

'Come in,' Sharni says warmly, taking our coats.

Sharni is an excellent hostess. I can't imagine how she finds the time but I suppose it helps not having children. The table is laid with assorted cheeses, ham, French bread, home-made Melba toast, pates, and small crispbreads topped with smoked salmon and cream cheese. Sharni hands us a mango Bellini while her husband, Tom, offers around a plate of canapés. I tell Sharni I'm not drinking but she's having none of it and says we're there to christen the house and what better way to do that than with champagne.

'One won't hurt,' Chris whispers.

I'm not at all used to champagne. I can't remember the last time Chris and I had some. I only ever drink it at weddings and we haven't been to one of those in a long time. It's not something we have in the house. A bottle of wine is a treat for us. The truth is I don't like to mix alcohol with diazepam. It's not that I can't. It's just I don't want to be incapable of taking care of Ben. Being a mum means everything to me.

'The house is lovely,' I say.

'You'd never think you'd just moved in,' agrees Chris, looking around.

Tom laughs. He's good looking. Not the kind of man I would have imagined Sharni to be with. He's dynamic and stands out whereas Sharni seems insignificant with her mousy brown hair and glasses. Tom has a very upper-crust accent, unlike Sharni who has a West Country lilt to her voice.

'You haven't seen the upstairs. Everything that hasn't been unpacked is up there,' says Tom.

He tops up my Bellini before I can stop him. Chris and I sit together on the white sofa. It feels hard and resistant beneath me, unlike our old saggy one where my body moulds into its softness. Sharni looks less tired than when I last saw her. Her hair is tidier and tied back into a neat bun. Large black dangly earrings hang from her ears.

There are 'Good Luck' cards on the windowsill. I've never been in the house before. An elderly couple lived here previously. I'd heard the work being done before Sharni and Tom moved in. The lounge wall is covered in black and white photos. Several are of Tom in a natural pose. I wonder if he's a model. He clearly knows how to pose for photographs. Alongside those are colour prints of another couple, older than us and I presume them to be Sharni or Tom's parents. Others are of country landscapes and the rest are of Sharni and Tom in loving poses. I stand up and study them.

'Nice photos,' I say, feeling the champagne relax me.

I feel Sharni at the side of me and sniff her perfume. It smells of lemons.

'I took them,' she says, pouring champagne into my glass.

'You did?' says Chris. 'They're brilliant.'

'Oh, no more,' I say, covering the glass with my hand. 'I really can't be drunk in charge of a two-year-old.'

'You're not with him now,' she says, removing my hand. 'I could take some photos of Ben if you like?'

I start at Ben's name. I don't remember telling her his name was Ben.

'You're a good photographer,' I say.

I'm beginning to feel heady.

'She should be. It's her job,' laughs Tom.

'Really?' says Chris. 'Who do you work for?'

'Chris is a town planner. He's always taking photos of roads. You know, for road improvements,' I say, taking a Melba toast. The champagne is beginning to make my head spin.

'It's not quite the same,' says Chris and for a moment I feel stupid and hate him for making me feel that way.

'I'm freelance,' says Sharni, helping herself to a salmon crispbread. 'I take fashion photos. I design the sets for fashion shoots. I do a lot of work for *Vogue*, do you know it? I have a studio in their London offices.'

'But mostly she gets to work from home, the lucky woman,' says Tom, kissing her lovingly on the cheek. 'Town planning, that's interesting,' he adds, turning to Chris.

I can't help thinking there's a patronising tone in his voice. I turn away and study the photos.

'These are excellent,' I say and wonder if my speech is slurred.

'It would be great to have a professional photo of Ben,' says Chris. 'Wouldn't it Clare?'

'I'd be happy to take photos of him,' says Sharni.

I watch in surprise as Tom uncorks another bottle of champagne. I don't think Chris and I have ever got through a whole bottle of wine in an evening let alone two bottles of champagne.

'What do you do Clare?' Tom asks.

'I'm a school teacher. I only do two days a week now.'

'She helps at the local nursery too,' adds Chris and I feel stupidly embarrassed that I don't have a high-powered job like Sharni's.

'That must be great for Ben,' says Sharni, but her voice sounds hollow.

'We like to get involved,' says Chris. 'We're key holders too so should there ever be a problem we're the first on the list.'

I roll my eyes at Chris. He's going over the top trying to impress them for some reason.

'Lucky you,' says Tom, clinking my glass with his. 'I feel like I do eight days a week.'

'Tom's a barrister, so it never really stops,' groans Sharni.

'That must be really interesting,' says Chris and I feel a spark of irritation. Does he have to suck up to them? After all, their house isn't much bigger than ours. In fact, I'm beginning to wonder, if they're doing that well, why are they living here at all?

'Clare is brilliant at interior design,' says Sharni.

'No, I'm not really,' I protest.

'You're too modest.'

'I'll get some beers,' says Tom.

'I'll get them,' Sharni says, taking me by the arm. 'I want to show Clare the kitchen.'

I glance down at my bag. I really should check my phone just in case Kathryn has texted. I'm pulled into a surprisingly messy kitchen. Used oven dishes clutter the counter along with empty packets of smoked salmon. Sharni peeks into the shiny new Aga.

'Can you pass the oven glove?' she asks. 'It's with the dishes.'

I turn to get the glove and stare at a crystal vase on the window sill. It's full of flowers.

'Is it not there?' she asks.

'Oh yes.'

She slams a tray of tartlets on to the counter.

'God, that's hot.'

I wonder if I should ask for my vase. She clearly doesn't need it, but I don't want to seem petty. I'll wait until we leave. She's no doubt got it somewhere ready to give me, when we do.

'The kitchen's a bit of a tip, I know. I thought I'd wallpaper, what do you think? I really value your opinion.'

'I think wallpaper would be nice.'

'I'm not sure. Paint is so much easier.'

'Yes, our kitchen is painted.'

'Do you want a beer?' she asks, opening the fridge.

I shake my head.

'Perhaps we could go to Liberty's together, take a look at the wallpapers. How about Monday? You don't work Mondays do you?' she says excitedly.

I stare at her.

'How do you know I don't work Mondays?' I hear the sharpness in my voice and regret it. She doesn't seem to notice and says,

'It was Monday when we moved in. You were home. I just presumed you don't work on a Monday.'

'Oh, of course, I forgot.'

'We could do lunch too,' she says.

'I'll have Ben,' I remind her.

'That's okay. It'll be great to take Ben out. I can take some photos of him. Kill two birds with one stone.'

'Well ...'

Before I realise, she has topped up my glass with champagne.

'Let's get these beers to the guys,' she says.

It's almost eleven. I'd promised Kathryn we wouldn't be later than ten-thirty but it's beginning to feel like the evening has only just started.

'Should I phone Kathryn?' I ask Chris. 'Tell her we'll be a bit later. Check it is okay?'

'I'm sure it will be but yes, give her a bell.'

'Can I use your loo?' I ask Sharni.

'Sure,' she says. 'It's upstairs, first on the left.'

I search in my bag for my phone. My eyes are blurry and I'm finding it difficult to see.

'You've dropped something,' says Chris.

My hand finally lands on the phone and I pull it out of the jumbled mess in my handbag along with numerous bits of make-up. Sharni must think I'm so disorganised.

I climb the stairs carefully, my head spinning from the alcohol.

'There's no light bulb,' Sharni calls as I reach the top. 'Turn the lamp on.'

I fumble around the little table on the landing until I feel the lamp. The soft light illuminates the landing. The lamp is identical to ours. It's the one Sharni admired in our lounge.

'I got it in John Lewis.'

Her voice makes me jump.

'Sorry did I scare you?' she says from behind me.

'It's okay,' I say shakily.

'I hope you don't mind. I love it so much. I thought I'd put it up here.'

'I'm flattered,' I smile.

'You girls okay up there? I'm making coffee,' calls Tom.

'Clare just saw our new lamp,' smiles Sharni.

'You shouldn't have such good taste Clare,' says Tom. 'Do you want a coffee?'

'I'm fine,' I say, 'we really should be going.'

I find the bathroom and step inside. Sharni must think I'm a right neurotic. I have to admit that I feel a bit annoyed about the vase but she's probably been rushed off her feet and has forgotten all about it. I'll ask for it in a few days. It's nice to be admired though. I can't remember when anyone has admired my ideas. Chris had never liked the lamp. I feel vindicated. It will be nice to go shopping with someone who has the same taste as me. It will be fun.

The bathroom is new. Shiny and squeaky clean, unlike ours with towels strewn everywhere. Here, the towels are neatly folded over a rail.

'Thanks for a great night,' says Chris, kissing Sharni on the cheek.

It's eleven-thirty and I'm feeling quite anxious about Ben. I've never left him this long with Kathryn before.

'We must do it again,' says Tom, hugging me.

'I'll see you Monday,' says Sharni, giving me a hug. Her lemon fragrance washes over me. 'I can't wait. I've got some great ideas for the house.'

'You must come to us next time,' says Chris. 'Come for dinner.'

We wave and Chris supports me by the arm.

'I've drunk too much,' I say.

'Good. I'll take advantage of you,' he laughs. 'Did you ask about the vase?'

'I forgot.'

He squeezes my bum.

'I'll get a taxi for Kathryn,' he whispers. 'And see you upstairs.'

'How have you been feeling this week?' Leah asked.

The tissue box is flowery this time. She wondered if Leah's other clients cried more than her. Do they relive their nightmares and hellish days in this room too? She sat with her hands in her lap and looked down at her bitten nails.

'The same,' she said flatly.

'Are the pills the doctor gave you helping?'

She sighed and looked to the floor.

'I don't like taking them,' she said. 'They make me forget things and I don't want to forget ...' she trailed off.

'No one wants you to forget,' Leah said softly, 'but we want you to heal. It's been nine months. It's important you help the healing process.'

The tears sprang to her eyes and ran down her cheeks. She didn't try to conceal them instead she demolished the flowery tissue box.

'How are things at home?'

Empty, everything at home feels empty.

'He's understanding and tries to be very caring.'

Leah nodded.

'He's suffering too. I know that.'

She blew noisily into the tissue.

But he's let me down, she thought. They've all let me down.

'I have to go,' she said getting up.

'You've only just arrived,' Leah said, but her voice was resigned.

'I'm not ready,' she said.

She doesn't think she'll ever be ready.

Chapter Four

'I'm not happy about continuing this medication, Clare.'

I open my mouth to protest. It's dry and my throat feels tight. I can feel my heart beating in my chest.

'I'm not going to stop it at the moment,' he continues. 'I just think we should discuss it. If you're still having anxiety problems perhaps we should look at other avenues.'

Dr Rawlins looks kindly at me. He must have seen the panic on my face.

I nod.

'Is your sleeping any better?'

'Some nights are okay but mostly ...'

He sighs.

'Diazepam and zopiclone on a regular basis is not something I'm happy about. These drugs are normally for short term only. It's not something I'm happy for you to have long term.'

I grit my teeth and wonder if he would feel this way about his own wife. If she were suffering would he deny her help?

'It's just some days ...' I begin.

'How many are you taking each day?'

My fuddled brain tries to remember.

'I'm ... I'm not sure,' I say honestly.

'You do realise that they can, in the long term, make the anxiety worse. The side effects are moodiness, and you can become more panicky. I understand you had a difficult time but you have Ben now. I think we should look at other ways to deal with your anxiety.'

'I don't want any more counselling,' I say firmly. 'I don't want to dredge everything up again.'

My hands tremble at the memory.

'Okay. I'm not going to force you to do anything you're not happy with. I'm not as familiar with your history as your previous doctor. Let's try reducing the dosage. Cut back a bit.'

I want to slap him. He has no idea what I've been through.

'Okay,' I say meekly. To argue would be pointless.

'Good, I'll give you a prescription and we'll see how you go.'

'Thank you,' I say, forcing a smile.

'Good and how is Ben?'

'He's fine,' I say.

'Hello little fella, you're coming along aren't you?' he says as he leans towards Ben.

I take the prescription and hurriedly leave the surgery. I check the time on my mobile to see if I can get to the pharmacy before meeting Sharni.

I wish I hadn't agreed to go out with Sharni. It's one of my free days with Ben and I'd much rather it was just the two of us. We could have gone to the park and then later, when Ben was napping, I would have made a curry for Chris. He likes my home-made curry. Instead we'll have to have breaded fish with oven chips. I don't even know Sharni that well. There is something about her that makes me feel uncomfortable. It's totally stupid to feel that way, I know. But the truth is I feel rather dowdy next to her, although I'm not sure why. Chris had laughed when I'd mentioned it. *She's not exactly a sex bomb,* he'd said, *especially with those glasses*. He's right of course. She isn't in the least glamorous, and her black-rimmed glasses don't do her justice. Her hair would look better with blonde highlights but her personality is so alive whereas I feel half dead. I glance in the pharmacy window at my reflection. My skin is a pasty white and I know there are black circles under my eyes. If only I could get one decent night's sleep. I'd do anything to lay my head on the pillow like Chris, and wake up in the morning refreshed. I envy him for that. *You must have a guilty conscience*, Helen had once said. *That's why you can't sleep*.

I hand my prescription slip to the assistant and then wander around the shop as I wait. Ben plays happily with his toy car. I wonder if I can cancel the trip to Liberty's with Sharni. I could tell her I have a migraine. I'm seriously considering this idea when my phone bleeps. It's a text but the number is not familiar.

Hi, are we still on for today? I just knocked but no answer. I'm a bit early. S x

How did Sharni get my mobile number? I'm sure I never gave it to her, or did I? My memory is getting bad lately. Maybe Dr Rawlins is right about the diazepam. I had drunk too much on Saturday too, and had a major hangover on Sunday. The fact is I can't remember much about that night at all.

Had to pop out, I text back. *At the pharmacy. Will be back in ten minutes.*

The assistant calls out my name and I collect my medication. I check inside the bag and sigh with relief. There is three month's supply of diazepam. I buy a bottle of water and swallow two tablets before leaving the shop.

My phone bleeps and I check the message.

Great. I'll walk down and meet you. We can get the bus outside the pharmacy. See you soon. S x

I tuck the pills into my handbag and push the buggy outside to wait.

'Here comes the bus,' says Sharni hurrying towards us. She's wearing a camel-coloured coat and long brown boots. They both look new. Before I can reach down to Ben she has him unbuckled and in her arms. She's a flurry of energy and I feel tired just being around her.

'I don't know how you fold these contraptions down,' she laughs, getting herself in a muddle with the buggy.

I try not to get anxious. I know she is just trying to help and she seems to have a firm hold on him but she's not familiar with children. I close up the buggy as Sharni puts her hand out to stop the bus.

'What a bit of luck,' she says climbing on.

I struggle with the buggy until the driver takes it off me and settles it into place at the front of the bus. I hurry down to Sharni and sit on the seat in front of her shoving all my toddler paraphernalia beside me. I put my arms out to take Ben but she says,

'He's all comfy. Can I hang on to him? I promise to hand him back when we get there.'

'Sure,' I say feeling the warmth of the diazepam envelope me. 'Sharni, I don't remember giving you my phone number.'

She smiles.

'You didn't. I asked Chris. You looked really ...' she pulls a face. 'Champagne is the worst. I don't know about you but I was pretty done for yesterday.'

'Was I that drunk?' I ask.

'I hope you didn't mind me asking Chris. I didn't want to be knocking on your door all the time.'

Ben reaches out to me and Sharni lifts him over the seat.

'He's had enough of me,' she says mimicking a sad face expression. I take Ben and cocoon him in the warmth of my arms. I can smell Sharni's perfume on him. Her hair is down and she runs her hands through it.

'Thanks for coming today. I really am grateful. I hate shopping for house things on my own, and Tom is hopeless.'

She rummages in her oversized handbag and produces a Nikon camera.

'I thought I'd get some pics of Ben. Natural ones are the best aren't they?'

'Thanks,' I say, sitting Ben on the seat beside me. 'That's a real professional camera.'

Chris and I only use our iPhones to take photos. I've been thinking about getting a proper camera. Maybe Sharni can advise me. I'm feeling relaxed about Liberty's now. It's been ages since I've been shopping properly. I pull a scrunch from my bag and tie my hair back while Ben leans over the seat to play with Sharni. I'm glad I didn't feign a headache. It's actually quite nice to be out, and with a friend. I'll get a bottle of wine to have with the fish tonight. At least that will make the meal more bearable.

She looked at the flowers on the coffee table. It was unusual to see flowers in the therapist's room.

'A client gave them to me,' said Leah by way of explanation.

It had never occurred to her to give Leah flowers. Why would she? She pays enough for these sessions as it is.

'They're very pretty,' she said.

'Do you like flowers?'

'Yes, but I don't often think to buy them for myself.'

'You're looking brighter today,' commented Leah.

'Am I? I don't feel any different.'

She stared at the flowers. Her mother had bought her flowers after the birth, a bouquet that had lasted weeks. She felt sad at the memory.

'What are they?'

'Chrysanthemums, I think.'

'Mum liked to arrange flowers and ...'

She trailed off as always. She wondered if she'd ever get a whole memory out into the open.

'Would you like to talk about your mother?'

That familiar ache in her heart returned and she shook her head.

'No, not yet.'

'What are you feeling right now?'

'Unsupported,' she said, surprising herself.

'By everyone?'

She fiddled with her wedding band. It looked strange sitting alone on her finger. Her hands were dry and the skin flaky. She'd decided to take her engagement ring off for a few days. She hadn't realised how naked she would feel without it.

'Not here,' she said. 'I feel supported here.'

But not believed, she thought. No one believes me. I'm all alone.

Chapter Five

I run my hands along the chiffon and turn over the price tag. It's more than I can afford.

'Why don't you try it on?' suggests Sharni.

I gently pull Ben's hands away from a scarf that hangs on a rail nearby.

'It is gorgeous,' I say.

'It would go great with this,' she says, reaching for a lemon cardigan.

I hesitate. I hadn't intended on buying clothes but the dress is nice and I am tempted.

'Go on, try it on. Ben and I can wait here.'

She points to a seating area.

'Okay,' I say, taking a size twelve from the rail.

It's been nice wandering around the shops with a friend. I'm exhausted but it's a pleasurable exhaustion. I slip the dress over my head and then struggle to pull it over my hips.

'How does it look?' calls Sharni.

I step gingerly from the changing room.

'It's a bit tight. It's a case of does my bum look big in this.'

She studies me.

'Hmmm,' she says thoughtfully.

I take that to mean my bum does look big in it.

'I'll get you the next size up,' she offers.

A size fourteen goes over the hips but hangs slightly loose on my breasts.

'It looks fabulous,' says Sharni.

I study myself in the mirror and slip on the lemon cardigan. It is nice and I don't often buy myself clothes these days. I check the price tag on the cardigan and gasp. I can't pay a hundred pounds for two items of clothing.

'Are you getting them?' Sharni asks as I come out of the changing room. Ben looks up at me and begins to cry.

'They're quite expensive,' I say.

'Oh, you must treat yourself sometimes,' she smiles. 'Isn't that why you work?'

I expect Sharni thinks nothing of spending a hundred pounds on herself. She's right, though. I hardly ever buy myself anything these days. Not since we've had Ben. I don't mind though. I'd much rather spend the money on him, but just this once won't hurt.

'You've talked me into it,' I laugh.

'They're gorgeous,' she says idly fingering the dresses on the rail.

I quickly pay before I have time to change my mind and then stroll back to Sharni. She has pulled out her camera and is snapping another picture of Ben.

'That's going to be beautiful,' she says, squinting behind the viewfinder.

I'd lost count of the number of photos Sharni had taken. Our arms ache from carrying our numerous shopping bags. My throat is dry. I should have bought a bottle of water. I glance at my phone to see it is three-thirty. Ben is wide awake and he should really have had a nap by now. If I leave it much later I'll be up half the night with him.

'I should try and rock him off to sleep,' I say.

I don't want Sharni to think I'm ungrateful for the photos she has taken but she is overexciting him.

'Shall we get a coffee?' she suggests.

'Sounds good,' I agree.

My feet ache and the thought of a sit down is heaven. I can rock Ben in the stroller as we have our coffee.

'I'll get them,' I say. 'You bought lunch.'

We find a table in the busy cafeteria. I drop my bags gratefully and throw my coat over the back of a chair. The stores are unbearably hot and I grimace at the odour under my arms. What must Sharni think of me?

'Okay to leave everything with you?' I ask.

'Sure,' she says, glancing at her shopping list. 'I must get some flowers before we go home.'

I open my mouth to ask about the vase but stop myself. It will sound so petty after all she has done today. I'll wait a few more days. Maybe buying the flowers will remind her about it.

I look down at Ben who is flaying about in his buggy. He throws off his blanket and squeezes his eyes tightly shut in a moment of frustration.

'He's tired,' I say with a sigh.

'He'll be fine,' she smiles.

'What would you like?' I ask, my heart sinking at the sight of the queue.

'A cappuccino for me,' she says.

I make my way to the endless line of people. I had completely forgotten about Christmas and the crowds had been a stark reminder of just how close it was. I look over to Sharni and Ben. She's rocking him in the stroller. I fish my phone from my bag and see there is a message from Chris.

I hope you're having a good time with Sharni. I'm going to be late. Unexpected meeting. Eat without me. Will keep you updated.

Disappointment washes over me. I'd bought a decent bottle of wine to have with our dinner.

Okay, let me know how you're doing I text back.

I find myself wondering how Chris can have an unexpected meeting and then hate myself for the thought. I really must not start that again. I've got Ben to think about now. I rub the back of my neck and move slowly forward in the queue. The clattering of cups and cutlery is making my head ache.

'Next, what can I get you?'

I look up at the assistant and then glance at the cakes and pastries on the counter. I never thought to ask Sharni if she wanted anything to eat.

'Erm ...'

The assistant fidgets impatiently.

'Two cappuccinos and ...'

I lift my head to look at Sharni. The table is empty. There is no sign of her or the buggy.

'Yes?' says the assistant.

I scan the seating area where I was sure I'd left Sharni and Ben. The loud swooshing noise of the coffee maker makes me jump.

'What else can I get you?' asks the assistant.

I don't understand why Sharni isn't at the table. I'm sure that's where I left them. A young couple are sitting there instead, sipping from their mugs. That can't be right. I'm sure they weren't there earlier.

'Two muffins,' I say absently while my eyes hurriedly scan the cafeteria. Maybe she's gone to the loo.

'Blueberry or chocolate?'

'What?'

The assistant sighs and I feel the air of tension behind me from the other customers.

'Do you want blueberry or chocolate muffins?'

'It doesn't matter.'

'I can't choose for you.'

'Blueberry,' I snap and immediately apologise. There's no sign of Sharni. My heart thumps in my chest. What was I thinking of, leaving my child with someone I hardly knew? Oh God, what if ... My mind begins to imagine all sorts of crazy things. What if they haven't really moved in next door at all? What if ... Oh God, what have I done? What mother leaves her child with a total stranger? I rummage for the diazepam tablets and swallow two. I ignore the assistant's raised eyebrows and lift the tray. I make my way hurriedly to the till. In my haste I push into the woman in front of me, spilling cappuccino into the saucers.

'I'm sorry,' I mumble.

My head is spinning and my trembling legs have difficulty walking to the table where the couple are sitting. I look for my coat on the back of the chair but it has gone. I feel dizzy and grab the chair for support. Should I phone the police? And If I do, what do I tell them? My neighbour has taken my child with my permission? Oh God, how could I have been so stupid. I place the tray on to a nearby empty table and wipe the perspiration from my brow.

'Are you okay?' the girl asks.

'I'm just a bit hot,' I say.

I fumble in my bag for my phone. I need to call Chris. Surely he will know what to do. Just as I go to punch in his number, it bleeps.

We're by the window.

I turn and see Sharni waving from the other side of the room. How could I have missed her? I felt sure I had looked there. I struggle to control my breathing and try to relax. Maybe I should try to cut down on the diazepam. Dr Rawlins did say it could make me more anxious. I feel beads of sweat run down my forehead but by the time I reach the table my breathing has calmed.

'You look really hot,' says Sharni, taking the tray from me.

'It's stuffy in here,' I say and wonder if she can hear the tremble in my voice.

'We had to move,' she explains. 'The draught there was awful. I didn't think it was good for Ben.'

'I wondered where you'd both gone,' I say, trying to keep my voice even.

'He's dozed off,' she smiles and covers him with his blanket. 'Ooh muffins,' she adds, looking at the tray.

Ben is cosy under his blankets. His sweet cherub face peeks out from beneath and his eyelashes flutter against his cheek. I want to scoop him up and hold him close to me for ever.

'I didn't know what you liked so I got blueberry.'

'Chocolate's my favourite,' she says, 'but blueberry is nice too.'

I stupidly feel that I have done something wrong and I flop into the chair. I turn the stroller around to face me.

'I can't believe it's almost Christmas,' says Sharni, spooning the froth from her coffee. 'What are you doing for Christmas?'

'I don't know, we haven't really thought about it.'

'Will you have your family come to you?'

I look down so she can't see my face.

'No, I don't really see my family. My mum ...'

'I'm so sorry Clare. Families are important at Christmas.'

'I have my family,' I say sounding defensive.

I decide to get a proper tree this year. Not that silly artificial bent thing that Chris bought the first year we were married. I can decorate it while Ben watches. He'll love that. I'll play Christmas songs to him.

We sit sipping our cappuccinos and listening to the Christmas music from the café speakers, both in worlds of our own.

'Why don't you come to us?' she says suddenly.

I'm so startled that I choke on my coffee.

'Are you okay?' she asks, her perfume drifting around me.

I see her through a haze of diazepam.

'It went down the wrong hole.'

She sits back down and scoops her hair back.

'It is hot in here,' she agrees. 'What do you think about Christmas?' she asks again.

'I ... Won't you have family?'

'Not this year.'

I don't like to ask more so simply say, 'I'll ask Chris.'

She must think I'm always saying *I'll ask Chris*. I check the time on my phone and gasp.

'It's gone four,' I say.

'Yes, it's getting late. You've got to get Ben home. Shall we go? We can get a taxi if you don't want to wait for a bus.'

I hesitate. A taxi would be heaven but in this part of London the fare would be criminal.

'I'll pay,' she says as though reading my mind. 'I'd rather get a cab to be honest. I don't know about you but I'm knackered.'

'Clare, is that you?'

I turn to the voice and see Helen. She pulls out a chair and flops into it.

'What are you doing here?' I ask, and realise that I sound accusing. 'I thought you'd be at school,' I add apologetically.

'I finished at three. I'm doing what I thought was early Christmas shopping. It seems I'm not the only one.'

'We were just leaving,' says Sharni, offering her hand. 'I'm

Sharni Wilson, Clare's new neighbour.'

'Hi, how are you settling in?'

'Good,' smiles Sharni. 'Clare is giving me some fab ideas for the house.'

'Great,' says Helen, glancing at her watch. 'I should run. The shops are only open for two more hours and you know how long Christmas shopping can take.'

Ben fidgets in his stroller and I rock it gently.

'I'll just get some flowers from the food hall and phone for a cab,' says Sharni, picking up her bags.

'She seems nice,' says Helen, watching Sharni hurry to the food hall.

'Yes,' I nod. 'I'll see you at school tomorrow.'

'It's your appraisal tomorrow isn't it?' grimaces Helen.

'I'm trying not to think about it.'

I hate appraisals. I'm feeling quite confident that everything will be okay but I have lost a few days this year when Ben was ill. I couldn't leave him at the nursery with a fever. The truth is I don't like leaving him at all but I have no choice. I need to work if Chris and I are going to keep up our mortgage payments. I kiss Helen on the cheek and bundle my bags under my arm.

'Good luck tomorrow.'

'Thanks Helen, I'm slightly anxious about it.'

'It'll be fine.'

The diazepam is taking effect and I feel calmer. I could shop some more but I need to get Ben home. I'll have a hot bath when I get back and treat myself to a glass of the wine I'd bought. Ben can play in his pen. Sharni approaches and points to a cab outside.

'Okay?' she asks.

I nod and before I can stop her she has lifted Ben from his stroller. I close it down and follow her, relishing the thought of my hot bath.

Chapter Six

I rock Ben back and forth, while he screams blue murder. My head thumps with every movement. I should never have let him sleep for so long but it had been so nice soaking in the bath with a glass of wine. It had seemed such a long time since I had relaxed like that. I just didn't want it to end. Now, I'm paying the price for my indulgence. Ben is wide awake and the wine which seemed so lovely earlier is kicking back and my head feels like it will burst with every one of Ben's cries. I've only slept for an hour and the cocktail of diazepam and wine has sent my head swimming. It doesn't matter what I do, Ben just won't settle.

I check the time on my phone and groan. It's three-thirty. My eyes are gritty from lack of sleep and the acidity in my stomach is making me nauseous. I look at the bedroom wall and wonder if Sharni and Tom can hear Ben's screams. I expect not. I can't help thinking of Sharni sleeping soundly next to Tom and find myself feeling irrationally resentful. It wasn't her fault. I should have been more insistent about Ben's nap.

'Christ Clare,' grumbles Chris. 'Can't you give him some Calpol?'

'That's not the answer Chris, and you know I won't give him that,' I say, feeling the irritation well up inside me.

'I've got to get up for work tomorrow,' he snaps, pulling the duvet over his head.

So have I, I want to snap, but I don't. Instead I climb wearily from the bed, hugging Ben close and make my way to the cold sitting room.

'Ben, please,' I plead. 'Just stop screaming.'

I fumble with the electric heater and click it on. I grab the throw from the back of the couch and wrap us both in it. I fleetingly wonder what Sharni would think of our interiors now. I lie back on the sofa and rock Ben in my arms. His screams jar in my head and I fight the urge to throw up. I hear the bed creak as Chris turns over. I close my eyes and think of the photos we'd have of Ben when Sharni prints them out. We don't have any decent pictures of Ben. I consider asking if she would take one of the three of us, a family portrait. It would look lovely in a frame above the fireplace. My eyes snap open as an awful thought occurs to me. *What if she publishes them in a magazine?* My heart races and my breathing becomes shallow. I struggle to take deep breaths. I can't take any more diazepam. Beads of sweat form on my forehead and I clasp Ben close. I'll ask her not to. It would be an invasion of our privacy. She would surely understand. I don't want anyone seeing photos of Ben. It's not worth the risk. But, I assure myself, she's a fashion photographer, not a baby and toddler photographer. I don't suppose she'll even keep the photos. Why would she? What interest would they be to her? My breathing slows and I realise that Ben has stopped screaming. I shift slightly and his eyes open.

'Alright sweetie, mummy's here,' I whisper, rocking him gently.

I consider taking two paracetamol but I can't reach my bag

without disturbing him. I close my eyes. I'll speak to Sharni tomorrow about the photos. Maybe I'll ask for the vase back too. After all, she can't possibly need it now. I gently feel Ben's forehead to check there is no fever. Thankfully his head is cool. My eyes close and I feel myself drifting into sleep.

'Clare, Clare.'

I open my eyes and a pain shoots through my neck. My arms are empty and I look for Ben.

'Where ...?'

'He's in his playpen. I let you sleep for a bit longer. Here's some porridge.'

Chris pushes a bowl into my hand.

I try to get up but my legs are numb.

'What's the time?'

'Seven. No need to rush.'

My head thumps and my eyes are blurry from sleep.

'You should have come back to bed,' he says.

'I was going to but I must have dozed off.'

'I've got to go. I've got meetings all day. Are you okay? You look rough.'

I put the porridge down and rub my eyes. Nausea overwhelms me and I take a deep breath.

'You're not working late again are you?' I say and wince at the accusatory tone in my voice. I couldn't bear another evening alone.

'No, of course not, I'll be home by six. I'll get a Chinese if you like. Save you cooking.'

I hug him gratefully.

'That'd be great, Chris. I have my appraisal today.'

'Oh yeah, I forgot. Good luck.'

He kisses me softly and strokes my hair.

'Don't worry so much. You've got a nice friend in Sharni. How did it go yesterday? Sorry I didn't ask when I got home. I was so knackered.'

I smile.

'It was good. She took some photos of Ben and ... I'll ask her not to publish them.'

He looks startled.

'Why would she publish them? We're not famous or anything.'

'I know,' I say as I realise how stupid I sound.

'See you later,' he says, grabbing his holdall.

'Chris, can you not give people my mobile number before asking me?'

'I haven't,' he says defensively, looking for his car keys.

'They're on the table,' I say. 'You gave it to Sharni.'

He grabs the keys.

'I don't think I did.'

'The night we went round there.'

He shakes his head.

'We did drink a lot,' I remind him.

'Yeah, maybe I did it without thinking. Sorry. See you later.'

I grab Ben and the playpen, and hurry up to the shower. I slam the door shut. I don't hear the phone ringing.

The ringing of the mobile made her jump.

'Sorry,' she said. 'I meant to turn it off.'

'It doesn't matter.'

'Do you have children?'

'You always ask that.'

'Not always.'

'Often.'

'And you always say it's not about you.'

'That's right.'

'I dreamt about it again last night.'

Her eyes are clear. She expects them to fill with tears but they don't. She's all cried out, that's why.

'What happened in the dream?'

'Everything was okay in the dream. The end was different. No one died.'

'So, you didn't really dream about 'it'?'

'That's what you say,' she whispers, fiddling with the tissue box. It's pink this time. She preferred the flowery one. It was more cheering.

'I won't let anyone take what I believe away from me.'

'How is it different to everyone else's beliefs?'

Everyone else is wrong, she thinks but doesn't say.

'I want to talk about my mother,' she says instead.

The therapist smiles, it's what she wanted to hear.

'Okay, why don't you tell me about her?'

Chapter Seven

I open the door and hear the shrill ring of the telephone. I grab Ben and hurry downstairs with the towel wrapped around me.

'Mrs Ryan?'

I recognise the voice immediately. It's Faye from the nursery.

'Yes, hello Faye.'

'I'm really sorry to tell you this but we've had to close the nursery today. There's been a flood. Someone blocked the sink and left the tap running. I did try you earlier.'

My heart misses a beat.

'I was in the shower. I have an appraisal this morning.'

My mobile trills and I grab it with the other hand. It's the school.

'Can you hold on one second Faye?'

'Sorry to be a pain Clare,' says the head. 'Can you stay a bit longer today? I know it's short notice but we've got two teachers off. I hope it's not too inconvenient.'

It couldn't be more inconvenient.

'Erm ... yes that's fine,' I say without thinking.

'Great. See you in a bit.'

'What's happening with the kids then?' I ask Faye.

'I'm afraid you'll have to make other arrangements for today.'

'But I don't have anyone,' I say, struggling to keep the panic from my voice.

'I'm sorry, but there is nothing we can do.'

'Thanks,' I say.

I replace the receiver.

'Shit, shit, shit,' I curse loudly. How can the bloody nursery be flooded?

Ben looks up at me wide-eyed. I tap in Chris's office number.

'Chris, the nursery is closed, they've had a flood. Can you work from home today? I've got my appraisal and we're short staffed.'

'I've got meetings all day Clare; I can't get out of them.'

'I don't know what to do,' I sob.

'Christ Clare. Have you tried Kathryn?'

'She's at college.'

'Shit.'

I feel tears prick at my eyelids.

'What about Sharni? She said the other night that we could ask her any time. She seemed very keen to help out with Ben,' he suggests.

'We hardly know her,' I say, surprised at the suggestion.

'She's not exactly going to kidnap him is she?' he says irritably. 'They've just moved in next door. Christ Clare, get a grip.'

I take a deep breath. I suppose he's right. Ben isn't going to come to any harm in one day. I could ask her. I've got no one else.

'If she can't then I'll have to take the day off and you realise if I do, I'll lose my job. I had that time off when Ben wasn't well and ...'

I'm accusing him but I'm not sure what of.

'I can't come home,' he says firmly.

'Okay I'll ask Sharni,' I say.

I dress and prepare Ben and then peek out of the window to see there is one car in Sharni's driveway. I wrap Ben in his jacket and grab all his nursery paraphernalia. I hesitate at her front door. I hardly know Sharni. How can I ask her to look after my child? I knock softly, in some vain hope that she won't hear. I'm about to turn away when the door opens and she stands there in a blue dressing gown, her hair askew.

'Clare,' she says. 'Is everything okay?'

'I'm really sorry,' I say and find I am annoyingly tearful. 'The nursery phoned and they've had to close for the day. I've got an appraisal at eleven and ...'

'You've got no one to have Ben,' she finishes for me.

'I'm so sorry to ask but ...'

'Of course I can have him,' she says, taking the bags from my hand. 'Come in, it's freezing out here.'

I'm pulled into her warm hallway and relieved of Ben. The hall smells of toast and fresh coffee. I remember my bowl of porridge, which I'd left on the coffee table, and sigh.

'You look terrible, are you okay?' asks Sharni.

'I didn't get much sleep last night. Are you sure about this, it'll be a long day.'

She doesn't seem to be listening to me and is already cocooning Ben in the warmth of her arms. His little fingers grasp at her fluffy dressing gown.

'We'll be okay, won't we Sweet Pea?' she says to Ben who laughs in response. He seems to like the words *Sweet Pea*.

'Don't worry, he'll be fine,' she says unbuttoning his jacket.

I pull a crumpled piece of paper from one of the bags. I

don't know why I still have it. It's my list of things that Ben needs during the day. I just feel safer handing it over each time to the nursery staff. After all, you never know when they'll have a new helper.

'It's all on here. His nap times and what time he has his lunch and ...'

'Great,' she says, smiling. 'We'll be fine.'

She whips the list out of my hand.

'That bag has his training pants and ...'

'We'll be fine,' she repeats, her voice firmer this time.

I twiddle with my necklace nervously.

'Are you sure?' I ask hesitantly. 'I can take him in with me.'

'That won't look very professional will it,' she smiles and for a moment I feel reprimanded.

'No,' I say.

She looks at the clock in the hallway.

'You'll be late'

I look longingly at Ben who is now playing with Sharni's hair.

'You can call my mobile as many times as you like,' she says with an encouraging smile and I feel like a child myself.

'Thanks,' I say, pulling up my collar. I turn to the door and then spin back round.

'Sharni, the photos you took ...'

'I'll print them today.'

'You won't publish them, you know, in a magazine or anything?'

I blush as I realise how silly I sound.

She laughs.

'Don't be daft. In this day and age, do you think I'm insane?'

I let out a sigh of relief.

'I'll phone you later,' I say, kissing Ben on the cheek. I've barely gone through the door when it is shut behind me. I climb into my car and am about to start the engine when her door opens and Sharni calls to me.

'Do you have a spare key to your house?'

'A key?' I repeat stupidly.

'Just in case, for toys and the stroller, so we can go for a walk.'

Shit. I'd forgotten all about the stroller. I'm going to be really late at this rate. I yank the door key off my keyring and hand it to her.

'The stroller is in the porch. His toys are in a box in the lounge. Oh, and his playpen is in the bedroom. I should have given you that. I'd better go.'

'Have a good day.'

I reverse the car and turn to wave but the door is already closed.

Chapter Eight

'We've been very happy with your performance this year Clare, aside from a few absences. I do, however, feel that sometimes you're not always focused and that your mind is elsewhere and not on your job. Of course, I'm very aware you have a young child,' says Geoff Markham, the head.

'Oh, I didn't realise. I'll try to be aware of that,' I say.

I'm finding it hard to focus. I'd turned my phone on to silent just before entering the meeting. At that moment it had flashed up a message and Sharni's name had popped on to the screen. One half of me tells myself if it was an emergency she would have phoned rather than send a text, but the other half can't stop worrying about it.

'I've been very happy,' I say.

Geoff looks at the form in front of him.

'There was a large absence and a couple of short ones after that. Is that likely to happen again? I know your child was unwell.'

'He had an allergy.'

'How is he now?'

'He's very well, back to normal.'

A sudden vision of Ben in an ambulance makes me break out in a cold sweat. Please God, let him be all right.

'Great. It's good you can do some extra teaching today. How would you feel about taking on more hours as a permanent arrangement?'

I gape at him.

'Oh,' I say, taken aback. The last thing I'd been expecting was an offer of extra work.

'If you could do Friday mornings too that would really help us and if you could possibly stay longer on your normal days that would be excellent.'

The thought of the extra money almost has me agreeing right away.

'I'll have to talk to my husband, Chris.'

'That's fine. I really need someone next week so do let me know.'

I nod.

'Wonderful. We're both happy then. Will we see you and your husband at the Christmas party?'

My phone flashes again and my heart races.

'Sorry,' I say.

'The Christmas party, I hope we're going to see you there with your husband?'

'Oh yes, we're looking forward to it.'

I must remember to tell Chris about the party.

'Excellent.'

I glance at the clock on the wall.

'Almost time for lunch,' he says, as though reading my mind.

I scrape my chair back and grab my handbag.

'Is there anything you want to discuss with me?' he asks.

'No, everything is fine. Thanks Geoff,' I say before dashing into the corridor and tugging the phone from my bag. I click into Sharni's message and realise I'm holding my breath.

Is Ben allergic to anything?

I feel myself sway. Oh God what's happened?

I blink to get the rest of the message in focus. My head thumps and I flop on to one of the chairs outside Geoff's office.

I thought I'd puree him some veg. I obviously don't want to give him anything he shouldn't have.

I wipe the sweat from my forehead. Maybe Dr Rawlins is right. Perhaps I do need therapy. But surely after what I've been through it's only natural to be protective. I fight the urge to take some diazepam although I'm sure just one at work wouldn't hurt.

'How did it go?'

I turn to see Helen.

'Blimey you look rough, was it that bad?'

'I was up half the night with Ben,' I smile. 'Actually the meeting went better than I could have imagined.'

'Let's get out. I'm desperate for a smoke. Those little buggers have driven me insane this morning. Let's get a pizza.'

I tap a message to Sharni and follow Helen out into the cold.

'Christ it's bitter. I reckon we've got snow coming,' she says lighting up a Benson and Hedges.

I'll phone Sharni when we get to Pizza Hut.

'She's looking after Ben?' questions Helen.

I can't tell if its surprise or alarm on her face.

'I didn't know what to do,' I say feebly.

'How can the sodding nursery have a flood?' she scoffs.

I pick at my salad.

'I did ask Chris if he could work from home today.'

'You're not worrying are you?' she asks.

I raise my eyebrows.

'You should get an award for worrying. She seemed great. I know what you mean though. You haven't known her five minutes ...'

'I'll give her a quick ring,' I say as the waiter approaches with our pizza.

Helen shrugs.

Sharni answers on the first ring.

'It's my lunch break,' I explain.

'Ben's absolutely fine. I'm giving him his pureed vegetables and then we're going to have his sleep.'

What I wouldn't do for a sleep. The thought of keeping my eyes open all afternoon feels like an enormous feat.

'You've had no problems?'

Helen rolls her eyes and cuts into her pizza.

'We're fine.'

I can hear the smile in Sharni's voice.

'All okay?' Helen asks as I hang up.

'She's very confident. She makes me feel a bit, I don't know ...'

'What does she do that she can be at home all day?'

'She's a professional photographer.'

'You're kidding. I'll look her up on Facebook.'

'Facebook?' I repeat.

Helen sighs.

'Facebook, you know that thing that everyone's on except you.'

I think of the photos Sharni took of Ben. I never asked her not to put them on Facebook.

'I am on Facebook,' I say. 'I just don't use it.'

'That's the same as not being on it,' she laughs and cuts into her garlic bread. 'Does she work from home then?'

'I'm not sure if it's every day.'

'We've got twenty minutes. No time for a pudding,' Helen says as she checks her watch.

I tuck into my pizza and realise I'm starving.

'I lent Sharni a vase,' I say casually. 'On the day she moved in. That would be a week ago. Her mother sent her flowers apparently so I lent her my best vase, the one that Chris bought me on our honeymoon. The thing is, it's a hand-painted original. I don't imagine we could replace it. She hasn't given it back but she's got flowers in other vases.'

Helen shrugs.

'Maybe she's put it away and forgotten all about it.'

'But you wouldn't put away someone else's vase would you?'

'Why don't you ask her for it?'

'I feel awkward, even more so now she's been kind enough to help out with Ben.'

'That doesn't mean you have to give her one of your vases,' laughs Helen.

'Maybe I'll ask for it tonight,' I say yawning.

We pay for our pizza and look out of the window at the first flurry of snow. I find myself hoping Sharni doesn't take Ben for a walk in this. He catches colds so easily.

'You can tell it's getting near Christmas,' says Helen. 'I can't wait to go to Ikea. I'm going to buy loads of candles.'

'It's quite heavy,' I say.

'Let's wait here for the bus,' suggests Helen. 'We can make a run for it as it turns the corner.'

I huddle in my parka and push my hands into the pockets. Helen lights a cigarette and I wave the smoke away. As I do so, I spot two men and a blonde woman leaving the restaurant on the other side of the road.

'Isn't that Chris?' says Helen.

'Yes,' I mumble.

'Hey Chris,' she yells but her voice is lost in the noise of the traffic.

'Bugger, he didn't hear me. Fancy that, you could have had lunch together.'

I barely hear her. All I can think of is how the woman had leaned close to Chris before throwing her head back and laughing. I pull the bottle of diazepam from my bag and swallow two.

'What are they?' asks Helen.

'Aspirin,' I lie.

'Here's our bus, come on.'

She grabs my arm and we hurry to the bus stop.

Chapter Nine

Chris frowned. He'd texted Clare four times now and still she hadn't replied. He could see the texts had been delivered. He wondered if he should phone her. But she might be in the middle of a class. He wouldn't want to bugger things up even more if her appraisal had gone badly, and if it had gone well he didn't want to ruin it by disturbing her teaching. He checked his phone again and then thought of phoning Sharni. He doubted anything was wrong with Ben but he couldn't think why else Clare wouldn't respond to a text. Supposing Ben had been taken ill and she hadn't had time to contact him? It seemed a bit unlikely. Surely she would ask Sharni to phone him. All the same ... He scrolled through his phone and realised he didn't have Sharni's mobile number. Damn, he didn't imagine their landline would be listed.

He struggled to remember the lawyer's office Tom worked for. After two minutes of searching Google, he had found it.

'Hey Chris, how's it going?' said Tom cheerfully.

'Yeah good. How about you?

'Not bad. I'm in court in five minutes.'

'Ah, I won't keep you. Sharni offered to take care of Ben

today as there was a problem at the nursery. I'm trying to get hold of Clare. She's not answering. I'm probably being silly but I thought something might have happened with Ben ...'

'Let me give you Sharni's number,' Tom interrupted.

'Thanks Tom.'

Seconds later Chris was calling Sharni on her mobile. He was surprised to see his hands were shaking.

'Hello.'

'Sharni? It's Chris.'

'Chris,' she sounded surprised. 'Hi, how are you?'

'I'm fine. I can't get hold of Clare. Everything's okay with Ben isn't it?'

He felt like kicking himself. Both she and Tom will think that he's as neurotic as his wife.

'He's fine. He's having a nap. I should wake him actually. I got carried away with work.'

'I'm sorry to have bothered you.'

'Don't be silly. I'd be phoning every two minutes if I'd left my child with someone.'

He forced a laugh.

'Oh, we're not like that. Has Clare been in touch?'

'Yes, earlier today.'

'Great, well, I'd better get back to work. Thanks for having Ben at such short notice.'

'Don't thank me. I've really enjoyed it.'

He hangs up and checks his messages again. He chews thoughtfully on the end of his pen and then calls Clare's number. The ringing tone seems to go on forever and jars on his nerves. A familiar feeling of anger builds within him. For God's sake, what is it now?

Chapter Ten

It's hot in Sharni's house.

'It's only because you've come in from the cold,' she says.

I step back in surprise. She smells of Jo Malone's *Grapefruit*.

'Is that ...?' I begin.

'Grapefruit,' she smiles. 'You rekindled the love in me. I had about a quarter of a bottle. It probably doesn't smell as fresh as yours though.'

It smells perfect on her. She leads me into the lounge where Ben is playing on her white fur rug. His playpen sits folded in the corner and a line of toy cars surrounds him. I gasp at the photographs that litter the floor. They're all of Ben.

'There are some from today and some from yesterday,' she says casually, scooping them up.

I look in amazement. They're beautiful. The kind of close-up photos I've always wanted to take but never been able to. The background has been expertly faded out.

'These are amazing,' I say. 'I can never get photos like this.'

She smiles indulgently.

'I'll put them into an envelope. You can choose the ones you want to frame.'

I stroke Ben's hair and check his forehead. Considering the house is so hot his head is cool.

'Has he been okay?'

'He's been a little angel, haven't you Sweet Pea,' she says, kissing him lovingly on the cheek. 'We've been playing with your cars, haven't we?'

I think her eyes mist over but immediately she is back to normal.

'He had a good nap and we went for a stroll to the park. I gave him pureed veg. I think it's good for their immune system, don't you?'

'Yes,' I say.

I never seem to get time to puree veg. I know I should. I'll dig the blender out of the cupboard. I know it's there somewhere.

'How did your appraisal go?'

'It went well. In fact they've offered me more work.'

I bite my lip. I hadn't intended telling her, at least not until I'd told Chris.

'That's great.'

I nod.

'Right, I'd better get Ben home.'

'Is the nursery sorted?' she asks. 'Or is it still flooded?'

'No, not yet but they say it will be fine for us to go Thursday. So we'll be okay.'

'Oh here,' she says, handing me the photographs. 'You know if ... well, I don't mind having him if you didn't want to pay out to the nursery. It would be a shame if all the extra money you earnt went to pay the nursery fees. I'm home and he's no trouble.'

'Oh, I couldn't ask you to do that,' I interrupt.

I can't help admitting the offer is appealing. The nursery

fees take most of my salary, but the extra hours will help. It isn't that Chris doesn't do well but by the time we've paid the mortgage and other bills there isn't much left.

'It's not a problem for me. Have a chat with Chris about it,' she says.

I bundle Ben up and open the stroller. It's easier to carry the bags over the handlebars.

'Oh here,' says Sharni, pushing the keys into my hand. 'Don't forget these.'

I am tempted to tell her to hang on to them but I am not really comfortable with someone one else having keys to our house. It is good of her to offer to have Ben, though. Surely Chris will agree that Sharni having Ben is a much better option than the nursery. We could save a fortune and I'd only have to pop Ben next door.

'Thanks,' I say and shove them into my handbag. 'Why don't I have a word with Chris about you looking after Ben?'

'Oh sure. No pressure. See you later.'

'Thanks Sharni and thanks for the photos. We ought to pay you or ...'

She looks offended.

'That's ridiculous.'

I push the stroller over the step and quickly say,

'You don't put photos on Facebook do you? It's just I'm a bit neurotic about Ben's picture being seen.'

'I hardly go on Facebook, let alone post photos of other people's children,' she says sharply.

Oh God, I really have offended her.

'I didn't mean ...'

'Oh there's Tom. He's early and I haven't even started dinner. Looks like a takeaway for us.'

The air seems to have cleared and I exhale gratefully.

'Hi,' calls Tom. 'I got let out early for good behaviour,' he jokes.

'I'll be off,' I say clutching the photos.

I look back to see Tom kissing Sharni before the door closes behind them. It's only then that I realise I had never told Sharni the nursery was closed because of a flood.

'I'm home,' calls Chris.

I busy myself folding the washing. I feel hurt and let down.

'Hi,' he says, kissing me. 'I got Chinese as promised. I've been texting you all day.'

'I know.'

I move past him into the living room and lay the table for dinner. I hear him take off his jacket and throw his briefcase on to the couch. I click off the television where Ben had been watching *Peppa Pig*.

'Hello mate,' he says to Ben, lifting him out of his high chair.

'I just settled him for dinner,' I say.

'So what have I done?' he asks in a tired voice.

I turn on him angrily.

'You tell me?'

'I would if I knew what it was.'

'You couldn't have your son but ...'

He raises his eyebrows.

'But you can fanny around with some blonde at lunchtime,' I finish.

He slumps on to the couch.

'You're surely not serious,' he says with a laugh. I feel the tears roll down my cheeks and have to fight the urge to slap him.

'I saw you, Chris. You came out of a restaurant. I was in Pizza Hut.'

I don't mention I'd just spent twenty minutes going through

his emails looking for anything suspicious. He shakes his head wearily.

'It was Toni you saw. We've had meetings all day. She's working along with me on the Hinski contract and we had to take the client out for lunch.'

'But I always thought Tony was a man.'

'Toni's a woman, Clare. I've told you that. I'm sure I have. Toni and I work together a lot.'

'What else do you do together?' I yell, snatching up his phone from the couch.

'For God's sake Clare, don't start that again.'

I scroll into his text messages and look for Toni. Chris sighs and walks to the kitchen.

'I'll dish up the Chinese,' he says.

I manically check his WhatsApp account and emails but there is no trace of Toni.

'You've deleted them,' I say accusingly. He walks back in and takes the phone from me. He scrolls into deleted items and hands it back.

'There's no fucking messages Clare, not to or from Toni. I'm not interested in Toni and she's not in the hell interested in me. She's got a boyfriend who adores her. Get a grip and for fuck's sake stop taking those bloody tranquilisers. They're messing with your head. Can't you see that? I can't deal with your jealousy again. I thought we were past all that.'

I drop the phone and burst into tears. Oh God, I feel so useless. I can't even puree vegetables for my child. I'm a neurotic drug-addicted mess and now my husband hates me.

'I'm so sorry Chris. I just ... I don't know what's happening. I feel so ...'

'You've got to get over this anxiety,' he says marching back into the kitchen.

I follow like a naughty child.

'I'm sure the pills make you worse,' he says.

'Dr Rawlins said I need to cut back.'

'Sounds like a good idea to me. Are you taking your other medication?'

I avoid his eyes.

He sighs.

'You should take it Clare. You might not need these bloody tranquillisers then.'

'I worry about Ben,' I say.

'Ben's fine.'

'I know I'm sorry, I overreact sometimes.'

'It's got to stop Clare. The only reason ...' he begins but the sound of the doorbell stops him.

'Can you get that?'

He nods and walks back into the living room. Seconds later he calls me.

'Clare, can you come in. It's the police.'

I feel myself turn cold. Why would the police be here?

'Hello,' I say coming in to the living room.

The policeman smiles and I relax.

'They want to ask you a few questions,' says Chris. 'It's about the nursery.'

'Oh, is everything okay?'

The policeman sniffs appreciatively.

'Dinner smells nice,' he comments.

'It's just a takeaway,' I say.

Now even the police know I'm a lousy cook and housewife.

'It was about the flood at the nursery. There's no sign of a break in. Nothing was taken. But there was a lot of damage so the nursery reported it.'

'Oh,' I say. 'That's ridiculous. Why would someone do that?'

'You tell me. Some people have a funny idea of fun,' he smiles.

'Quite,' says Chris.

For a moment he sounds like Tom.

'They wanted to check we still had our key, as we're official key holders,' says Chris.

'Yes, it's in my bag.'

'Do you always keep it with you?' asks the police officer. 'You haven't lost it at all?'

I hesitate. The truth is I'd stumbled on them this evening. I'd spilt some fruit juice and found them under the couch when cleaning up. But if I tell him that, he'll think I'm irresponsible with them. I don't want that getting back to the nursery.

'Yes, they're always in my bag.'

It's not a lie. They usually are. I don't know how they got under the couch.

'Can I ask why you're a key holder?'

'Our boy goes there twice a week and Clare helps out on a Wednesday morning. We're one of the closest parents so if the place needed opening in an emergency we could do it.'

'I see. That's great, thanks. Well if you should remember anything. Someone you've seen hanging around the place.'

'Do you think they're dangerous?' I ask before I can stop myself.

Chris shoots me a look.

'No, don't you worry Mrs Ryan. It's nothing like that. Thanks for your time.'

Chris sees him out and I finish dishing up the dinner.

'How did your appraisal go?' Chris asks coming up behind me.

He's trying to sound upbeat but I can hear the weariness in his voice and hate myself.

'Geoff offered me more hours,' I say, taking the wine from the fridge.

'He did?'

'Yes, I think it might be worth it but I'm not sure. I said I'd need to talk to you about it.'

He takes the plates and puts them on to the table. I take Ben's food from the microwave and feel consumed with guilt. I should have pureed something. Just some potato and greens would have been okay, but instead I test the processed carrot mix on my tongue.

'Would we have to pay more at the nursery?' he asks.

'Sharni has offered to look after Ben.'

'When did she do that?'

'When I picked Ben up, she asked about the appraisal and I told her I had been offered extra hours.'

'That's nice of her but what about her job?' Chris says as he holds a spoonful of carrot stew to Ben's mouth.

'She said it's not a problem.'

He looks thoughtful.

'I guess it's up to you but it sounds perfect. We could save a lot of money.'

I hand him the envelope with the photos. The Chinese is greasy. I must make more effort with the cooking. I'll do an internet shop later. I'll order plenty of veg and ask Chris to dig out the blender from the top cupboard.

'God, she's good isn't she?' he says sifting through the pictures. 'We'll have to get some frames.'

'I'm going to Ikea with Helen, I'll get some there.'

He smiles and I feel safe again. I'll take the extra hours and ask Sharni how much she'll charge. I'll cut back on the diazepam tomorrow. While Chris washes up I check how many I have left. I decide to start keeping a note on how many I take.

'Geoff asked if we were going to the Christmas party,' I call.

'Are we?'

'I'd like to.'

'Let's go then.'

I hug Ben. Everything is going to be okay.

'She believed me,' she said. Her voice was accusing but she didn't care.

Leah met her eyes but didn't speak. She reached for her glass of water. She sipped slowly and then said,

'She knew me better than anyone. I don't hallucinate. I don't see things that aren't there.'

Leah nodded.

'You were unconscious when the ambulance arrived though,' she said carefully. 'We sometimes make up things in order to make sense of them.'

She laughed and realised she sounded slightly hysterical. She sipped more water and then pulled her pills from her bag.

'Are you taking them regularly?' asked Leah.

'Only when I feel tense,' she said, swallowing two.

'Are you feeling tense now?'

She was feeling angry. Angry with everyone but she was particularly angry with him. He of all people should have believed her.

'I'm angry,' she said.

'How did you feel knowing your mother believed you?'

'It felt like I was finally understood, like I was being treated like a normal person instead of a nutcase. I felt like I was banging my head against a wall. I was telling them, telling all of them what happened and they looked at me as if I was a crazy woman. But I wasn't. It was all so clear. I didn't imagine it ...'

The tears came like a torrent, like they always did. Would she ever get past this? Why was she still banging her head against a wall? What was the point?

'Let's take a little break,' said Leah.

Chapter Eleven

'Christ, I needed this day off,' says Helen, lighting another cigarette. 'I'm not so sure Ikea is a great way to relax on my day off though.'

I laugh. I'm feeling happy.

'How do you think you'll find doing those extra hours next week? That little group is hellish let me tell you. I get them on a bloody Wednesday.'

'I'm looking forward to it,' I say.

Sharni had been delighted to have Ben and refused to take a penny. She said she'd be insulted if I paid her. We're friends, she'd said. It doesn't seem like two weeks since Sharni and Tom moved in next door. It feels as though they've been there forever.

'They're great aren't they?' Chris had said this morning. Chris and Tom were playing badminton after work. I can't remember the last time Chris played badminton. Tom and Sharni are the first real friends we've had since ... I shake the thoughts from my mind and fumble for the diazepam. I stop myself in time and see Helen looking at me.

'We should go back to the fray,' she says, nodding to the

entrance of Ikea.

I smile and check Ben is still asleep under his covers.

'I just need Christmas decs and a few other bits and then we can have Swedish meatballs and chips from the restaurant,' she laughs.

Ben cries softly and I give him a big smile. Faye had been great about me taking Ben out of the nursery and had promptly asked for the keys back. Only parents could be key holders she explained.

'I need to get photo frames. Sharni took some brilliant photos of Ben,' I say enthusiastically.

'Oh yeah, I looked her up. She is on Facebook. I requested friendship but she hasn't accepted. She's got a brilliant web page. It's all photos mind you, nothing else,' says Helen as she throws some Christmas baubles into the trolley.

My heart races and I clutch the handlebars of the stroller.

'She hasn't got photos of Ben on there has she?'

Helen gawps at me.

'Of course not, they're all fashion shoots. Let's get your frames, worry guts.'

I throw some Christmas cards into the trolley.

'Why don't you come over on Saturday?' I say. 'We're reciprocating Sharni and Tom. It'd be lovely if you could. Just a little drinks party.'

She pulls a black diary from her handbag.

'Let's see if I can squeeze you in,' she laughs.

We make our way through the fragrant smelling candle department and my eyes land on a vase. Helen follows my gaze and pulls a face.

'Didn't you get yours back then?'

'No, not yet, anyway, but I'm sure we will.'

Helen tuts.

'I reckon she's lost it. Ooh, I must get some Christmas

candles.'

Surely if Sharni had lost the vase she'd own up. She'd know I'd ask for it eventually. I feel a pang of uncertainty about asking her now. I don't want to rock the boat, especially now she has agreed to have Ben for nothing. Chris and I could barely believe our luck. We'd both figured she'd ask for something.

'She's going to have Ben for me on my teaching days,' I say, looking at the candles. 'I asked her this morning.'

'What! What about the nursery?'

'This is Ben's last week at the nursery. Sharni will do it for nothing, so I'll be saving money too.'

Helen scoffs.

'What about her job?'

I shrug.

'She said it wouldn't be a problem.'

'Huh, I think I'd be suspicious of a woman who offers to have my kid for nothing. It's bloody hard work isn't it? That's why nurseries charge so much.'

I take a deep breath.

'She's had him before,' I say but as usual I sound feeble.

The strong fragrance from the candles is making my head ache.

'I'm sorry Clare. Don't listen to me. I've never had bloody kids and never will. Ben's cute and all that but I just can't understand anyone volunteering to look after one. Anyway, Saturday's fine. I've got this new fella. If I'm still with him can I bring him along?'

'Yes, of course. That would be great. I'm going to make Melba toast.'

'Fucking hell. It's worth coming for that.'

We laugh and I follow her to the cafeteria. I'll pop into Sharni on the way home and ask for the vase. I'm sure she won't mind.

'Oh hi again,' Sharni says.

She's surprised to see me. Her hair has been cut. Her long brown hair is in a bob, similar to mine.

'Your hair looks different,' I say.

'Do you like it? I thought your style was so tidy. Mine was such a wreck.'

She leans down to Ben.

'Hello, Sweet Pea.'

Ben smiles and reaches up to her.

'I liked your hair,' I say.

'Ditto,' she laughs. 'Do you want to come in for a coffee?'

I point to my Ikea bags.

'Helen and I went to Ikea. Both Ben and I are knackered.'

'God, you're brave. I never go to Ikea.'

I can smell paint and sneak a look behind her.

'I've been painting the kitchen. I know we looked at that great wallpaper but ... Anyway come and have a quick look. Tell me what you think.'

'Okay,' I say, scooping Ben out of the stroller.

When she said 'I've been painting,' I, of course, thought that was what she meant. I stop in surprise at the sight of a hunky blond Adonis wielding a paintbrush.

'Oh,' I say.

'Hello,' he smiles.

The wall is the same colour as ours. In fact if it weren't for the Aga and new kitchen table, it could easily have been our kitchen.

'Sorry, did you think I was doing it? I'm giving out the orders. This is Jack. If you ever need a painter I can recommend him, he's the best. Are you sure you don't want a coffee? I'm just about to make one.'

'I'm fine, really. You've gone for the same colour as ...'

'Yes, I couldn't think of a better one,' she says casually.

Ben reaches his arms out to her and she looks at me.

'Is it okay?'

Before I can reply she has picked him up.

'Hello darling,' she croons.

I fumble in my handbag for my keys, breaking a nail in the process.

'Damn.'

'Everything okay?' asks Sharni.

'This damn handbag, I can never find anything in it. I can't find my keys now.'

'I'm sure they're there. But you know if you ever do get shut out you can always come in here. There's a spare key under an old paint tin in the garden. That's how Jack gets in if I'm not around.'

I pull out my keys and sigh with relief.

'Actually I'll use your loo if that's okay. I've been holding it forever.'

'Yeah, of course, you know where it is.'

I can't believe I haven't asked for the vase. The idea of knocking had been to ask Sharni for that. But the whole thing seems so petty somehow. Maybe Chris can ask Tom. Then again I don't really want Chris to know that we still haven't had it back. He's no doubt forgotten about it too. I pass the master bedroom and my eye catches something familiar. It's the bedside lamp, there's something about it. I tap the door gently and it swings open. I clap my hand over my mouth and stifle a gasp. I feel my legs go weak at the knees and I have to hold on to the door handle to support myself. The bedroom is identical to ours.

'Slow down, you're talking too fast,' says Chris with a sigh.

'It was *our* bedroom in their house!'

'What do you mean *our* bedroom?' he laughs.

'Everything, everything was the same. They had the same bed as ours. The bed covering was the same. That cream set I bought in Ikea but Sharni said she never goes to Ikea. The bedside cabinets were identical and even the lamps. Oh, and she's reading the same book as me, *The Lovely Bones*.'

'Christ, is that a book title?'

'Chris,' I shout and then lower my voice when I realise Sharni and Tom might hear us through the wall.

'It's not a crime, Clare. She thinks you've got great taste.'

I clench my hands.

'We've never discussed books.'

He rubs his chin.

'You may have done. Perhaps you've forgotten.'

I feel sure Sharni and I have never talked about books.

'Isn't it a bit odd though? She's even having the kitchen painted the same colour.'

'She's never even seen our bedroom has she? So, it's obviously her just following your advice. You seem to have a lot in common with her.'

I struggle to remember when Sharni had been upstairs.

'She had our key that day,' I say shakily. 'That day of the flood at the nursery, I gave her my key.'

Oh God, I'm sounding paranoid again. I go into the kitchen as calmly as I can and open my little notebook. I check my diazepam intake and sigh with relief. I can take another one.

'You're not going to take more of those are you?' says Chris from behind me. 'It's not a big deal Clare.'

'She must have gone into our bedroom the day I gave her the key,' I say feeling a chill run down my spine.

'Oh come on Clare. Are you saying she's recreated our

bedroom in that short time? They've only been here just over two weeks.'

'Well ... I ...' I say flustered.

'Are you sure it was exactly the same?'

'The bed linen and ...'

'It's from Ikea, thousands of people go to Ikea, Clare and ...'

'But she said she didn't go to Ikea,' I argue.

'For Christ's sake, there are loads of cream duvet covers. It's not that odd and I'm sure the bed is not identical either.'

'Not identical,' I say, beginning to feel stupid.

Now I think back there were some things that were slightly different. Maybe the cream duvet cover wasn't exactly the same.

'Get some perspective Clare. You should be flattered,' he says tiredly. 'One minute you've got no self-esteem and the next minute you've got someone looking up to you in this way and you're still anxious. Perhaps she lacks confidence in house decorating.'

I open my mouth to argue but feel somehow deflated. I try to remember if I'd said I was reading *The Lovely Bones*. I decide not to tell him about Sharni's haircut as I know he wouldn't understand.

'I was going to ask about the vase,' I say and wait for his reaction.

'What vase?'

'The one we lent her.'

He looks surprised.

'I thought she'd given that back.'

I shake my head.

'We'll ask her on Saturday about the vase and their bedroom if you like. What were you doing in their bedroom anyway?'

'I just happened to see,' I say blushing.

He pulls me into his arms and I sniff his jumper. The warm smell of Aqua De Parma washes over me.

'Everything is going really well Clare. You need to calm down. You have a new friend. Extra hours at work and we're going to save some money. We've got a bit more of a social life and Ben is thriving. We're going to have a brilliant Christmas. We've got your school party. Most importantly you're getting off the diazepam and sleeping pills.'

I snuggle into the warmth of him.

'Sharni invited us for Christmas,' I mumble into his jumper.

'Yes, Tom mentioned it. I'd rather have Christmas Day just the three of us, wouldn't you?'

I nod happily.

'Let's see how we feel. We could always pop in for a drink Christmas evening.'

I look up at him.

'You think it is okay for Sharni to still have Ben.'

He laughs.

'Clare, come on. Decorating a bedroom like ours doesn't make her a child molester does it?'

I shrug.

'We'll ask her on Saturday. I'm sure she didn't do it to upset you.'

'Okay,' I agree.

'We'll also ask what she's done with that bloody vase.'

Sometimes she wondered if her mind had played tricks. It would be easier to believe that. At least she could move on if she did. There would be some kind of closure.

'You're right,' she could agree. 'I imagined it. Most likely the shock caused it.'

And some days she did wonder. Had she imagined it? Could she have been hallucinating? Was everyone right and she wrong?

But, no ... she knew. They could try as hard as they liked to make her think otherwise. She had been there and she knew.

'Of course you know dear,' said her mother. 'They should believe you. He should believe you too.'

Tears sprang to her eyes. Christ, would this ever stop? She thought. Is this bloody therapy helping at all?

'I didn't imagine it.'

Leah didn't reply.

'You don't believe me either.'

'Do you feel guilty about what happened?'

She laughed.

'What do you think? Of course I do. The guilt is killing me.'

But I didn't make it up.

'But supposing someone else did the bad thing? Wouldn't that make you less guilty?'

'I'm guilty. I don't deny that. I should have left before it got dark.'

'Shall we talk about that? Why you didn't leave?'

'It won't change anything,' she said flatly.

She knew she couldn't go back and fix things. But she could go forward and just possibly put things right.

'It's important for you to accept what happened? The truth of what happened.'

How dare she tell her what was the truth, she thought angrily? She was the only one who knew what the truth was.

'You need to reclaim your life.'

She stared at the tissue box. It occurred to her for the first time that it might be easier to give in. To give up the fight and do as they say.

'I miss him,' she said simply.

'Of course,' Leah said sympathetically.

She looked at the clock on the wall. Ten more minutes and she could leave. She'd have stayed the full hour.

Chapter Twelve

Sharni waves at me from her place on the floor. She'd talked me into a Pilates class. I'm not sure it's my thing but Sharni assures me it's the best way to get my core muscles in shape.

'It's brilliant for toning up any flabbiness.'

My feelings must have shown because she'd quickly added, 'I'm not insinuating you're flabby or anything.'

But I'd become acutely aware of my pear-shaped body. Chris had always said I was cuddly but I don't think that is very complimentary. I wave back to Sharni and try not to look at her perfectly toned body. I wish I could stop comparing myself to her. It's not like she's glamorous or anything, especially with her dark-rimmed glasses, but she does have an air about her that I don't have. I look down at my chubby thighs in the black leotard and sigh. It's freezing in the Methodist church hall too. I can't think what Sharni likes about it. I yearn for the peacefulness and warmth of my little living room.

Cheryl, the teacher, barks orders to us, saying we should 'focus on our breathing' and 'pull our muscles in'. I'm dying for a pee and the cold hall isn't helping.

'Focus on the breath,' she orders.

Sharni smiles from across the room. There's something odd in the way she smiles at me but I can't put my finger on what it is. She turns away and laughs at something the woman next to her is saying and then I realise. When she laughs with other people the smile reaches her eyes, but when she smiles with me it's as though her eyes are dead. I shake my head in irritation. What a stupid thought.

'Keep those knees straight, Clare,' orders Cheryl.

I strain to see the side room where the crèche is being held. I'm sure I would have heard Ben if he was unhappy. There is a pause in the session and Sharni tells me that she will check on him. I nod. I would check on him myself but Cheryl is pulling at my leg.

'Breathe slowly Clare, I've noticed you have a tendency to shallow breathe,' says Cheryl. I feel the stares of the other women and become more self-conscious about my pear-shaped body. Why do they all have to have perfect flat stomachs and slim thighs?

I look at my reflection in the mirror. My blonde streaked hair is messy from the exercise. I drag a brush through it and dab some blusher on to my cheeks. I pull my jumper over my tummy and sigh. I need to lose some weight. I must start cooking some proper meals. It's just so difficult with Ben and work. When I'm not teaching I'm preparing lesson plans. There never seems to be enough hours in the day. There's going to be even less time when I start the new hours.

'Shall we get a coffee in Costa?' Sharni asks with a smile.

I realise I am right about her smile. It really doesn't meet her eyes at least not when she smiles at me. I pull my hair back and secure it in a band.

'Don't you have work to do?' I ask.

'I've got a meeting in town at two, so I've got plenty of time,' she says, taking the stroller from me.

I think of the lesson planning that awaits me.

'Just a quick one,' I say.

Costa is quiet and we find a table easily. I decide to let Sharni get the drinks this time. At least I can keep a close eye on Ben.

'Do you want a cake or anything?' she asks.

Before I can answer she says,

'I'll get a chocolate brownie, they're lush in here,' and she hurries to the counter. My thighs hurt from the stretching and I groan as I lift Ben out of the stroller. Sharni returns with the coffee and brownies.

'I should try and lose some weight,' I say, tying Ben's bib and handing him his beaker.

'Really?' she asks. 'Did Chris say something?'

'Chris?'

'It's just he mentioned that you might like Pilates.'

'He did?' I say surprised.

'Not to me,' she laughs.

I study her eyes. There's no sparkle there. Maybe there wasn't a sparkle when she laughed with the other woman. I could have imagined it.

'Tom mentioned that I go to Pilates and Chris said you might like it because you wanted to tone up,' she says, peeling a banana for Ben.

'Oh,' I say.

It's not like Chris to say something like that. I have mentioned wanting to lose a bit of weight and needing to tone up but he'd always said I looked fine as I was.

'It's not good to carry too much extra weight,' says Sharni, taking a bite from her chocolate brownie. 'Chris is very fit isn't he?'

I stare at her.

'Fit as in healthy fit,' she smiles.

I nod.

'He likes to exercise,' I say.

'Yeah, so does Tom. Well, I do too. It's not good to let yourself go.'

I look down at the brownie. Is she trying to say that's what I've done? Is that what Chris has said?

'It's difficult to find time for exercise with Ben,' I say and hate that I sound so feeble.

'I'll always have him if you want to go for a run.'

I really can't imagine me pounding the streets of London with my flabby bits flopping all over the place. I push the brownie to one side.

'You're coming to Pilates, that's a start,' she says before I can reply.

'I ought to get back,' I say, standing up. 'I've got tons of lesson plans to do.'

She checks the time on her phone.

'Yes, I should get going too. I need to shower before my meeting.'

She kisses Ben on the cheek and hugs him tightly.

'Ooh, what to get you for Christmas.'

'You don't have to get him anything.'

'You can't come round Christmas Day and we not have presents for Ben.'

Shit. I thought Chris was going to have a word with Tom about Christmas Day.

'The thing is ...' I begin.

'I'd better fly,' she says.

She wraps a scarf around her neck and looks up and again I get that feeling that I have met her before.

'Sometimes you look familiar,' I say without thinking.

'I do?' she says, grabbing her bag. 'I guess there are a lot of women like me, brown haired with glasses.'

She pulls her satchel bag over her shoulder and I see what she means. She is quite plain and not at all eye catching. Perhaps Chris is right. Maybe she does lack confidence. I should be flattered that she thinks I have good taste with interior design.

'Do you need help on Saturday?' she asks.

Oh no, that's the last thing I want.

'No, everything's in hand.'

She nods.

'Shall we go,' she says and before I can stop her she has grabbed the stroller. We reach the door and one of the waitresses goes to open it, kneeling down to pinch Ben's cheek as she does so.

'He's so gorgeous,' she says looking at Sharni.

'Thanks,' she smiles.

'How old is he?'

I open my mouth but Sharni says, 'almost two.'

'He's a credit,' says the girl, opening the door.

'He is,' smiles Sharni and this time the smile reaches her eyes.

Chapter Thirteen

I check the notebook again and then recount the pills. It doesn't make sense. I'd been really careful. I know I have. I curse silently. I'm so uptight about this evening. I really needed something to calm me down. My heart has been racing for hours. Just one would help. I know I'd got upset about Sharni's bedroom but I'm certain I didn't take any that evening. Chris had talked me out of it. I lock the bathroom door and guiltily empty the cabinet but there's nothing. I count them again and then with trembling hands grab my phone and google 'diazepam and memory loss'.

You could experience amnesia when taking this medicine in high doses.

I stare in horror at the bottle. Had I been forgetting to write it down? I take one and swallow it with water from the tap. I can't entertain in this state. I write it shakily in the book and date it. I must remember to put the date in future. I push the bottle to the back of the cabinet. I'll make an appointment with Dr Rawlins. He's very understanding. Maybe I need something else to keep the anxiety under control. I look at myself in the mirror and then pull out my make-up bag. There are dark circles under my eyes and my complexion is dull.

'Do you want a glass of Prosecco?' calls Chris. 'I've just opened a bottle to get us in the party mood.'

One glass won't hurt. At least I'll be relaxed when they arrive.

'Great,' I call back. 'I'm just doing my hair.'

I wonder if Chris will notice Sharni's new hairstyle. I spray dry shampoo on to mine to give it a lift and then put on my make-up. Chris tries the door and I groan when I remember I had locked it.

'Sorry,' I mumble.

'Why are you locking the door?' he asks.

'Force of habit,' I say, taking the Prosecco.

'You look nice,' he says kissing me on the cheek.

'You don't think I'm fat do you?'

He looks surprised.

'Fat, no of course not. I like a woman with a bit of meat on her.'

'So, you do think I'm fat?'

'No, you're fine.'

I sigh.

'Is Ben okay?'

'No, he won't go down, at least not with me. Is there anything else I can do?'

I shake my head.

'The table looks great,' he adds, kissing me. 'Well done.'

'The Melba toasts aren't as good as Sharni's,' I say. 'Do you think I should take those off the table?'

'Of course not. Honestly you women,' he says, hurrying down the hall. 'Ben's screaming. Don't be long will you?'

I throw back the Prosecco and take a look at myself in the mirror. I look half dead. I'd been undecided about what to wear.

It had occurred to me to wear the new dress I'd bought with Sharni but decide to wear my black cocktail dress instead, with a red shawl to brighten it up. That might help my sallow complexion.

'This is bloody impressive,' says Helen, saluting me. 'I couldn't do this to save my life.'

She smells of tobacco and Body Shop's *White Musk*. Chris takes her coat and I offer her a mini salmon quiche.

'Wine or Prosecco?' Chris asks.

'Ooh Prosecco, darling, what else?'

'Where's your new fella?' I ask.

'Ah,' she laughs. 'That didn't work out.'

She looks at the new photos on the wall and I feel myself swell with pride.

'They're good,' she says, taking a closer look.

'Our neighbour, Sharni, took them,' says Chris proudly.

'Yeah, I've heard about her. The neighbour from heaven isn't she? Will she come with a halo tonight?'

'Helen,' I reprimand.

'That's your teacher voice,' she laughs.

'What do you mean?' asks Chris. I can almost see the hairs prickle on the back of his neck.

'Well, she is a bit perfect isn't she?' says Helen. 'Aside from giving you your bloody vase back.'

'Helen's just envious because she'll never be the neighbour from heaven,' I laugh, attempting to ease the tension.

'The neighbour from hell, that's me.'

'Well, we're going to ask about the vase tonight,' says Chris, forcing a smile.

'Where's Ben?' asks Helen, settling herself on the couch.

'In bed and I hope he sleeps through,' I say. 'I'm knackered.'

'I'm still getting over our Ikea trip. Those frames look good though.'

There's a light tap at the front door.

'That'll be Sharni and Tom.'

Butterflies flutter in my stomach and I realise that I'm nervous, and even slightly intimidated by Sharni.

'Come on in,' I hear Chris say.

Helen stands up and we both wait expectantly. I can't imagine how silly we look. It's not like royalty have just arrived. Sharni strolls in and the smell of her perfume reminds me that I had forgotten to put mine on. Just as well because I was going to put on *Grapefruit* too. Hers doesn't smell in the least old. Chris takes her coat and I have to fight back a gasp. She's wearing my flowery chiffon dress and the lemon cardigan. What's even worse is that she looks spectacular in them. Long dangling earrings complement the look. She smiles at me. I can't believe she is wearing that dress. How could she? I stupidly feel like crying. I'll never be able to wear it now without thinking of Sharni.

'I hope you don't mind,' she says.

'No, of course not,' I say, my voice emotionless.

The dress that once felt special now feels pointless and extravagant.

Her new bob is glossy. She looks different somehow. The new hairstyle seems to have changed the shape of her face. The diazepam hasn't kicked in as much as I'd have liked and my palms feel sweaty. Why would Sharni buy the same dress? I consider taking another diazepam to calm myself down. After all, one more won't hurt.

'This looks beautiful,' says Sharni, looking at the table. She kisses me and envelopes me in the warmth of her scent.

'Thanks for inviting us,' says Tom, handing me a bunch of flowers.

'That's so kind,' says Chris.

'Hello,' Sharni says to Helen. 'I think we met in Marks.'

'Good memory,' Helen nods while taking a Melba toast. 'I've been admiring your photos of Ben.'

Sharni looks at the walls and a smile beams across her face.

'They look terrific in those frames.'

'Let's get you both a drink,' says Chris.

'If you'll excuse me,' I say hurrying to the kitchen with the flowers. I lay them in the sink and dash upstairs to check on Ben. He's sleeping soundly and I sigh with relief. One more diazepam won't hurt. I lock the bathroom door and sniff under my armpits. I'm so hot and my palms are sweatier than ever. I take a pill from the bottle and swallow it, reminding myself that I must write it in the notebook before I go to bed.

'Clare made them. I think it's the first time she has,' Chris is saying as I walk back into the room.

'We were just complimenting you on the toasts,' says Tom, patting me on the shoulder.

I try not to glare at Chris. He didn't have to tell them it was the first time I'd made them. I refill my glass.

'I had a bit of time to spare,' I say.

'I hear you're going to be looking after Ben when Clare teaches,' says Helen.

'Yes, I'm looking forward to it,' replies Sharni.

Helen bites into a Melba toast.

'These are bloody good,' she grins.

I'm beginning to wish I hadn't made them.

'So, you don't work full-time as a photographer then?' Helen asks. She has a glint in her eye and I try to give her a warning look.

'I work from home,' says Sharni, before sipping her Prosecco. 'Ben is no trouble.'

'It's very good of you. I said to Clare, not many women would have another woman's child free of charge.'

'What are friends for but to help out?' smiles Sharni.

'As long as you don't take on too much,' Tom says, kissing her on the forehead. Helen raises her eyebrows and then holds out her glass to Chris.

'I've got some chilli on the stove,' I say more hurriedly than I meant. Why doesn't the damn diazepam kick in. 'I'll bring it in. Chris, can you get the nachos?'

'I can do that,' Sharni says.

'Heaven,' mutters Helen and I give her a scathing look.

I must tell Chris not to give her any more Prosecco.

'Personally I think social media is a bloody waste of everyone's time,' slurs Helen. 'I don't get what Instagram is all about except for all the narcissists to show off. What's your take on Instagram Sharni? You're a photographer after all.'

'I'm not on Instagram,' smiles Sharni.

'You're on Facebook though,' says Helen quickly.

'You'll never get me on Facebook,' says Tom.

'Nor me,' agrees Chris.

'I barely go on it,' smiles Sharni.

'Ah, I wondered,' says Helen blatantly. 'I sent you a friend request.'

'Oh really,' says Sharni warmly. 'I'll have to take a look.'

'I'll get the dessert,' I say.

'You ought to put those flowers in water,' winks Helen.

'Let me help,' says Sharni.

'It's okay, you relax.'

I want to snap I don't need any help.

There's a hiccup from the baby monitor and I use that as an excuse to go upstairs. Ben is still sleeping and I hesitate outside the bathroom door. I shouldn't take another diazepam. I'm obviously taking too many if they're not working.

'If you're not going then I will. I'm dying for a pee,' says Helen from behind me.

'Helen, what are you up to?'

'What do you mean? I'm not up to anything.'

'I feel like you're baiting Sharni.'

'Well, she's too good to be true if you ask me and what's she doing with your hairstyle. Jesus, she'll have your husband next.'

I feel like she has slapped me and I reel backwards.

'Don't be ridiculous.'

'I'd ask for the bloody vase if I were you.'

She closes the bathroom door and I stand transfixed for a few moments. I take a deep breath and go back downstairs.

'I'll put the flowers in water, can you get a vase Chris,' I say pointedly and nod towards Sharni while fighting the annoyance that threatens to overwhelm me. Chris frowns at me but turns to Sharni and says nonchalantly,

'Ah, Sharni, now you and Tom have the house a bit straight would it be okay to have our vase back, or do you still need it?'

Helen nudges me as she walks into the room.

'I gave Clare the vase,' Sharni says simply, looking directly at me. I prickle under her stare.

'Oh, well there you go then,' says Helen. 'Why don't you put the flowers in that?'

I grab a bottle of wine and empty the contents into my glass. I know I shouldn't drink any more, not with the diazepam but I'm finding the whole evening a big strain.

'I don't think you did Sharni,' I say, throwing back the wine. 'I'd have remembered. It's a special vase.'

The air is now thick with tension.

'Well, someone's got it wrong,' says Helen.

'I came round with it Clare, don't you remember? I was a bit late bringing it back, I apologised for that. You were having trouble with your washing machine at the time.'

I remember that. The water wouldn't drain and I was getting irritated because the door wouldn't open. I'd gone to find a screwdriver when I'd heard the doorbell. Sharni had stood with a packet in her hand. I'm sure that was all she had in her hand. Surely I would have remembered if she was holding a vase.

'The postman knocked but you obviously didn't hear him,' she'd smiled. I'm certain there was only a package in her hand. It had been the book Chris had ordered from Amazon.

'I remember you brought a package,' I say.

Sharni holds my gaze.

'I gave you the vase and you put it under the sink,' she insists.

'Let's get it then,' says Helen as she marches into the kitchen.

'Clare ...' says Chris, laying his hand on my arm. I shrug it off and follow Helen into the kitchen. I wouldn't have put it under the sink. It's a special vase. I always put it on the top shelf on the Welsh dresser. Chris knows that.

'I wouldn't have put it in the cupboard under the sink,' I hiss.

'Perhaps you were in a rush,' he says.

'You don't believe me?'

I realised I've raised my voice and feel my face grow hot. Helen rummages in the cupboard while Sharni stands with her arms folded. I throw back the rest of the wine in my glass and say,

'I wouldn't bother Helen, it isn't ...' But I'm stopped as her arm is pulled back and she holds up the vase, the colourful hand-painted vase from Ireland. I fight back a gasp.

'Is this it?' she asks, her cheeks red. 'It was in a carrier bag'

'But ...' I begin.

Helen hands me the vase.

'Can I go out the back for a smoke?' she asks.

'Sure,' says Chris as he nods to the back door.

'I'll join you,' says Tom.

Sharni and Chris look at me. The door slams and I watch Helen offer Tom a cigarette. My shoulders are hunched and I feel an ache in my neck.

'I didn't know Tom smoked,' I say to break the awkwardness of the moment.

Chris opens the fridge and grabs a bottle of wine that is chilling. He tops up our glasses and says, 'I think I'll join the smokers. I could do with some air.'

Sharni watches him leave and throws back some of the wine.

'Tom and I had a bit of an upset some years back. We almost broke up in fact. We found different ways to cope. Tom took up smoking and I gave myself the luxury of a breakdown.'

I clench my hands.

'I'm so sorry.'

She shrugs.

'It's past.'

She nods at the vase.

'I'm sorry about the vase mix-up. I don't know why you don't remember.'

'I get anxious,' I say. 'I ... I lost a child and ever since ...'

Tears fill my eyes and I grab some kitchen towel. I don't know why I'm telling Sharni this.

'I'm sorry Clare, when did that happen?' she asks, looking genuinely surprised.

I avoid her question and say with a smile, 'Anyway, I have Ben now.'

'Yes, you do,' she says, and the emotion disappears from her face. Her tone is hard and almost resentful. I feel myself shiver.

'If there's anything I can do ...' she adds as she puts her arm around me, but her embrace is stiff and I sense she is uncomfortable.

'They're coming in, why don't you go upstairs and freshen up. I'll make coffee,' she says removing her arm.

I nod and pull away. I go upstairs and check on Ben. I can't go on like this. It isn't fair on Ben. I'm forgetting too many things. I'll make an appointment to see the doctor first thing Monday. But I don't understand why I would put the vase under the sink. I just wouldn't do that.

Chapter Fourteen

'I really don't remember her returning it,' I say.

'Then how do you explain it being there?' Chris says throwing his shirt over a chair.

'I honestly don't think I would put it there,' I shrug.

'What are you saying Clare?'

I pull the duvet up and snuggle down in bed. The electric blanket is on and it's cosy and warm. I could feel really relaxed if only I didn't have this niggle in my head.

'I don't know. I only know I would have put it on the dresser if I had it. It's too special to be pushed under the sink. I remember her coming round and I remember her bringing a package that the postman couldn't get through the letterbox, but I don't remember the vase.'

'So you're saying she put it there when you weren't looking? She hid the vase under the sink and waited for us to ask for it so she could make you look stupid. Why would she want to do that?'

He pulls back the duvet and I shiver.

'Helen thinks she's a bit too good to be true,' I say in attempt to defend myself.

'Oh great,' he laughs, pulling me towards him. 'And we trust her opinion do we? Compared to Helen everyone is too good to be true.'

I snuggle into his chest.

'Did you know Tom smoked?' I ask.

'Yeah, he smokes after a game of badminton.'

His hand fondles my breast.

'Did you know their marriage nearly broke up?'

He shakes his head.

'That's why he started smoking. Sharni had a breakdown apparently,' I say.

He stops fondling and looks at me.

'What happened?'

'I don't know, she wouldn't say. Just that they had an upset and ... Do you think Tom had an affair? He's good looking isn't he? I can imagine the women chasing him.'

'We don't know what it was,' Chris sighs.

I stroke his thigh and say, 'I think I'd prefer Ben to stay at nursery. If they can't have him I can find another nursery. I think there is one ...'

He puts his hand over mine.

'Are you serious? You were all for Sharni having him.'

'I'm not sure about her,' I say lamely.

'You were dead keen to have her,' he reminds me.

'I know, but ...'

'For God's sake,' he says impatiently. 'This is all because you forgot she gave the vase back? What's wrong with you these days?'

I decide not to mention about the diazepam.

'I know, it's just that and the bedroom thing and ...'

'And what?'

'It's just the other day when we went for coffee she gave the waitress the impression that Ben was her child.'

His face clouds over.

'I'm sure you just imagined it.'

'Do you think?'

'You're always reading stuff into things.'

'Maybe.'

I can't mention her smile not reaching her eyes. He'll think I've totally lost the plot.

'This is ridiculous. We've got a chance to save some money and you're going to throw it all away because the woman admires you. I thought you'd be flattered. She looks up to you. I can't believe she copied the bedroom. It's not possible. She's taken those great photos and doesn't want anything in return. Honestly Clare, it's crazy what you're saying. She's a well-known photographer. She's got a big feature in *Vogue* this month, did she tell you that?'

I shake my head.

'Tom told me. You should buy it.'

'Are you happy for her to have Ben then?' I ask.

'Of course, I think they're a nice couple. You shouldn't listen to Helen, what does she know? She can't keep a bloke for five minutes.'

'Well ...' I hesitate.

I think of the chiffon dress in the wardrobe and sigh. It feels like Sharni has stolen that from me too. Is Helen right, will she steal my husband next?

'So, what do you want for our anniversary, aside from my body?' he says, putting his arms back around me.

I'd completely forgotten about our anniversary. I can't believe we've been married for seven years. It seems like only yesterday that Chris had chatted me up at Fenella's New Year Eve's party. I wonder what happened to Fenella? I suppose I could look her up on Facebook. Everyone seems to be on Facebook, even Sharni.

'A nice meal with you,' I say. 'We could get Kathryn to babysit.'

'Or ask Sharni. She'd probably do it for nothing.'

'We can't just use her Chris.'

His hand moves up my thigh and I shudder.

'Okay, but I can use you, can't I?'

I open my legs willingly and pull him closer.

Chapter Fifteen

Chris scrunched up the paper into a ball before aiming it at the bin across the room. The door to his office swung open as he did so and the ball hit Sharni on her chest as she entered.

'Oh,' she said. 'Was that a reject?'

'Hey,' he said.

He was taken aback to see Sharni. He hoped Clare was aware of the visit. He didn't want another scene with Clare over it.

'I hope it's okay for me to call in. The girl at reception said it was your lunch break,' she said shyly.

Chris noticed her hair was cut in a style similar to Clare's. It didn't somehow suit Sharni.

'Yeah, of course. Is everything okay?'

'Yes fine. I've just been to get some copies of *Vogue*.'

'How did you know where I worked?' he asked casually.

'Tom told me.'

'Oh right.'

'What do you think?' she asked, handing him a copy of the magazine.

'Clare would like to see a copy,' he said. He didn't know why he felt the need to mention Clare. He just wanted to remind Sharni that he was married for some reason. Clare's jealousy had made him paranoid too.

'She said it was your anniversary in three weeks. Seven years together.'

He didn't know whether to invite her to sit down or not.

'Yeah, a whole seven years. I would have got less for murder,' he smiled and then wondered if it sounded like a complaint.

'You know what they say about seven years,' she said tapping him on the arm.

'Oh right,' he said, realising what she meant.

'That's why I popped in to see you. I thought it would be nice to take some portraits of you with Ben, as a gift for Clare. Father and child photos are really popular these days; I think Clare would love it. I thought we could set a time when you are free and I've got Ben.'

'Do you think so? That sounds great, thanks Sharni.'

'Give me a text tomorrow when I've got my diary in front of me and we'll fix a time,' she said as she handed him her business card.

Toni tapped lightly on the door.

'Sorry to interrupt, but we have a meeting in three minutes.'

'I'm just off,' Sharni said as she moved towards the door.

'I thought she'd be more glamorous. I suppose because she takes fashion photos, you just expect that,' Toni said as she watched her walk down the corridor.

'Yeah,' said Chris, trying to sound disinterested. He really didn't want Sharni dropping into the office like that again. He'd never be able to make Clare understand there was nothing in it.

Chapter Sixteen

Helen wrapped a woollen scarf around her neck and pulled on a pair of matching gloves. Her eyes stung from the sharp wind.

'Christ, can it get any colder?' she grumbled.

'Hopefully we'll have a white Christmas,' Julia said, looking at the leaden sky.

'Who needs a bloody white Christmas?' moaned Helen as she rummaged in her bag for a packet of cigarettes.

'You're such a bah-humbug,' smiled Julia

'You music teachers are all the same,' laughed Helen. 'Full of good cheer and bloody awful carols.'

Julia grinned.

'I'll be glad when the term ends,' said Helen, blowing smoke from the corner of her mouth.

'I think that woman is waving at you,' said Julia, pointing across the road.

'Oh Christ, she's weird,' Helen groaned.

'Who is she?'

'Clare's neighbour. She looks after Clare's kid when she's teaching.'

'She's coming over.'

Helen stubbed out her cigarette.

'I'm glad I caught you,' said Sharni.

Helen struggled not to stare at Sharni's haircut. It was just too weird. Why would anyone copy someone else's hairstyle? She really doesn't understand why Clare puts up with it. She'd certainly never leave any kid of hers with this woman.

Julia pointed to a bus.

'That's mine,' she said. 'I'll see you tomorrow Helen.'

'Nice to have met you,' she smiled at Sharni before running for the bus.

'Well, it was nice seeing you,' said Helen, 'But I've got to hurry for a bus too.'

Sharni looked disappointed. 'I was hoping we could have a coffee,' she said.

Helen raised her eyebrows. She had no intention of having a coffee with Sharni.

'I wanted to talk to you about Clare.'

'What about Clare?' Helen said brusquely.

'It's her and Chris's anniversary soon. It's seven years and ...'

'So, you're going to get them both a medal?' Helen said scathingly.

Helen watched Sharni's lips tighten.

'No, actually I was going to arrange a little dinner party for them, at a nice restaurant in London. I thought I could ask some of her other closest friends to come as a surprise for her.'

'You want to arrange a dinner party for their anniversary?'

Helen sighed as her bus drove past. Shit, the next one isn't for another twenty minutes.

'Clare's not close friends with anyone, except me,' Helen said bluntly. 'I don't think she and Chris would appreciate a dinner party.'

'Oh Chris knows,' Sharni said gleefully.

Helen tried not to show her surprise. What was wrong with Chris? Too afraid of upsetting their great friends Tom and Sharni, she thought. Helen pulled her cigarettes from her bag.

'Couldn't we just discuss it over coffee?' asked Sharni.

'I'm not a great dinner party guest to be frank and I'm even worse at keeping secrets. It's probably best not to involve me.'

She lit her cigarette and threw her bag over her shoulder. A flash of anger again passed over Sharni's face.

'That's a shame,' she said.

'I'd better shoot,' said Helen. 'Thanks for thinking of me.'

Without giving Sharni a chance to reply Helen turned and walked away.

It was the last thing she wanted to talk about but she knew she couldn't put it off forever. There were no flowers today and the tissue box was Tesco's Value. It stupidly made her feel cheap. The tissues were thin. She grabbed two and dabbed at her watery eyes.

'I panicked,' she said.

She heard Leah's encouraging tone but all she could see was the bridge in the glare of her headlights. It had been raining heavily ever since she'd left her mother's. The rain was hammering on the windscreen. The wipers had made her dizzy with their incessant whirring. They seemed to make no difference. All she could see was a mist of rain. She should have left earlier. Why hadn't she? Any responsible person would have. She didn't think she'd ever feel good about herself again, unless ...

She clung to the thought. It gave her hope. It was surely possible. She would be alone though, with no one to support her.

'What's going through your mind?' Leah asked.

You don't want to know, she thought.

'Do you remember that moment?'

She nodded.

'I panicked,' she said flatly. 'And the car skidded.'

Leah didn't say anything.

'I was stupid,' she said, pulling out several tissues. Her hand knocked over the glass of water and the glass shattered on the floor. The sound made her jump and her neck jolted back.

'Oh God,' she sobbed. Like her recurring nightmare she felt the car go over the bridge again.

'I'll get a cloth,' said Leah.

Shards of glass lay scattered on the floor. Like the broken pieces of my life, she thought.

Chapter Seventeen

Chris pulls on his trainers and then rummages in the cupboard for his badminton racquet. I sigh as I put down the paper. I feel resentful. Sundays used to be our family day. We would read the Sunday papers in bed with Ben sleeping between us. Ever since Sharni and Tom moved in our weekends have changed. I push my feet into my slippers and shuffle to the kitchen to make another coffee.

'What are you going to do this morning?' Chris asks.

He feels guilty. I can tell by his face. He wants me to make things easy for him.

'I'll finish the papers,' I say. 'Then I might go to Oxford Street and do some Christmas shopping. Maybe I'll phone Helen, see what's she doing.'

He laughs, 'You'll be lucky if she's up.'

'Then I'll go on my own.'

'I'm sure Sharni would go with you.'

I fight the urge to roll my eyes.

'I'm sure she's got loads of work to do,' I say.

He glances at the *Vogue* magazine on the table.

'They're brilliant photos aren't they?'

I nod. The truth is I haven't looked at the magazine since Sharni dropped it in. I'm still annoyed with Sharni for making me feel stupid about the vase. I am sure she was purposely trying to make me doubt myself, but I don't know why. I am sure my memory isn't that bad, that I would forget her giving the vase back, especially as Chris and I went on about it so much.

'When are you seeing Dr Rawlins?' Chris asks, zipping up his holdall.

'Tomorrow, he's been on holiday for a week.'

'Good, tell him about your memory lapses.'

I want to argue that I don't have memory lapses but I bite my tongue. I sigh and dunk a digestive in my coffee.

'What time will you be back?'

He shrugs.

'About one, we usually go for a pint after.'

I pick up Ben and nuzzle him to my chest.

'Let's get ready, shall we?' I say kissing the top of his head.

The front door slams and I watch from the window as Chris climbs into Tom's Audi. I notice Sharni's car isn't there and wonder where she has gone. I dress Ben and throw on some warm clothes. Ten minutes later we're both kitted out in scarves and hats to face the cold weather.

I stop at the end of Sharni's driveway. Ben giggles and kicks off his blanket. I throw it back on and walk purposefully around to Sharni's back door. The kitchen blind is down. I tap on the door and wait. After a few minutes I hesitantly turn the handle. The door is locked. I feel my heart thump in my chest as I fumble under the old paint tin. I lift it carefully and see the key. I take it and with trembling hands turn it in the lock. The door creaks open and I nervously step inside.

Breakfast dishes are stacked in the sink and a cold cup of coffee sits on the worktop. I can smell Sharni's perfume in the air. It isn't *Grapefruit.* If she discovers I was here I'll say that I couldn't find my keys and that Ben was getting cold and that I felt sure that she and Tom wouldn't mind if Ben and I stayed warm. I step into the living room. Everything is neat and tidy. I peer out of the window and check that her car isn't there. I'm not sure what I'm looking for or why I felt the need to come in.

'Let's check out that bedroom,' I whisper to Ben.

I tiptoe stealthily up the stairs and past the small bedroom that is packed with boxes, and make my way to the master bedroom. I have to fight back a gasp as I open the door. On closer inspection I realise that the bed is different to ours but the duvet cover looks identical to mine. Even the cushions are arranged like ours. I place Ben on the floor and go to the bedside cabinet where her copy of *The Lovely Bones* sits. Next to it is a jar of night cream. I don't recognise the brand and it isn't one I use. It looks expensive. I put my hand on the drawer handle and hesitate. If Chris ever found out he'd go mental. I can almost hear his reprimand. *'What on earth did you think you were doing going through their stuff? Tom's a bloody lawyer. There may have been confidential papers there.'*

I remove my hand from the drawer and study the items on the dresser. There's a new bottle of *Jo Malone's Grapefruit*, still in its box. Why did Sharni say she had an old bottle? *The Lovely Bones* looks barely touched. I look again at the drawer, hesitate, and make myself leave the bedroom.

The door to the second bedroom is open. It's Sharni's work room. Photos are scattered over her desk with a laptop and printer to one side. Back copies of *Vogue* are piled on a bookcase. I glance through the window to check Sharni hasn't come back and then put Ben on the floor. Photos of Ben are lined up on the window sill. They are not the ones Sharni gave us. I study them intently. They seem to have been taken in Sharni's back garden. A narrow wardrobe stands opposite the desk and I open it gingerly and reel back in shock at the pile of baby clothes on the shelves. Below on another shelf are baby toys. My breath catches in my throat when I see a plain blue box marked *Nathan.* I'm about to open it but am stopped by the sound of a car on the gravel driveway. I close the wardrobe door and grab Ben. I hurry down the stairs, my heart banging against my chest. I fly out of the back door just as I hear the key turn in the lock. I quickly lock the door, shove the key under the paint tin and drop Ben into the stroller. A loud knock on the window makes me jump out of my skin. I turn to see Sharni smiling from the other side of the window and before I can think she has opened the door. Did she see me put the key back? I can hear my heart beating in my ears.

'Hi,' she says.

My mouth is so dry that I can barely speak.

'Hi,' I say breathlessly.

'I've just got back,' she says, looking at me intently.

She wants to know what I'm doing in her back garden. My original excuse has fled from my mind.

'Yes, I saw your car wasn't there. I just wondered if you had a hard brush. I almost slipped on the leaves on our path,' I say, but it sounds so bloody feeble. She surely doesn't believe me.

'There's one in the shed,' she says.

She opens the door and steps outside. She's still wearing her coat and I can smell her perfume. I wait while she gets the broom from the shed.

'Thanks,' I say, taking it from her. 'I'd better get on.'

'Do you want a coffee?'

'No, thanks, I'm meeting Helen in a bit,' I lie.

'Okay. I'll see Ben on Tuesday then?'

I nod. I feel my body trembling as I walk down the path. I wonder what Chris will say when I tell him about the baby clothes. I can't tell him I went into their house when they were out. I suddenly feel very alone. I don't feel anyone believes me, even Chris thinks I am losing it. I'll talk to Helen, but then I don't really know Helen that well. How did I get to be so isolated? Maybe I can say what I am feeling to Dr Rawlins but then he may think it's caused by the diazepam and that I'm just being delusional. Maybe I am.

I scroll into the contacts on my phone and call Helen.

'Do you fancy shopping in Oxford Street?' I ask.

'There's a table,' Helen says. We push our way to the one free table and I flop down gratefully.

'You'd think they were giving it away. Bloody Christmas,' says Helen, throwing her bags on to a spare chair. I clear the dirty coffee mugs and wipe over the table with a tissue. The place is packed with hungry Christmas shoppers.

'Just a drink?' she asks.

I nod. Ben is crying. He hasn't stopped for forty minutes and I feel like I could scream. I push a beaker of juice into his hands and encourage him to drink but he just spits it out angrily and bawls some more. I try rocking him to sleep but he's having none of it. Helen returns with two mugs of hot chocolate and grimaces.

'I don't know what's wrong with him,' I say.

'He's had enough of bloody Christmas shopping I reckon.'

I nod and lift him from the stroller. He screams for a bit longer and then relaxes in my arms his hand clutching my necklace.

'You want to be careful he doesn't break that,' says Helen.

'He often holds it,' I smile. 'I think it comforts him.'

'It's gorgeous, where did you get it?'

'Oh, it's a Celtic harp. I bought it years ago at an antique fair in London. It was a long time ago.'

'It's unusual. You don't want it to get broken.'

Ben hiccups softly and I stroke his hair.

'Are you all ready for Christmas?' asks Helen.

'I think so. I just need to get a sports top for Chris. I can't see anything that I think he'll like. But then I'm done. What about you?'

She makes a tutting sound.

'Me? What do I care about Christmas? I'm on my own anyway. Boxing Day I'm at my sister's but that's just bloody duty.'

'Why don't you come to us on Christmas Day?' I say impulsively. At least that way we can't go to Sharni's no matter how hard she tries. Helen widens her eyes in surprise.

'Don't you have family?'

I shake my head.

'Chris's family are in Canada and well ... I don't see mine.'

'How come?'

Helen's bluntness has always grated on me and today is no exception. After all, it isn't any of her business. I force a smile.

'There was a bit of a rift,' I say. 'And my mum ...' I trail off. It was too difficult to talk about.

'Oh I'm sorry, Clare, I hadn't realised.'

I shrug.

'Will you come then?'

'That's nice of you. Will it be okay with Chris? I don't want it to be too much for you.'

I laugh.

'We'll never get through a whole turkey just the two of us. No, do come, it will be lovely.'

'You're sure Chris won't want you all to himself?'

'No, he sees me all the time.'

'Sharni and Tom aren't going to be there are they?'

'Sharni and Tom?' I say surprised.

'You two seem very matey with them.'

I sip my hot chocolate.

'Not really.'

'Funny about your vase wasn't it?'

'I really don't remember her bringing it back but, you know, I do get anxious sometimes.'

'I didn't know that could affect your memory,' she says dryly.

'I saw her bedroom,' I say suddenly. 'It's almost identical to ours.'

Helen looks startled.

'You're kidding?'

It feels such a relief to be able to share it with someone and not feel I am the only one who thinks it odd.

'She also has the same lamp as us on her landing.'

'And your haircut,' adds Helen.

'And my perfume,' I say.

'Christ,' she exclaims. 'Not to mention your kid twice a week.'

My hand trembles and I put my mug down.

'Chris thinks I'm paranoid about her,' I confide. 'But I really don't think I want her to have Ben any more.'

'I don't blame you,' she agrees and I feel more confident about talking to Chris. 'There must be another nursery you can take him to. Have you asked about taking him back to his old one?'

'I could ask tomorrow,' I say feeling comforted that Helen also doesn't think I'm totally nuts. 'Chris says it's just because she admires me.'

'But she's a top photographer with a lawyer husband. I imagine they're not short of a bob or two either. Don't get me wrong, you're nice enough but what can she be coveting of yours that she doesn't already have herself?'

I meet Helen's eyes and we both look at Ben.

'Seems too crazy to be true,' says Helen finally.

I nod in agreement.

'Yes, I'm sure she just wants ideas for decorating the house, that's all.'

'Yeah,' agrees Helen but her expression says she doesn't think that's true.

'Anyway, there's no harm in checking out the nurseries is there?'

'None at all,' agrees Helen. 'We should get back, Chris will be wondering what's happened to you.'

I release Ben's hand from my necklace and settle him into the stroller. I'll talk to Chris when I get home.

'Shall we continue?' Leah said as she handed her another glass. She took some painkillers from her bag and swallowed them with the water.

'My head aches,' she says.

'Shall we continue?' Leah repeats. 'You were talking about the accident.'

She leaned back in the couch and rested her head.

'It was my fault,' she said.

'You almost hit a deer, you couldn't help that.'

'But if it hadn't been dark. If I'd left earlier, in fact, if I hadn't even gone ...'

'That's a lot of ifs,' smiled Leah.

She wanted to wipe the smile from her face. There is nothing to smile about. She wondered if she would ever smile again.

'I don't see the point in talking about it.'

'We need to talk about your guilt. It was dark, that wasn't your fault ...'

'I should have left earlier.'

'Why would you have thought of leaving earlier? You've driven in the dark before. You've made that trip before. There'd been no reason for you to think things would be any different.'

She licked her lips.

'I knew that bit of the lane. I knew the bridge was there and ...'

'You didn't know a deer would jump out?'

She shook her head. 'No,' she agreed. 'There were these flashing headlights and ...'

'Can you talk about it and face what really happened?'

'I know what really happened,' she said firmly.

'The car went over the bridge, you remember that?'

'It hung on the edge of the bridge.'

'The rescue services found the car in the water, do you not remember?'

She shook her head emphatically.

'It didn't go over the bridge. It hung on the edge,' she repeated.

Leah sighed.

'The car was submerged in water. You know what that meant?'

She grabbed her bag.

'You don't know what you're talking about, none of you do.'

The clock clicked as the hand moved to two o'clock.

'My time's up,' she said and walked to the door.

Chapter Eighteen

I can see Tom's Audi in their driveway but our house is in darkness. I park on the drive and kill the engine. I unstrap Ben from the car seat with him still sleeping and unlock the front door. The house is cold and I turn up the heating. Ben begins to stir. I had hoped Chris would take over so I could get a break from Ben's crying. The clock says five and I feel a wave of anxiety wash over me. Where could Chris be? He and Tom must have finished badminton ages ago. I fish my phone from my bag and send him a text.

I'm home, where are you?

It isn't delivered which means his phone is off or he has no signal. Ben begins to cry and I feel the first stirrings of a headache. I decide to prepare dinner and then, if I haven't heard anything, I'll phone him.

Ben cries as I prepare pork chops and roast potatoes. Even his toy car doesn't appease him. I check my phone again and see my text message still hasn't been delivered. It's now five twenty. The pangs of anxiety are getting stronger and I think of the bottle of diazepam upstairs. I check the notebook and count the number I have taken, and am pleased; my use of the pills has reduced. I feel a rush of relief and hurry upstairs to take one. I check my phone on my return but there's nothing. It's now five thirty. It's unlike Chris not to make contact. Signal is low on my phone and I decide to call him from the landline. There's no reply. I wrap Ben in a blanket and leave the house. I knock on Sharni's door and wait. Tom opens it and a blanket of warmth from their house envelopes me.

'Hi Clare we ...'

'Chris isn't back and I was just wondering what time you two finished ...?'

'Chris is here,' he interrupts.

'What?' I say surprised.

'Come in.'

He steps to one side and I see Chris standing in the kitchen.

'Clare,' he says with a smile.

A sudden anger overwhelms me. For some reason I feel ganged up on.

'I sent you a text,' I say, my voice hard. 'And I just tried to phone you.'

My teeth clench together. How dare Chris make me look foolish like this.

'Oh, I've probably got no signal,' he says casually.

Ben is screaming and I feel like joining him.

'Hi,' says Sharni cheerfully, popping her head around the kitchen doorway.

'Here,' I say, thrusting Ben on to Chris. 'He's been like this all day and I've got a splitting headache. He's all yours.'

'Can we ...?' begins Tom.

'No, you can't,' I say brusquely and walk to the front door. 'I'll see you back in *our* house,' I say angrily before striding back home.

I have to fight back the tears of anger. What is wrong with him? He must have known we would be back by now. Why didn't he text me? How bloody dare he? I rush upstairs and take another diazepam. No wonder I'm on bloody tranquilisers. Anyone would be if they had to put up with what I have to put up with. The front door slams and I hear Chris calling me. I stomp down the stairs and face him in the hallway.

'Oh, you've decided to come home have you?'

'What the hell was all that about?' he demands.

'Think about it,' I snap.

He rolls his eyes.

'Don't roll your eyes at me,' I scream. 'How dare you.'

'Calm down for Christ's sake Clare, do you want them to hear you?'

'I don't give a fuck if they hear me,' I shout.

'You're making a fool of yourself and you're upsetting Ben.'

Ben screams uncontrollably and I feel like banging my head against a wall.

'Why don't you fuck off and move in with them,' I shout.

'You're not helping Ben,' he says calmly.

The diazepam start to kick in and I take a deep breath to help.

'How could you just ignore my texts and phone call?' I ask tearfully. 'I was really worried about you.'

'I didn't get them,' he says quietly. 'I came home and you weren't here and ...'

'What time was that?' I snap.

'It was about three I think. I figured you'd gone out with Helen like you said. I went into the garden to tidy the shed and Tom saw me and asked if I'd like a beer. So, I popped in. I wasn't going to stay long and I was keeping an eye out to see when your car pulled up ...'

'Weren't you worried about me?'

'You were out shopping,' he says tiredly. 'Why are you

making such a fuss? You were out with Helen so I had a drink with Tom.'

'And ignored my messages,' I say angrily.

'I didn't get them. I must have lost signal. I didn't notice.'

'Too preoccupied,' I say angrily, dropping into a kitchen chair.

'This is madness,' he says, putting Ben in his highchair and checking dinner. 'How many diazepam have you taken today?'

I can't admit to him that I've just taken two.

'I'm cutting back.'

'Is that why you're so edgy? I'll be glad when you see Dr Rawlins.'

'I don't want Sharni to have Ben,' I say.

'Not again,' he sighs.

'Helen agrees with me.'

He rolls his eyes.

'I'm not discussing anything with you while you're in this state, especially about anything that Helen agrees with.'

'He's my baby,' I say and burst into tears. Chris gives me an odd look and I walk away from him to get some kitchen towel.

'We'll discuss this after dinner when you're calmer,' he says and goes into the living room with Ben.

Chapter Nineteen

I try to grab the bottle out of Chris's hands.

'Clare, you were given a three month supply of pills only three weeks ago. How many have you been taking?'

'I've been cutting back.'

He makes me feel like a failure.

'You've been taking more,' he says. There's disappointment written across his face.

'I've been writing it down.'

'Please don't raise your voice. I've just got Ben to sleep.'

'I'll show you.'

I hurry downstairs and grab the notebook. He studies the pages and then looks at me solemnly.

'This can't be right Clare. You've taken far more than this.'

'No I haven't,' I say shaking my head. 'Maybe I've forgotten to put it in the book a few times, but not that many.'

'You had eighty-four tablets. There's only twenty-four left.'

'That's not possible,' I say.

'You know they're addictive. The more you take the more you need.'

'I don't understand,' I say. 'I'm sure I've been cutting back.'

'You've got to get your anxiety under control. We can't go on like this. I can't go on like this.'

The feeling of frustration overwhelms me and I clutch his arm.

'Can we please talk about Sharni and Tom?' I ask.

He sighs.

'If you don't want to be friends with her, that's fine but I can't agree with you about the nursery. It's only two and a half days Clare. Why should we pay when Sharni is offering to do it for nothing? She takes good care of Ben doesn't she? He's better looked after with her than he would be at a nursery.'

I struggle not to clench my hands.

'But what about those things I told you? The bedroom and our lamp and there's more Chris ...'

He stops on the stairs.

'More what?' he asks impatiently.

'Didn't you notice the kitchen?'

'It's being decorated,' he frowns. 'What's wrong with that?'

'The same colour as our kitchen,' I say pointedly.

He rolls his eyes.

'I didn't even notice.'

'She's even wearing the same perfume as me too, and her haircut is the same as mine. Surely you noticed that?'

'Yes, I noticed the hair,' he agrees.

'I saw her study,' I say hesitantly. 'She's got baby clothes in there.'

'Maybe they're trying for a baby,' he shrugs.

'You don't buy baby clothes in advance,' I say impatiently.

'What are you trying to say Clare?'

I relax my shoulders.

'I don't know. I don't understand any of it. There was a box with the name *Nathan* on it.'

'Christ Clare, have you been prying through their private things?'

'I ...'

'I think you're becoming obsessed with her.'

I gape at him.

'I'm becoming obsessed with *her*,' I repeat. 'Surely it's the other way around.'

'I just think you're overreacting.'

He's silent for a second and then says, 'Maybe you should go back on your medication.'

I stare at him.

'You keep telling me to stop it.'

'You know what medication I'm talking about.'

I look down at the floor.

'I'm fine,' I say. 'I won't be able to look after Ben. I'll feel half dead. I can't go back on that.'

'Get things in perspective and cut back on those other pills.'

'Fine,' I say resolutely.

I decide there and then that if Chris won't support me then I'll do it alone. I'll check out nurseries in my lunch break tomorrow.

Chapter Twenty

'We don't have any vacancies until the New Year I'm afraid.'

I try not to show my disappointment.

'You can't fit him in for a few weeks?' I ask. 'He's no trouble,'

'I'm very sorry. We will have a vacancy at the beginning of February. I can put your name down for that.'

I shake my head. I have no option but to try Ben's old nursery. Faye lets me in and I can see her smile is forced.

'I'm afraid Ben's place has been taken Clare.'

'Couldn't you squeeze him in?'

'It's impossible I'm afraid.'

I decide it is futile to plead and hurry to school. I reach the doors just as the bell sounds.

'Running late Clare?' says a voice behind me.

I turn to see the head.

'No, I'm here,' I say, opening the classroom door.

The morning drags and all I can think about is Ben. I shouldn't have agreed to the extra hours. I have a splitting headache from trying to work out a solution. I pull my phone from my bag and check for messages. There's a text. My heart skips a beat as it always does.

We've had to change Ben's appointment this morning to 11.30. Please let us know if you can't make it. The GP surgery.

'Shit,' I say aloud and the children snigger. That can't be right. I felt certain the kitchen calendar said Ben's appointment was next Monday. I'd never have made an appointment for a Tuesday. I can't ask to leave early. I've only been doing the extra hours for a short time. How could I have forgotten?

'Ah, Mrs Ryan thanks for calling back,' says the receptionist pleasantly.

'I've only just seen the message,' I say. 'Otherwise I would have phoned earlier.'

'It's not a problem, we phoned your husband when we didn't hear from you. Your friend, Sharni, brought Ben. Your husband arranged it. We got Ben in for 11.30 after all. All done and dusted.'

'I'd have preferred it if you'd asked me,' I say calmly but my hands are shaking with anger.

'We understood from your husband that you were both happy for Ben to have his vaccination.'

I bite my lip. If I argue I will sound like I put my pride before my child's health.

'Thanks for your help,' I say.

I'm shaking and have to fight to gain control before going back into the classroom. How dare Chris arrange for Sharni to take Ben to the surgery without asking me, especially after our argument yesterday.

'I've finished miss,' says Matthew, raising his hand.

'Me too,' yells another.

'Okay great. Right let's move on,' I say in my best teacher voice.

'You don't think you're overreacting?' says Helen as she puffs on her cigarette. I am tempted to ask her for a cigarette even though I don't smoke. I'm so wound up and I know I can't take any more diazepam. I'm seeing Dr Rawlins at five and I really want to be calm.

'Surely she helped you out by taking him?'

'Do you think I'm being paranoid?'

Helen shrugs and checks the time. It's our afternoon break and the time is dragging. I just want to be home and with Ben.

'I don't know. I'm thinking maybe she does admire you and just wants to please. I mean, what else could it be? It's not like taking Ben for his jabs was doing a bad thing was it?'

'I suppose not.'

She stubs out her cigarette.

'I wish the nursery had a space,' I sigh.

'Oh well, at least you can take him in the New Year. February isn't that far off is it? She can't do that much harm between now and then. Besides, we'll be breaking up for the holidays soon.'

I nod and search my bag for my diary. I'll make a note to phone the nursery the first week of January. As I open it the card with Ben's appointment printed on it flutters to the floor. I stare at it. The appointment was for next Monday at 11. I didn't get it wrong. I would never make an appointment for a Tuesday. It's one of the days I work.

I wait impatiently as the receptionist studies the screen.

'Yes, here we are. There is a message on the system. It says Mum phoned to rearrange the appointment. It was originally for next Monday but you asked for it to be this week. We're very sorry for having to rearrange the appointment. It was lucky that your friend was able to bring him,' the pale-faced receptionist says.

'I didn't phone and change the original appointment,' I say firmly.

'It's here on the system,' she argues.

'I didn't phone the surgery to change the appointment,' I repeat. 'I certainly wouldn't have made it for a Tuesday. It's one of the days I work.'

The receptionist frowns.

'It says here that you spoke to one of our receptionists,' she says stubbornly. 'It states quite clearly, Mrs Ryan phoned.'

'But I didn't phone. I always bring Ben myself. I wouldn't have made an appointment for a day that I couldn't bring him.'

'I can only tell you what's on the screen.'

'But ...'

I stop and grab the counter. Oh God. Did Sharni make the call? She could have seen the appointment on the calendar and pretended to be me. She must have phoned the surgery and changed the appointment.

'Okay, thanks,' I say to the receptionist, feeling numb.

I find a chair and sit down. My legs are weak. I know if I tell Chris he won't believe it. I can't tell Dr Rawlins either. There's no one left to turn to. I struggle to compose myself. I need Dr Rawlins to give me more diazepam. I sit with my hands folded in my lap and try to ignore the looks from the receptionist. People are coughing and sneezing all around me. I hope I don't catch something and take it back to Ben. I really can't afford to take time off and I certainly don't want Sharni looking after Ben when he's ill. I'm relieved when Dr Rawlins finally calls me in.

He checks my notes on the computer before turning to me and asking, 'How can I help you today Mrs Ryan?'

'My anxiety has got worse. I'm very edgy and a bit weepy. I seem to be forgetting things,' I say and immediately regret it. He's bound to make the connection with the diazepam.

'I'm not sleeping well,' I add quickly.

'Ah,' he nods.

'I've been taking the diazepam to help me sleep,' I lie.

'So, you're taking more diazepam?'

I blush.

'But less zopiclone, if any.'

'I see. Why are you more anxious do you think?'

If I tell him about Sharni's house he'll think I'm mad. I'm beginning to think that even Helen thinks I am paranoid.

'I've had a few upsets,' I say, trying not to clench my hands.

'Is Ben okay?'

'He's fine.'

'Perhaps we should try you on some anti-depressants.'

'No,' I say more sharply than I mean to. 'I'm not depressed.'

'Just anxious?'

I nod.

'But you don't know what about?'

'I can't find a nursery for Ben and my neighbour is caring for him and I don't know her very well and that's been worrying me.'

I sound so ridiculous.

'I see. You were supposed to be cutting down on the diazepam ...'

'I have, at least during the day.'

Please let me have more. Please. He looks thoughtful. My heart is pounding so forcibly I feel sure he must be able to hear it.

'I'll give you some more and an anti-depressant to take at night. It's been known to help people sleep but I urge you to reduce the diazepam. Try taking one and a half a day and after two weeks reduce to one a day. Don't increase that dose at any time and keep a record of what you're taking. I would also suggest some counselling ...'

'I don't want counselling,' I say sharply.

'It can ...'

'I've had counselling. I don't want it again.'

It's so easy to say things you don't want to say in counselling. To remember things you don't want to remember.

'Think about it,' he says curtly. 'We can't dismiss it. You can't stay on diazepam. We have to get you off that. Long-term diazepam increases anxiety and that's what I think is happening to you. I'm not saying stop altogether, but you must start reducing. Therapy is a great way to look at your anxieties.'

I nod without committing myself. I wait patiently while he prints out the prescription, the sense of relief overwhelming me. I will calm down. Chris is right. I'm getting everything out of proportion. I must get off the diazepam, they're making me paranoid. But I didn't phone the surgery. That phone call never happened. Despite what the receptionist said it was not me that changed Ben's appointment.

Chapter Twenty-One

The car bumped up on to the driveway and Chris swung his legs out of the car. He was late. The meeting had gone on longer than he'd thought, but he'd managed to get away by two o'clock. What a fantastic outcome. He hoped his breath didn't smell of alcohol. He'd only had the one glass of bubbly. He'd get another bottle on the way home and celebrate with Clare later.

He'd barely reached the front door when Sharni opened it.

'Hi, sorry I'm late,' he said apologetically.

'I didn't notice the time,' she smiled.

'I have to be back at four.'

'No worries, it won't take long.'

He saw her looking across the street. The old woman from over the road was watching from her window.

'She clocks everything, doesn't she,' said Sharni.

He raised his eyebrows. God, it looked a bit odd though, him going into the neighbour's house while her husband and his wife were at work. Shit. He couldn't even tell Clare, not if these photos were to be a surprise. Hopefully the old girl wouldn't say anything. He didn't think Clare knew her anyway. Oh well, he thought, if she did he'd have to open up about the photos. Sharni would admit to taking them and that would be that. Clare couldn't be jealous of Sharni. She was being so supportive by looking after Ben.

He walked into the living room where Ben was crawling on the floor. Sharni scooped him up and tossed him expertly over her shoulder. Sometimes he had to admit that Sharni had a confidence with Ben that even Clare didn't have. She certainly seemed more balanced than Clare at the moment.

'I was going to make a coffee, do you want one before we start?'

'Great, thanks.'

The living room was scattered with photographs and outlines of interiors.

'Ignore the muddle. I'm working on a fashion shoot for L'Oréal.'

'Wow, that's impressive,' he said coming up behind her and taking Ben's little hand in his.

'Not really, it sounds more impressive than it is.'

She handed him Ben and emptied the kettle into a cafetiere.

'Thanks for earlier. I don't know why Clare forgot.'

'It happens to the best of us,' she smiled at Chris.

'Not with Ben. She's normally on the ball.'

'Is that right?' she said and he detected a hint of sarcasm in her voice.

'Has he been all right since the jabs?'

'We've had lots of cuddles, haven't we Ben?'

Ben reached out his arms to her and Chris handed him over.

'You're certainly a hit.'

'You hang on to him. I'll get the camera.'

Something in her tone made Chris uneasy. He remembered the things Clare had rambled on about. He shook his head in annoyance. Her paranoia was rubbing off on him. There was no doubt about it. He read somewhere that living with an unbalanced partner was not only toxic but left its mark. '*It can damage an otherwise healthy level-headed partner.*' He needed to detach himself from her paranoia. Sharni was just being businesslike. Getting the job done and after all hadn't he said he needed to be back by four?

'Naked photos are best,' she said as she assembled a white backdrop.

He blinked in surprise but Sharni seemed unfazed.

'Naked?' he repeated.

'Just your shirt off,' she said casually, taking Ben from him and removing his top.

He looked at Sharni's window. She didn't have nets and if that old dear was still looking. Sharni didn't seem worried and he didn't want to make a fuss.

'Right,' he said pulling off his shirt. 'Clare will love these.'

Sharni didn't reply but busied herself attaching a lens to her camera.

'I've found a great restaurant. It's French, in the West End. I've booked a table for your anniversary. Tom and I would like to take you out. I thought eight would be a good time. I'll surprise Clare with the photos,' she says without looking up.

Chris struggled not to look taken aback.

'Ah right,' he said. He had hoped to spend the anniversary alone with Clare but felt it would be rude to say no to Sharni. 'That's great I'll tell her. We'll need to get a sitter.'

He couldn't bring himself to say that he and Clare wanted to spend their anniversary alone. He didn't want to seem ungrateful. It felt strange to be half undressed in Sharni's living room and he hoped Sharni wouldn't take much longer.

'Okay, if you stand here,' she said. 'I'll do a few of you first to get the light right. I don't want to be fiddling around when I take Ben's photos or he'll get agitated.'

'Oh right,' he nodded. She told him how to pose and for the next five minutes she snapped like crazy.

'Best to get everything planned before we put Ben in the picture,' she smiled.

Chris nodded but he felt uncomfortable posing like a model.

'Okay,' she said finally. 'Let's get Ben in.'

Ten minutes later they were done.

'Thanks for that,' said Chris.

'I hope Clare won't mind the secrecy, but I'm sure she'll be okay. We've all had secrets at some time in our life, right?'

Her eyes seemed to bore right into his. He turned away and looked at his watch.

'I better go. I've a meeting at four.'

He kissed Ben on the forehead and moved to the door.

'Thanks for taking those, and for taking Ben to the doctor.'

'My pleasure,' she smiled but it seemed to him that her smile didn't reach her eyes.

Chapter Twenty-Two

I shove the appointment card under his nose.

'It's here in black and white. I didn't phone the surgery. Why would I want to change it to a Tuesday?'

'Maybe they got the day wrong.'

'For Christ's sake Chris,' I sigh.

'Why would Sharni change Ben's appointment, and besides, how could she have known when the original appointment was for?'

'She had my key the first day she had Ben. She would have seen it on the fridge calendar.'

'This is sounding so paranoid Clare,' he sighs.

'Who made the phone call?' I say, raising my voice. 'I didn't, and I certainly wouldn't make an appointment for a day when I'm working.'

'You don't seem to remember much of what you do these days.'

I stare at him open-mouthed.

'I can't believe you said that.'

'Clare ...'

'I don't want her to have him any more,' I say firmly.

Chris looks at me with pleading eyes.

'Please Clare, not again, okay?'

I force myself to calm down. I've got to cut back on the diazepam. Dr Rawlins will insist on counselling if I don't.

'The nurseries are full. I checked today,' I say, trying to sound calmer. 'They haven't got space until February so it looks like I don't have any choice, but in February he goes back to nursery.'

'Okay,' he agrees, but I can tell that he is hoping that by February I will have changed my mind.

'Have you been drinking?' I ask. I can smell alcohol on his breath. Very slight, but it's definitely there.

'That's what I've wanted to tell you but you were at me as soon as I walked in the door.'

'Okay,' I say.

'They want me to take charge of the Hinski contract.'

'That's wonderful,' I say.

'I bought some Prosecco.'

'I'm so pleased for you.'

'It'll mean some overtime,' he smiles. 'So what with your extra hours and this ...'

'The dinner,' I say as I rush to the kitchen.

'What did Dr Rawlins say?' he asks.

'He thinks I need to go on anti-depressants.'

'Oh.' He pops the cork. 'What did he say about the diazepam?'

'He gave me some more and said to continue with the reduction programme.'

He raises his eyebrows.

'Did you tell him you that you have been forgetting that you'd taken them?'

'He talked about therapy and you know ...'

'Let's celebrate,' he says changing the subject.

I clink my glass against his.

'Congratulations Chris,' I say.

'It does mean I have to go to Amsterdam for a few days.'

My hands tighten around the glass.

'When?'

I tell myself not to sound anxious. Don't ruin the good news by getting worked up. I'm already struggling to fill my lungs with air.

'In a few weeks, I'm not sure exactly when. I'll only be gone a few days. I have to go. It's down to me to work out the details with the customer.'

'I know,' I say squeezing his arm.

'We'll have Christmas to look forward to.'

The mention of Christmas reminds me that I'd asked Helen over for Christmas Day. I'm beginning to wish I hadn't now.

'I asked Helen if she wanted to come to us on Christmas Day.'

'What? Why?' he groans.

'She's going to be all on her own.'

'Oh, Clare.'

'I'd rather that than go next door,' I say irritably.

'Okay, let's not ruin the evening. Can't we just celebrate without disagreeing?'

'Sorry,' I say meekly.

He wraps his arm around me.

'After dinner and when Ben's gone to sleep why don't we watch a movie? Have a real chill out.'

I nod. I can't think of anything nicer.

'We ended the last session talking about the car accident. I think we should revisit that,' Leah said.

She gave a sarcastic laugh. The word 'we' was ironic. If only there had been a 'we' at the time. At least then she'd have been believed. No one believed her, they all dismissed her. She struggled to breathe.

'Are you okay?'

'When I think back I feel panicky, it's the feeling of helplessness.'

'Try to remember what actually happened.'

She knows what actually happened, she didn't have to try. She could hear the wind battering the car and the rain hammering on the windscreen. She could smell the dampness of the night and she could see the dazzling headlights that blinded her. She hadn't got far to go. Her hands had gripped the steering wheel and even now she could feel the ache in her shoulders. She knew the bridge wasn't far away, knew she had to be cautious going over it. She'd cursed again for leaving so late, but who could have known the rain would come down like that? The deer had come out of nowhere. She was squinting at the flashing headlights and, it was there, its eyes wide and frightened.

'There were headlights,' she said.

'It's dark in the country,' said Leah.

'He was beautiful and so scared.'

'You didn't hit him.'

She'd turned the steering wheel so violently that she'd torn the ligaments in her wrist. Her foot had slammed on to the brake but the car skidded. She was going too fast. The world spun around her until she could do nothing but scream.

'I thought I'd gone over the bridge,' she says. 'I couldn't see. My head throbbed and ...'

'You crawled out and the car went over the bridge.'

'How can you tell me what happened? I was there.'

She struggled not to raise her voice.

'Do you need some water, maybe a tablet?' asked Leah.

'I was pulled from the car. I couldn't move.'

'You were unconscious when they found you.' Leah's voice was soft.

'Everything was hazy but the car was hanging over the edge of the bridge. Someone came. They helped me, they got us out of the car and then ...'

'There's no evidence of anyone being there. You had a really bad knock on the head and ...'

'I saw ...'

'The mind plays tricks.'

The hand on the clock clicked. She looked up in surprise. It was two o'clock. She turned back to Leah. She was looking at her diary.

'Next Thursday okay?'

'Fine,' she said, but I haven't finished she wanted to shout. I can't put my life on hold until next Thursday.

Chapter Twenty-Three

'You look gorgeous,' Julia says.

I fiddle with my hair self-consciously.

'Thanks, I wasn't sure what to wear.'

I was nervous stepping into the foyer. It was the first time I'd been to a big school function and also the first time for years I'd attended anything like this with Chris. He looks handsome in his crisp white shirt and bow tie. I bought the pale blue evening dress especially and spent ages curling my hair only to change my mind and tie it back.

'It's going to be a good night,' says Julia, looking at Chris.

'This is my husband,' I say.

'Hi,' says Chris, shaking her hand.

Music pours from the sound system in the hall and small groups of partygoers jiggle to the music as they sip their champagne. I'm feeling relaxed. The champagne reception is helping. I've allowed myself one drink and then I'm sticking to diet coke. I'd agreed to drive. A cab would have been extravagant.

'No holds barred tonight,' laughs Julia. 'I think the champagne was donated by a parent.'

'Rich parent,' laughs Chris.

The mention of money reminds me of the uncomfortable moment earlier when we'd been about to leave the house. Kathryn had arrived, early as usual, and I'd opened the door to her just as Tom and Sharni were getting into their car. Sharni said I looked nice but I felt a reprimand in her voice. It was almost as if she was angry because she didn't know we were going out. I'd told her we were off to the school Christmas party but I felt embarrassed and didn't know why. She'd glanced at Kathryn and said in a hurtful tone that they would have babysat. The presumption that we would always give Ben to her annoyed me. I told her that I hadn't thought of asking and almost apologised, but of course I had thought about asking Sharni. When I closed the door my face was red. I'd felt guilty and had no idea why.

Chris was more worried about upsetting Sharni and said that we don't want to offend her, especially as she is having Ben on my teaching days, and that it would have saved paying Kathryn. I'd gaped at him and said that I'm not going to be blackmailed. I felt the irritation rise up inside me. It seems every time Sharni's name is mentioned we argue.

'Let's have a good time shall we,' Chris says, interrupting my thoughts. I take his arm and we move into the hall where tables are laid for dinner. I look around the crowded hall for Helen.

'Good to see you,' says Geoff.

'This is my husband Chris,' I say proudly.

'Glad you could make it. Have a nice evening.'

I pull Chris over to the table plan and sigh with relief when I see we're seated with Helen.

'Oh brilliant,' groans Chris.

The party is in full swing and I watch as Helen glides around the dance floor. The disco lights flash around us. I sip my diet coke before texting Kathryn.

Is everything okay? We'll be leaving soon.

Kathryn texts back a thumbs up and smiley face. I push my phone to Chris.

'It's almost ten-thirty, we should go soon.'

'You're not going already are you?' Helen says, lurching towards us.

'We have to get back to the babysitter,' I say, finishing the last of my coke.

'You'll miss the speeches,' slurs Julia.

'I'm sure Sharni would be happy to have him for another hour,' grins Helen.

'Sharni isn't babysitting,' I say.

'Best to stay for speeches,' says Chris. 'I'll get another beer.'

'Why couldn't Sharni babyshit?' Helen asks, causing Julia to burst out laughing. I sigh. There's nothing worse than being sober when everyone else is drunk.

'She's great is Sharni,' Helen tells Julia. 'She babysits for free.'

I look to the bar. I really think it's time to leave.

'That's good of her,' says Julia, rubbing her eyes.

'They're good pals, aren't you?' says Helen loudly.

I strain to look for Chris.

'I'm just going to get Chris,' I say as I stand up.

'She's even arranging an anniversary dinner for them. Seven year special. How nice is that? Getting all their mates to come and ...' Helen clamps a hand to her mouth.

'Whoops,' she giggles. 'You probably don't know about that yet.'

I must have snapped my head around so sharply for I hear a crack and feel a pain shoot down my shoulder.

'What anniversary party?'

'Clare?' Chris says from behind me. There's concern in his voice. I spin round. His face tells me everything.

'You know about this?'

'I haven't had time to talk to you ...'

'Oops, sorry,' says Helen, wincing.

I must stay calm. It's a nice thing that Sharni wants to do, but for Helen to know and Chris ... Why hadn't someone told me?

'She asked me if I could make it,' says Helen, placing her hand on my arm. 'She wants to make it nice for you. Have all your friends there and stuff.'

I meet Chris's eyes.

'She wants to take us to *Chez Pierre* in town. She wanted to ask you if the restaurant was okay. I said I'd ask you and what with the Hinski contract I forgot.'

'What a nice thing to do,' says Julia, slurping her coffee.

'Anyone else for coffee?' Helen asks.

'I think we should get back to Ben,' I say.

'It's a nice thought,' says Chris in the car.

'Yes,' I say. 'I guess it is, although I would have preferred to have gone out just the two of us.'

'You shouldn't have told her it was our anniversary then,' he says pushing his head back against the seat. 'It was a good do tonight.'

'I thought you told her,' I say, my hands gripping the steering wheel.

'Me, no, I barely remember it myself, let alone remember to tell someone else.'

'I don't remember telling her,' I say.

'Your memory,' he laughs.

My hands tingle and I release the pressure on the steering wheel. I didn't forget that I'd told Sharni about our anniversary. I don't forget things I don't say, and I didn't tell Sharni it was our seventh anniversary. The only person who could have told her is Chris, but why would he lie?

Chapter Twenty-Four

'I don't know of anyone, Mrs Ryan. I'm really sorry,' apologises Kathryn.

'That's okay, thanks anyway.'

I click off the phone and chew my fingernails. Ben grabs my necklace and tries to put it into his mouth. I gently remove it and sigh. I'm feeling desperate. I really don't want to face Sharni this morning but I can't seem to find anyone else to have Ben. I feel trapped. I wish there was somewhere else for Ben to go. There is no point talking to Chris. He is taken up with his new contract. I'm starting to wish he'd never got it, which is horrid of me, but he is so preoccupied with it these days.

I check the time and sigh. It's no good. I'll have to take Ben to Sharni. I lock the front door and push the stroller up her driveway, my feet crunch on the gravel, announcing my arrival. She opens the door before I'm even halfway.

'You're late,' she says, her eyes flashing.

'We overslept,' I lie. How dare she tell me off? I am tempted to turn on my heel and take Ben to work with me, but the thought of Chris's anger stops me. I take a deep breath and ignore the pounding of my heart. I lift Ben from the stroller and she takes him from me.

'Sharni, about the anniversary dinner you've arranged ...'

'Is that restaurant okay?' she asks, with her head tilted.

'It's just I really wanted to spend that evening on my own with Chris.'

Her lips tighten.

'Oh, of course, I should have realised. I'll cancel it.'

'It was nice of you to ...' I begin.

'Not a problem. Maybe we could all do something on the Saturday. I obviously misunderstood Chris. I thought it was all okay.'

'Misunderstood?' I question.

'When I saw Chris at his office the other day, we were joking about the seven year itch and all that, so maybe I just misunderstood what he said. I thought he was keen but I must have got that wrong.'

My head begins to spin. What was she doing at Chris's office, and why didn't he mention it? And why in God's name was he talking about the seven year itch with her?

'He said he would tell you.'

'He did tell me,' I say.

'Well, not to worry. Did you have a nice time on Saturday?' she asks.

Ben had leaned over and was clutching my necklace. She pulls him back a bit too quickly and the Celtic harp comes off the chain.

'Oh no,' she says.

I prize it from Ben's hand.

'Leave it with us and we'll get it repaired,' she says, reaching to take it.

'It's okay,' I say.

'It's the least I can do,' she says, taking it out of my hand.

'I know a jeweller who can do it. We'll see you later then,' she smiles, but the smile doesn't reach her eyes.

I hurry to my car and angrily tap a message to Chris.

When was Sharni in your office?

I rummage through my bag with shaky hands and pull out the diazepam. I need to find somewhere else for Ben. I'll ask around the school. Surely there is someone who can have him. Anyone would be preferable to Sharni.

'Isn't Sharni great,' says Helen as she greets me in the staffroom.

It's the last thing I need to hear.

'What?' I say. The last person I expected Helen to call great was Sharni.

'The bloody photographer we booked for the Christmas photos has let us down. No bloody reason. I emailed Sharni. She phoned me first thing this morning. She's going to do them at cost price.'

I gape at her.

'When did you email her?'

'Yesterday, I did mean to text you but it got a bit chaotic here. Julia's gone down with a stomach bug.'

'She didn't mention it but I was a bit late this morning. Helen, I need someone else to look after Ben.'

She looks surprised.

'Oh, I thought you couldn't find anywhere,' she says clicking on the kettle. 'Christ, is that the time? I thought I had time for one coffee. Where does it go?'

'I don't feel I can trust her and ...'

She lifts her coffee mug, 'Do you want one?'

I shake my head.

'She seems okay,' she smiles. 'Maybe it is us not being charitable enough.'

'But I thought you didn't like her? You used to say she was too good to be true.'

'Yeah, but, she's been good to you hasn't she? Taking Ben for nothing and wanting to arrange something nice for your anniversary. I wish I had a friend like that. I honestly thought she'd tell me where to go when I asked about the school photos. I mean, I have been a bit off with her but she was as nice as pie.'

I grind my teeth.

'That's what she's like. Too nice. You said so yourself.'

She shrugs.

'I don't really know her. All I know is she's got us out of a right fix, so I'm dead grateful.'

The rehearsal is running late. I haven't heard back from Chris and haven't had a second to message him again. It's almost four-thirty and my class haven't had their run through yet. They're fidgety and irritable. Geoff sees me looking at my phone and comes over. I shove the phone into my bag and smile.

'Everything okay?' he asks.

I nod.

'No problem. I just need to let my sitter know I'm going to be late.'

'Yes, I'm sorry we're going overtime.'

I hurry into the hall and phone Sharni. Her phone rings and rings. I click off and send a text.

Running late, school concert rehearsal going over time, I hope all is okay.

I watch but it isn't delivered. Damn. I copy the text and send it via WhatsApp and wait for the blue tick to show it has been read. It doesn't. I try Chris's phone but he doesn't answer either. I throw the phone into my bag and return to the hall.

'I can't get hold of Sharni,' I tell Helen. 'My texts aren't being delivered.'

I go to fiddle with my necklace and remember it isn't there. Where the hell is Sharni and where is Chris? I take a deep breath.

'I'm sure everything is okay,' Helen says, sensing my anxiety. 'She seems very capable.'

'But it's gone four-thirty and it's getting dark. She wouldn't be out with Ben at this time.'

'Perhaps her battery has died,' she says, but Sharni doesn't strike me the type of person that would let her battery die.

'I don't think you should get so worried. Anyone would think you'd left your child with a psychopath. Oh, you're up.' She points to the stage where Geoff is beckoning to me. I usher the kids forward and see that my hands are shaking.

'Okay, let's wrap this up shall we. We have some impatient parents waiting outside,' he laughs.

I strain to see my phone but it's at the bottom of my handbag. I sit through the rehearsal with a knotted stomach. I try to smile at the right times and encourage the little shepherds, but all I can think about is Ben. The hall feels stuffy and hot, and the high-pitched voices of the children singing nativity songs seem to last forever. Finally Geoff winds things up and the children rush for their coats and scarves and hurry out to their parents. I pull my phone out and see there are no messages or missed calls.

I grab my coat and hurry to my car only to find I'm blocked in by one of the parent's cars. I try Chris's phone again and finally he answers.

'Where have you been?' I yell. 'I've been trying to get hold of you.'

'Clare, what's the matter? Has something happened?'

'I've been messaging you. I'm running really late. I can't get hold of Sharni. When will you be home?'

'I've only just seen your messages. I had a meeting and there was no reception. As for Sharni ...'

'Where was the meeting?' I demand.

'What?'

'Where was your meeting? Who was it with?'

There's silence. Is he struggling to think of a reply?

'Chris,' I say angrily.

The parent whose car has blocked me in is chatting to another parent. They laugh loudly and I feel my blood boil.

'Can you move your car? I need to get home,' I shout from the window. 'We haven't all got time to waste.'

'Clare, calm down,' Chris calls down the phone.

'Oh sorry,' says the parent, looking embarrassed. 'I didn't realise.'

I close the window and take a deep breath.

'I don't like being interrogated,' Chris says in a hurt voice. 'I can't go through this jealousy thing of yours again, Clare. I really thought having Ben would ...'

'When will you be home?' I butt in.

'I'll be leaving soon. I'm seeing Mike to discuss something to do with the Hinski contract and then I'll leave.'

'That bloody Hinski contract,' I snap and click off my phone before shooting out of the car park. I look down at the phone. My messages to Sharni still haven't been read.

Chapter Twenty-Five

I'm shaking so much that my foot slips off the accelerator and the car jerks. I let out a small sob and pull into a lay-by where I rest my head on the steering wheel. What's happening? Ever since Sharni and Tom arrived it feels like my life has been spiralling out of control. I can't remember things and when I do Chris makes me doubt myself. I'm leaving my child with a woman I can't trust. Did I ever trust her? I struggle to think. Is it me? Am I losing my grip? I was anxious even before Sharni moved next door. While Ben is young I am going to be anxious and even fearful, like when the police came to the house. It's always going to be there, although I know it's stupid. I have every right to happiness. I deserve it. I'm a good mother, not like some who neglect their children. I'd never do that, not ever. Women like that don't deserve children. I clench my hands until my nails dig into the palm. My heart begins to slow and I wipe the perspiration from my face. I have to find somewhere else for Ben, but where? I'll look at nurseries outside Kensington. It'll mean leaving earlier but I can cope with that. Chances are they'll be cheaper too. I sigh. The children might be rougher though, and I really don't want Ben mixing with mean kids.

Most likely their mothers are neglectful. Why did I listen to Chris? I fight to get things in perspective. Sharni hadn't done anything to hurt Ben and now even Helen is growing to like her. Maybe it is me. Maybe she is just keen to please. But I can't help feeling Sharni is more interested in my life than she is in her own and that seems wrong. My phone rings and I look down to see it is Chris.

'I'm worried about you,' he says.

'I'm okay.'

'Are you driving?'

'I stopped to answer your call.' I don't want to tell him I had to stop to calm down.

'There are a few issues Mike wants to iron out with the Hinksi contract. I know you can't stand it but ...'

'Okay,' I say, feeling defeated.

'It's my job Clare.'

A tiny voice in my head whispers that he's with Sharni and I try to ignore it.

'I'll try not to be too late.'

'I'll see you in a bit,' I say.

'Try to calm down.'

'Yes.'

I hear him sigh.

'I don't know what's going through your head Clare, but I can tell you it's all stupid.'

I hang up and check my messages. There's no response from Sharni. It's now quarter to six. It's way past Ben's tea time. I start the engine and drive home.

Sharni's house is in darkness. There are no cars in the drive. I hammer on the door while knowing no one will answer. I walk to the back door and let myself in with the key under the paint pot. I hurry into the living room. The room is tidy; no sign of a child having been there. I rush upstairs to their bedroom calling Ben's name as I do so. Where the fuck is she? What has she done with my child? I grab my phone to call Chris and then stop. What do I tell him? Sharni isn't back with Ben and she hasn't let me know what's happening. He'll say I'm overreacting. I'm about to throw my phone back into my bag when it rings. It's Sharni. I feel sick. I click it on and mumble, 'hello'.

'Hi Clare, it's me.'

Her voice is bright and cheery. Surely if anything had happened to Ben, she wouldn't sound like this. Relief floods through my body.

'I've had no signal. I had to pop into the office. They had a crisis and I had to help out. We were in the basement. Ben's great. He's had loads of attention and loads of new toys. Ooh, and I got your necklace repaired. I'm really sorry we're late. I've given Ben his tea and ...'

'When will you be back?' I interrupt.

'In twenty minutes but traffic is really bad.'

I'm so relieved to hear her voice that I can barely muster up any anger. I sit on her bed.

'Okay,' I mumble.

'See you soon.'

'Okay.'

I look at the phone and burst into tears. How can I complain about her now she has phoned, got my necklace repaired and also fed Ben? Why does she always manage to get the better of me? Why is it I always look like the crazy one? I realise I am still in her house and pull myself off the bed and straighten the duvet. It's brushed cotton, different to ours after all. I glance at *The Lovely Bones* on her bedside table and wipe the tears from my cheeks. The book still looks unread.

I get home and I've barely got the key in my door when Mrs Riley rushes over with a package.

'Woo hoo, Mrs Ryan. This came for you today. Your neighbour was out too so they asked if I'd take it.'

It's an Amazon delivery, a CD I'd ordered for Chris. I thought I would give it to him on our anniversary. Sharni's words about the seven year itch play on my mind again.

'She looks after your boy then?'

'What?' I say, pulling my mind back to the present.

'Your neighbour, she looks after your boy?'

I nod.

'Thanks for this.'

'Saw your husband going in there the other day. She likes your menfolk doesn't she?'

My stomach flips.

'Oh, what day was that?' I say casually, trying not to let my voice shake.

'The day you were at work,' she says and turns to walk back to her house.

I go to punch in Helen's number and then it occurs to me that Helen may not believe me either. It's then I realise I don't have anyone to call. I'm alone and no one believes me. Everyone thinks I'm overly anxious. Even my doctor thinks I'm neurotic. The house is cold and it takes ages for the heating to kick in. I make tea and take a diazepam. I don't bother writing it in the book. There seems little point.

Sharni knocks on the door twenty minutes later and I can't

look her in the eye. She smiles. I notice Ben is holding another new toy.

'Sorry we're late,' she apologises. 'The traffic was crazy. He's great though and here's your necklace.'

I don't trust myself to say anything so just mumble a thank you.

'Is Chris not home?' she asks casually.

I shake my head.

'He's going to be late.'

'You look knackered,' she comments.

'It's been a long day.'

'I'll leave you to it then. Bye bye Sweet Pea,' she says, leaning forward to kiss Ben, but I pull him away and take off his hat. He struggles and I again pull him to me. He cries and lashes out at my face.

'Mama,' he says, reaching out to Sharni and a knife twists through my heart. In that moment I want to twist a knife in Sharni's stomach.

'Bless him,' she says.

I nod and then thankfully she is gone.

Chapter Twenty-Six

'I've looked everywhere,' I shout over Ben's screaming. 'You'll have to go next door and get it.'

'It must be here somewhere,' argues Chris, rummaging through the wardrobe.

'It's not and he'll never go to sleep without it. You know what he's like about his comfort blanket.'

'Can't you phone her?'

'For fuck's sake Chris, what's the problem? You don't mind going round there to see her when it suits you, do you?'

His shoulders tense and he looks uncomfortable.

'What are you talking about?' he asks hoarsely.

I sigh heavily. I really don't want to talk about it now, not while Ben's playing up. Why the hell didn't Sharni give me the comfort blanket?

'Can you please just get the bloody blanket?'

I move the linen basket to check it hasn't fallen behind it. The room is a muddle. I've felt so knackered lately that it has felt like too big an effort to clean through the house too.

Chris trips over one of Ben's toys and then I hear his footsteps on the stairs. The front door slams and I exhale heavily. Ben hasn't stopped screaming since Sharni dropped him off. He won't go to sleep and his screams are giving me a migraine. I carry him downstairs and wait. I strain my ears to hear what is happening next door but all is silent. Minutes later Chris returns with Sharni. I feel the hairs bristle on the back of my neck.

'Sharni doesn't have it,' says Chris simply.

'I gave it to you,' Sharni says. 'When you picked Ben up, I gave you everything.'

She's lying, she has to be. The blanket isn't here and I know I gave it to her this morning. Chris gives me that look. The look I'm getting to know so well. I know damn well she didn't give me the blanket.

'Try his rabbit,' she says. 'He loves it. He cuddled it all afternoon.'

'That won't work,' I snap.

Chris looks apologetically at Sharni and I fight back the urge to slap him. Does he have to make it so bloody obvious that he fancies her?

'Here you are Sweet Pea,' she says, moving close to Ben. 'Shall we sing to it?'

She wipes a tear from his cheek and Ben calms down. He makes a little whimpering sound and cuddles the rabbit.

'I think you should move in,' jokes Chris.

'And I'll move out,' I say caustically.

'I didn't mean ...' begins Sharni, looking at Chris.

I scoop up Ben and brush past them both and up the stairs to the bedroom.

I wring my hands and stare at Chris's iPhone. Its past midnight and I can't sleep. I tap in his password and with my breath held scroll through his text messages. Sharni's name seems to scream at me and I want to march upstairs and throw the phone at him and call him a lying deceiving bastard. Sharni is in his contacts. I read the thread with my hand gripping the phone so tightly that my knuckles turn white.

I can pop round tomorrow for about an hour. Will you be around?

'Yes, great, look forward to it.'

Oh God, he'd actually been round there when Ben was with her. I check his call log and see he has phoned Sharni several times. There's nothing to indicate he was with her today though.

I take two diazepam tablets and pull a bottle of wine from the fridge. I try to ignore how few pills are left in the bottle. It feels like my life is crumbling. I can't believe Chris is having an affair with Sharni. I should write the number of pills into the notebook. I throw back some of the wine and shudder. It's acidic and sharp on my tongue. Tears prick my eyelids. I don't know what to do. I've got to find somewhere for Ben. Maybe things aren't what they seem. I'll speak to Chris in the morning. I must stay calm. I need to get some perspective but after another glass of wine I find myself standing at the foot of the bed shouting abuse at him. Ben wakes up and screams.

'Mama, mama,' he cries.

'Mama's here,' I say. But when I take him into my arms, he struggles.

'Mama,' he bellows.

'I hate you,' I scream at Chris. 'You've been lying to me.'

'You're upsetting him, for Christ's sake calm down.'

'You were with her tonight weren't you?'

'With who, what the hell are you on about?'

He rubs his eyes tiredly.

'Sharni,' I say sharply.

'Don't be so ridiculous,' he laughs, switching on the bedside lamp.

'I've seen her messages on your phone. Don't lie to me,' I scream.

He winces.

'She came to your office,' I say grabbing his arm. 'Didn't she? Don't lie to me. She's already told me how you discussed our anniversary and the seven year itch.'

'Christ,' he moaned. 'It's not like you're making it sound.'

'What was it like then?'

'Sharni wanted to take a portrait of me with Ben. She wanted to give it to you for our anniversary. That's why she came to the office and that's why I texted her. The only other time I phoned her was when you forgot to take Ben for his jabs.'

I glare at him.

'I didn't forget. What are you saying?'

'You do forget Clare. Look at yourself. What kind of a mother are you. Screaming like a mad woman in front of Ben. Taking too many tranquillisers and now accusing me of God knows what. You're totally paranoid Clare. Everyone is trying to help and that includes Sharni. Your memory is going. You need to get help and I don't mean from Dr Rawlins or at least try and pull yourself together.'

'You were in her house, the lady over the road saw you.'

'She was taking photos of me and Ben. I'm not having an affair with anyone, but God knows Clare, the way you are, it wouldn't be hard not to.'

'But why didn't you tell me?'

'This,' he says pointing at me. 'This is why I don't tell you.'

He takes Ben downstairs and I burst into tears.

Chris had barely spoken to me this morning. He was livid.

'I can't even discuss the things you said last night,' he'd said quietly. 'If you want to believe I'm having an affair with Sharni, then you can think it, but it's bloody lunacy. You look terrible, you should get some sleep.'

Ben is asleep on the couch and I curl up beside him. My head thumps but I have to find somewhere to take Ben tomorrow. I make a feeble effort to tidy the kitchen and then open my laptop and search for nurseries in our area. I'm about to phone them when there is a loud rapping on the front door. I peek out of the window to see it is Tom and I wince at his angry expression. I back away from the window but he's seen me. I've no alternative but to answer the door.

'Can I have a word?' he asks bluntly. He's wearing a dark suit and carries his briefcase. I realise that I barely know Tom. I really don't want to ask him in but it's cold and a gust of wind blows into the house.

'You'd better come in,' I say reluctantly.

He steps in hesitantly.

'I'm not going to beat about the bush Clare. It wasn't pleasant listening to your vulgarity last night. The walls are fairly thick but if you're screaming like a banshee then we're all likely to hear.'

I feel myself blush. I won't defend myself. Why should I? It's his wife that's the bloody slut. She's clearly after my husband.

'I don't know what we've done for you to behave like this. But Sharni is very upset. All she wanted to do was give you a nice photo of Chris and Ben.'

'You know about the photo?' I say, surprised.

'Of course I do.'

I remember all the horrible things I had said to Chris and feel my body turn hot. Tom's jaw twitches.

'We don't have secrets,' he says. 'Sharni is a very caring woman ...'

'I don't think we're talking about the same Sharni,' I say and quickly bite my lip.

'I'm aware you've got issues Clare and ...'

'How dare you. She lies all the time. She never gave me the vase back. I don't even know why she asked for it. She has plenty of vases she could have put her mother's flowers in.'

'What are you talking about? Sharni's mother is dead.'

'What, but she said ...'

He shakes his head sadly at me.

'I think it's more a case of you've got bad listening skills. The flowers weren't from her mother. She wouldn't lie about that. Sharni has done a lot to help you. You could do with helping yourself. Perhaps getting off those drugs might be a start. It can't be good for Ben.'

I let out a small gasp. Did Chris tell him about the diazepam?

'I don't know what you're talking about,' I stutter.

'Sharni saw the diazepam notebook when we were here for dinner ...'

'Ben is fine,' I say defensively.

'They are clearly affecting you. I'm sorry you've got problems Clare, but I don't appreciate hearing through the walls you accusing my wife of all sorts. It's just not right.'

He looks at me pityingly and for a fleeting moment I think how handsome he is. I've been so focused on Sharni that I've never really seen Tom. It occurs to me that with a husband like Tom why would Sharni be interested in Chris.

'I can assure you that my wife is not having an affair with your husband. She's feeling quite hurt this morning. I don't know what she's done for you to treat her this way.'

'She ...' I begin but he interrupts me.

'If not for yourself then for Ben's sake get your drug addiction sorted. You don't want this to get out of control.'

'What do you mean?' I say nervously. My head thumps with every beat of my heart.

'I think I've probably said enough. Sharni didn't want me to come round but I can't let something like this pass.'

'I ...'

'Sharni is very happy to have Ben as usual but obviously ...'

'I'm checking out nurseries,' I say quickly.

'That's your decision.'

He opens the door.

'Have a good day,' he says before striding down the path.

I close the door behind him and lean against it. What did he mean? His words seem to echo around the hallway, *If not for yourself then for Ben's sake get your drug addiction sorted.* He made it sound like I was on cocaine. What if they report me to social services? I wouldn't put anything past Sharni. I wring my hands nervously and then text Helen.

Chapter Twenty-Seven

Helen watched as Sharni expertly guided the children into perfect poses for their photograph. It had been Sharni's idea to create a Christmas backdrop. Helen was impressed with her patience. She made the children feel at ease and managed to get a smile from each child as she clicked the shutter. It was quite true, Helen thought, you should never judge a book by its cover. Maybe Clare had it all wrong about Sharni.

'A great find,' Geoff smiled.

'We should hire her,' said Helen. 'She's got the patience of a saint.'

'All credit to you for finding her.'

'Oh, I didn't find her as such. She lives right next door to Clare.'

'How about a group teacher photo,' Sharni called.

'Ooh, one of us. That makes a change,' laughed Helen.

'It's not normally what we do,' said Geoff uncertainly. 'But I agree it's a good idea. We don't have all the staff in today though.'

'We could phone around,' said Helen. 'We're only three down. Do you want to call Clare?' Helen asked Sharni.

Sharni's face clouded over. 'I'll leave that to you,' she smiled but Helen sensed her discomfort.

The other teachers laughed amongst themselves.

'Are you sure you don't mind?' asked Geoff. 'I don't imagine we'll be able to do it until after the kids finish at three.'

'That's fine,' smiled Sharni. 'I'm enjoying it.'

'I'll take Sharni for lunch shall I?' Helen said hopefully. It would make a change for her to take someone to lunch on school expenses. Geoff got to do it all the time so he couldn't very well say no.

'Of course, just put it on expenses. We'll see you after lunch to do year three.'

'Great, let's go to the little place around the corner,' said Helen, helping Sharni to pack up her equipment. 'Best put all this in the head's office.'

'God, you've got some patience,' said Helen, lighting up a cigarette and inhaling deeply.

'I like kids,' laughed Sharni.

'That's more than I bloody do.'

'But you're a teacher.'

'That doesn't mean I have to like the little darlings. Here we are.'

She led Sharni into the small restaurant. It smelt of fry-ups and Helen wrinkled her nose.

'It's normally quiet in here.'

She led Sharni to a table in the corner. They ordered a bottle of water and Helen said without preamble, 'So, what's happened between you and Clare?'

Sharni gave her a look of surprise.

'Has Clare said something?' she asked, avoiding Helen's eyes.

Helen pulled her phone from her bag.

'I had a text this morning. She seemed upset. I said I'd give her a ring at lunchtime but I don't want to be all excited about you taking a teacher photo and stuff if things are not good between you.'

Helen watched as Sharni sipped her water. She wasn't quite as plain as Helen had once thought. In fact, if that hair was highlighted and contacts replaced those hideous glasses she imagined Sharni could be quite pretty. A frown flickers across Sharni's forehead.

'I'm not really sure what I've done but she's got it in her head that I'm having an affair with Chris. It's my fault. I should have known she was insecure. I thought I'd give her a portrait photo of Chris and Ben for her anniversary. Father and son portraits are very popular. Tom told me where Chris's office was, and I popped in to see what Chris thought of the idea. He said he'd text me when he could come round and have the photos done.'

She shrugged.

'So that's what we did. It was all very innocent.'

Helen nodded and muttered, 'Ah.'

'But from the screaming that came from their place last night it sounded like she went through Chris's phone and saw his text to me. It was harmless. It was just us arranging a time for the photo shoot.'

'Oops,' said Helen, handing the menu to the waiter.

'I'm having a jacket potato.'

Sharni nodded.

'The same for me.'

Helen pushed her chair back and stretched.

'That seems a bit over the top,' she said. 'Mind you, she does get very anxious, especially over Ben.'

'I think she was cross with me yesterday. I didn't get Ben back until late. I had to go in to work. I didn't text because I thought we'd be back in time, and Ben was fine but I got waylaid. We were in the basement and there's no signal there and ...'

'She was pretty edgy. I tried to calm her,' remembered Helen.

'She takes a lot of medication doesn't she?'

Helen's head snapped up.

'She said it was aspirin.'

'It's Valium. I don't think they're good for her.'

'Christ, she's always popping the things.'

'Last night Chris came round in a bit of state. Seemed Ben was screaming and Clare couldn't find his comfort blanket. But I'd given it to Clare earlier. I remembered doing it.'

She shrugged.

'Still ...'

'Look,' said Helen. 'I've got to phone her. Let me see if I can talk her around. Maybe you two can talk after the photo session.'

'I don't think she'll come.'

'I think maybe those pills are affecting her. I'll be honest with you, and I am a bit outspoken, I thought you were a bit odd at the beginning. You know that stuff with the vase and ... anyway. I'm starting to think that maybe Clare's not well and probably needs our help. I'll call her now.'

Chapter Twenty-Eight

I check my phone again. Helen had texted that she would phone at lunchtime. But there's still no message. It rings and I grab it gratefully.

'Oh, Helen thanks for phoning. I didn't know who to turn to.'

'What's going on?'

'I'm not sure what's going on but Sharni is doing an awful lot of things behind my back. She's got Ben's comfort blanket for a start and she's got Ben calling her mama. It was really late when she got back yesterday and she's been going to Chris's office. I lost it last night with Chris and ...'

I burst into tears and fumble in my handbag for some paracetamol. I'd been crying on and off all morning and my head is thumping.

'Christ, it sounds like you've got yourself into a right old state. Honestly Clare, are you sure you're not getting everything out of proportion?'

'I don't know any more. I feel sure that Tom threatened me this morning too.'

'What? In what way?'

'He kind of hinted I wasn't fit to take care of Ben.'

'Well if you lost it with Chris I imagine they heard you.'

'Oh God, Helen, I accused Chris of having an affair with Sharni. You don't think he is, do you?'

'No I don't and look, don't take this the wrong way, but Sharni has been here this morning taking the kids photos and, well she's pretty upset and doesn't seem to know what she's done.'

My stomach churns. Helen has been talking to Sharni? Have they been talking about me?

'You've spoken to her?' I say numbly.

'Yes, this morning. Look Clare we're all having a staff photo taken. A Christmassy thing and it would be great if you could be in it. Geoff is waiting until this afternoon to see if we can get all the staff in. Please say you'll come.'

I feel like I'm suffocating. I thought Helen would be on my side. I struggle to breathe.

'I ...'

'You could chat to Sharni with me there. Surely it would be better to get things sorted.'

I grip the phone tightly and glance at Ben. He is playing with the bunny rabbit that Sharni bought him.

'It'll be such a shame if you're the only one not in the picture,' Helen continues.

I feel like everyone is manipulating me. Helen, who was supposed to be a friend has now been brainwashed by Sharni. How could she be so weak? How can all of them be so weak as to fall under her spell?

'I'll try,' I say. 'I'd better go. Ben's getting fidgety.'

'Great, see you at three.'

I hang up and struggle to breathe. I know I have no choice but to go to school and join in the photo. I know what everyone will say if I don't. I feel trapped. I'd spent the morning searching for a nursery until my neck went stiff. The only one that could take Ben was in Knightsbridge and cost the earth. I just can't imagine Chris agreeing to that. It occurred to me that the only way I could keep Ben with me was to take the rest of the year off sick. There was no way Geoff would put up with that. I drop my head into my hands and sob.

I stare at the vase on the dresser. Chris had tried to buy it secretly. I'd giggled like a schoolgirl when he'd said,

'Wait here. I'll just be a minute.'

I knew he was going to buy the vase. I'd pointed it out the day before. The small shop sat on a hill overlooking our hotel and we passed it every day. I'd looked longingly at the vase knowing we could never afford it. Our priority was our first home and not hand-painted vases. But Chris had managed to get a second and I couldn't have been more thrilled. I'd hugged him tightly. He was apologetic that it was not perfect but I said it was as perfect as it could ever get.

I held the vase in my hands and turned it around. I'm not sure what I expect to find. I stupidly tip it upside down, but nothing falls out. I don't know what I was hoping for; a little note to fall out perhaps, or a sign of some sort. I sigh in irritation and am about to put it back when something catches my eye.

I rummage through the kitchen drawers. Damn it. I'd seen the stupid magnifying glass numerous times when I hadn't needed it and now that I did it was nowhere to be found. I grab the vase again and hold it up against the light from the window. The vase had a ring of tulips around the base, but my vase had one imperfect tulip. I had always loved that slightly imperfect tulip because it reminded me of myself, imperfect and delicate.

I scrabble through Chris's toolkit and find the magnifying

glass and study the vase carefully. There isn't one imperfect tulip. This is not my vase. Sharni hadn't returned my vase at all.

I place it carefully on the hall table and calmly wrap Ben in his coat before throwing mine over my shoulders.

The driveway is empty. I know that Tom won't be back until this evening and Sharni is at the school until three. I let myself in with the key from under the paint pot, struggling with Ben's playpen as I do. The smell of fresh paint lingers in the air from the kitchen that looks more than ever like my own. I make my way to Sharni's office. The door is open and scattered around her printer are photos of Ben. I open the playpen and lift Ben in. I pick up a photo and gasp at the others that lie beneath. They're of Ben and Sharni together. Some have been taken on her bed, while others have been shot on the couch. I feel tears prick my eyelids. I pull myself away from the photos and turn to the wardrobe. Ben whoops and throws his rabbit into the air.

I touch the baby clothes which are neatly piled on the shelf. They're all neatly folded and smell of conditioner. My hand rests on the box marked *Nathan*. My heart is beating so hard that I can hear it in my ears. It blocks out everything. To the side of the box is another pile of photos and I pull them towards me carefully. I reel backwards in shock. They're black and white shots of Chris, and behind the photos is Ben's comfort blanket.

'Oh God,' I moan. She did lie. I wasn't wrong.

I flick through the photos. Chris is naked and smiling at the camera. Smiling at her, at Sharni, oh God, was she naked too?

I push them back with trembling hands and roughly swipe away the tears. I won't cry. I won't. Any sympathy I may have felt for Sharni losing her baby has gone now and I pull the lid off the box and stare in disbelief at the items inside. A lock of hair lies on a pair of tiny bootees, and I feel tears run down my cheeks. The box is full of memento's belonging to a child. Did Sharni lose a baby in tragic circumstances? Perhaps she is out of her mind with grief. Is that why she wants to be so close to Ben? On the other side of the box is a photo album. It's titled *Nathan*. I open it and let out a strangled cry. The photos inside are all of Ben.

'I almost didn't come,' she said.

'Why did you?' asked Leah.

'I've nowhere else to go,' she said with a sardonic smile.

'How have things been?'

'Better. I'm feeling more positive.'

'Do you feel more accepting?'

She picked up the box of tissues.

'Do you buy them?'

Leah looked confused.

'The tissues? No the association does.'

'People should bring their own.'

'Let's talk about you?' said Leah. 'In what way are you being more positive?'

'I've decided to take action.'

Leah stifled a sigh and sat back in her chair.

'Is that a good idea?'

'I think so.'

'Have you discussed this with your doctor, and with your husband?'

She laughed.

'They wouldn't agree with me.'

'Do you still think you're right?'

'I know what I saw.'

'It's not just easier for you to have someone else to blame.'

She shook her head and took a tissue from the box and slowly began to fold it.

'No, I know the accident was my fault. But I know what happened after.'

Leah sat forward in her seat.

'This doesn't help your grief, you know that?'

'What I don't understand is why no one believes me ...'

'Because they didn't find anything. The mind can do strange things in grief. I want to help you work through this. Everyone did their best. The police were thorough. You have to stop doing this to yourself.'

She stands up and pulls a box of tissues from a carrier bag. It has a floral design, the design she liked.

'This is my gift. To say thank you. You helped me see I wasn't mad. Everyone thinks I am, even you, but I know I'm not, and you've shown me the way forward. You've shown me that I will not get anywhere with talk, because no one will believe me. I know that I can't rely on anyone for help. I know I will have to do this on my own.'

She looked at the clock. It was two minutes to two. She put on her coat and stepped out of the room, forever.

Chapter Twenty-Nine

Sharni

I feel my legs tremble beneath me. I've prepared so long for this and now I'm about to do it, I feel I can't. I should have worn my coat but I want to look vulnerable. I push my finger on the doorbell. There's silence and I'm about to turn away when I hear her footsteps. I shiver with nervousness. The door opens and I'm face to face with her. The moment isn't what I expected. It feels too normal. She looks down at my breasts. She seems uncomfortable and I pull my cardigan around me. I swallow and say,

'Hello, it's freezing isn't it?'

I can't stop looking at her. She's wearing jeans and a thick jumper and studies me for a moment. That's fine. If she's going to recognise me it will be now, but she doesn't. There isn't even a flicker of recognition.

'I'm Sharni,' I say. 'We've just moved into number 24, next door.'

I point to the removal van.

'I'm Clare,' she says. 'It's nice to meet you.'

I feign embarrassment.

'I'm sorry to be a pain, already,' I smile. 'But I've been sent some flowers and I can't seem to find a vase anywhere. There are just so many boxes and ...'

'Oh, of course, come in.'

She opens the door wider.

'It's lovely and warm in here,' I say as the heat hits me.

'Do you not have heating?'

'Oh yes, but with the door open all the time it's impossible to stay warm.'

'I'll get you a vase,' she says and beckons me to follow her into the living room. 'Would you like a coffee?'

I see him and tears rush unbidden to my eyes. I quickly turn away and rub my eyes on my sleeve.

'I'm steamed up,' I say. 'A coffee would be great.'

She leaves the room and I hear her fumbling about in the kitchen. I bend down to Ben and stroke his hair.

'Hello my lovely. Aren't you gorgeous? Are you making rabbits?'

He smiles in response. I fight the urge to pick him up and hold him close to me. My hand trembles in his and I swallow the lump in my throat. I kiss his tiny hand and wipe my eyes.

'I'll help too,' I say.

Clare comes back with the coffee and a vase. It's pretentious and garish, a heavy ceramic thing with no style.

'Oh, that's lovely,' I say.

Ben guides my hand to the rabbit he wants me to colour.

'My husband bought it for me when we were honeymooning in Ireland.'

'If you're sure?' I ask, 'I'll bring it back tomorrow. It's just I don't want the flowers to die.'

'That's fine,' she says.

She pushes some papers off the coffee table and places a mug in front of me.

'He's adorable,' I say.

'He is.'

I stroke the top of his head and then reluctantly pull my hand away. She sips her coffee.

'You have a lovely home,' I add.

'Thank you.'

'I'm keen to get ideas. I want our house to look really nice. You've done a great job here.'

She's done a fucking lousy job and it's all I can do not to tell her so. I touch the art deco lamp on the side table and smile.

'Do you mind if I ask where you bought this?'

'John Lewis if I remember. They have lovely things there.'

Ben lets out a burp and we both laugh.

'How old is he?' I ask.

'Almost two.'

He struggles from her arms and attempts to walk towards me.

'He's just discovered his legs,' laughs Clare.

I quickly catch him before he falls.

'Do you have children?' she asks.

She may as well have kicked me in the stomach. Why am I not surprised she is so thoughtless? She sits in her motherhood smugness without a thought for anyone else.

'No,' I say.

She's uncomfortable and fidgets in her seat.

'Are you in interior design?' I ask to change the subject.

She laughs. She has white even teeth.

'Me? No, I wouldn't know where to start. I'm a teacher, well, only part-time now that we have Ben.'

'But this room is gorgeous, you have excellent taste. I'll have to pick your brains when I start decorating ours.'

'It'll be nice to have neighbours of our own age,' she says.

This is my opportunity.

'I've got a great idea, why don't you and your husband come

over Saturday evening for house-warming drinks. We can get to know each other better.'

'But you'll be up to your eyes won't you?' she says looking surprised.

'We'll need a break. Do say you'll come.'

'I'll need to check with Chris my husband, but I'm sure it will be okay.'

'Great,' I say getting up from the couch. 'Shall we say about eight? If you can't get a sitter then bring the toddler with you.'

She looks uncertain. She wants to ask if she can bring him but doesn't want to look too clingy. I need to get out before I do something I'll regret.

'Thanks,' she says finally. 'Enjoy your flowers.'

'Flowers?' I repeat and then I remember. Shit.

'The ones you needed the vase for.'

'Oh yes,' I say, picking up the garish vase. 'My mum sent them. Thanks Clare. See you on Saturday.'

Chapter Thirty

'Just taking a break,' the removal man shouts from the van. The men sit in the cab with steaming mugs of tea. I nod as I pass, enter the house and close the door firmly behind me, my hand gripping the vase. I'm shaking.

'Fucking bitch,' I hiss before throwing the vase with all my strength on to the kitchen floor. The vase smashes sending pieces of colourful ceramic scattering across the room. I grip the sink as my stomach heaves and wait for the nausea to pass. From the corner of my eye I see my phone flashing on the kitchen counter. I force my trembling legs over to it. There's a message from Tom.

I'm on my way back. Shouldn't be too long. How's it going?

I hear the removal men chatting at the front door and look around for the dustpan and brush.

'Had an accident?' the removal man says as he points to the floor.

'Yes, a vase. I don't think it can be repaired.'

'The perils of moving,' he smiles.

I sweep up the bits and then study the bottom piece before

placing the rest in a carrier bag. A quick search on Google brings up the pottery shop.

'If you send some pieces we can recreate it,' says the man at the other end of the phone.

'Fabulous,' I say. 'It's for a photoshoot for *Vogue* magazine. It has to be the identical to the original.'

'How exciting; please have the vase on us.'

'That's very kind, thank you.'

I click off the phone and go upstairs. The house is freezing. I search through a suitcase and find a thick jumper. My hand lands on the box and I pull it out carefully. The lid prises off easily and I stroke my cheek with Nathan's lock of hair. I rest my back against the foot of the bed and allow the memories to engulf me. It seems like only yesterday I had gripped Tom's hand.

'How much longer?' I asked through ragged gasps.

I could see the hopelessness in his eyes.

'Almost there,' said my mother but not before I saw her giving the doctor a concerned look.

It had been almost sixteen hours. I knew that some labours went on a long time but surely something should have happened by now.

'We're going to have to do a C section,' the doctor said.

I turned my head to look at him. Perspiration had run into my eyes and he became a blur in a white coat.

'No,' I said, but my voice wasn't as strong as I would have liked it to have been. Fifteen hours of labour had taken its toll.

'I don't want that,' I whispered to my mother.

'We have no choice,' said the doctor.

'They know best,' said Tom.

I could see he wanted it to be over. I felt another contraction starting and grabbed Tom's hand.

'It's going to be fine,' he said.

'Let's go,' I heard someone say and felt a prick in my arm and then, there was nothing.

Mum brought a huge bouquet of flowers.

'I'll have to take them to the cottage,' I said. 'They won't let me have them here.'

'Have we got enough vases for that lot?' laughed Tom.

'He's perfect,' said Mum holding up Nathan.

And it was true. How did they manage to produce something so perfect?

'He looks like you,' said Tom.

I squeezed his hand. He looked tired and his unshaven face made him look older than his thirty-six years.

'You look how I feel,' I smiled.

'I felt every contraction.'

'Sweetheart,' said Mum, stroking my arm 'There's something you need to know.'

Tom looked away but not before I saw the tears in his eyes.

'No,' I said quickly before Mum had a chance to say more. I could feel things were wrong. A woman knows.

'They had to remove your womb.'

I tried to block out the words. I shook my head emphatically. If I didn't accept them, they wouldn't be true.

'You can't have any more children.'

My cheeks felt wet and I realised I was crying. Mum clung to my hand and I thought how pale she looked.

'Couldn't it have waited?' asked Tom.

'I'd rather she heard it from us than the doctors.'

'It's okay,' I mumbled.

Mum's tears fell on to my hand.

'We'll visit the Lakes together,' I said as though she'd never spoken. 'As soon as I'm out of hospital that's what we'll do, you me and Nathan, okay?'

Mum nodded. I hugged baby Nathan close to my breast. I wouldn't think about other babies. Not yet.

Chapter Thirty-One

'I don't know why you're going to so much trouble. We barely know these people.'

'They seem nice. It will be good to have friends nearby,' I say, checking the Melba toasts. 'What do you think of the new lamp?'

'It's okay, if you like it that's what matters.'

'I saw it at Clare's. I think it looks good on the landing. We ought to get that light fitting fixed Tom.'

'I've got an electrician coming,' he smiles. He lifts the glasses from my face and pushes them to the top of my head.

'I wish you'd wear your contacts. You look so much prettier.'

'My eyes get sore,' I lie. My stomach churns. With every lie to Tom another piece of me dies.

'I know,' he says, turning to the champagne bottles on the table.

'I'll crack one open shall I?'

'Great,' I say fiddling with my earrings. 'Tom, don't tell them about ...'

'Of course not,' he says.

'Or about the cottage.'

'Why would I?'

I nod. Of course he wouldn't but it's best to be sure.

'By the way, Rachel said she's been trying to get hold of you.' He looks at me closely.

'Yes, I keep meaning to call her back.'

I have tried to call her back. I just never quite manage to hit that final digit.

'She said she misses seeing you.'

'I miss her. It's just ... well you of all people should understand Tom.'

He nods.

'I'll get the glasses.'

I take a deep breath and check the toasts in the oven. I'll phone Rachel tomorrow. I reach for the tray and burn my finger. I jerk back and lick the burn. A memory rushes into my head and I hear Rachel's voice.

'Are you okay?'

'Shit,' I muttered. 'I burnt my hand on the tray. I've got no bloody coordination these days.'

'Here let me,' she said, and pulled out the tray of muffins with ease.

'Nothing to it,' she'd laughed.

I pushed the pram into the middle of the garden and breathed in the scent of the honeysuckle. The cottage windows were wide open. I loved it here. The Lakes had always been special to me. Tom marvelled that the sun even shone. It's supposed to always rain in the Lake District, he'd joked.

Tom always complained the cottage was too small but I'd loved it from the first day we'd set eyes on it. I didn't mind the small living room. It was cosy and warm, even cosier now that Tom had set up a little desk in the corner.

'I'm off soon,' he said, coming up behind me. 'It's going to be another hot one isn't it?'

I looked up at the clear sky. It was ten in the morning and the sun was already scorching.

'Yes, Rachel thought we might take Nathan to Silecroft beach. Shoot some photos.'

'Sounds perfect, I wish I could join you.'

'Good luck today. I'm sure you'll win.'

'Nothing is certain but I think I've a good chance,' smiled Tom.

I loved that Tom was so confident. I kissed him warmly and then watched his car disappear down the country lane. Nathan was sleeping peacefully and Rachel and I decided to take the opportunity to get a few jobs done in the cottage.

'Let's fortify ourselves first with muffin and tea,' she said pouring from the teapot.

We drank from china cups and felt blessed that we had such fulfilled lives. Later we left Nathan in his pram in the sunshine while we filled vases with fresh flowers that we'd cut from the garden. I could see the pram from the kitchen window. I knew he was safe. It was so quiet that if Nathan hiccupped I would hear him.

Rachel's gaze drifted to the holiday cottage. She could see someone moving in the garden. I never bothered to introduce myself to holidaymakers. There seemed little point.

'Don't you ever wonder about them?' Rachel asked.

'Not really.'

Rachel sketched while I tidied the garden. It was an idyllic lifestyle. I knew it wouldn't last forever. Soon I'd have to return to work but for the moment I was making the most of it.

'Christ, it's hot isn't it?' complained Rachel, wiping the sweat from her brow.

I poured more water into our glasses.

'I like it.'

'You're probably not feeling it. Your hormones are up the creek ...'

She stopped and I felt her discomfort. My hormones would of course be up the creek. They'd taken away my womb. I fought the resentment I felt at the doctor. I knew he was only doing his job.

'They sure are.'

'What I meant ...' began Rachel.

'It's fine,' I said in an attempt to put her at ease.

'Listen, would you and Tom like to come bowling tomorrow? Nachos and beer on us.'

'I don't think I'll make a great team member but yes, sounds great. I'd better check with Tom though.'

'Ooh yes, it's a big case he's on isn't it? Is he ahead?'

'He thinks so.'

'Fabulous. Shall we say seven, unless I hear from you to say otherwise? God, I hope it bloody rains soon.'

I wiped the perspiration from my own forehead. I couldn't help agreeing that a storm would clear the air. My eyes strayed to the holiday cottage. The couple staying there were strolling down the lane. It wouldn't be much fun for them if it poured with rain. My hair was stuck to my neck and I pulled it back and clipped it with a slide.

'Shall we go to Silecroft Beach?' Rachel asked. 'It will be peaceful there. You can take photos while I sketch.'

I push the memory from my mind and stare at the tray. I ought to get ready, they'll be here soon. I'm really not looking forward to spending an evening with the bitch but I've no choice if my plan is to work.

'I'll make Bellini's,' Tom says as the doorbell chimes.

I take a deep breath and open the door. Clare's perfume wafts over me. It has alcohol undertones. Clearly she's only just put it on.

'You're wearing *Grapefruit*,' I say. 'I love Jo Malone.'

'It's one of my few luxuries,' she says.

'Come in,' I say as warmly as I can.

I take them into the lounge where I've laid the table. Tom offers around the canapés. Clare protests when I offer her a mango Bellini.

'I'm not drinking,' she says in her feeble voice.

'Don't be silly, you're here to christen the house with us, what better way than with a champagne Bellini?'

She looks around the lounge, just as I hoped she would. She'll be looking for her vase. I see her glance at the cards on the windowsill and then at the photos on the wall.

'Do sit down,' I tell her, pointing to the couch. I miss our old couch with its handmade crocheted blankets. I miss everything. I shake my head. This is not the time for memories.

'The house is lovely,' Clare says.

Tom laughs. He knows how hard I've been working to get the place to look just right.

'You haven't seen the upstairs. Everything that hasn't been unpacked is up there,' he says.

Clare studies the photos on the wall.

'Nice photos,' she says.

I step closer to her. Her perfume overpowers me.

'I took them,' I say, pouring champagne into her glass.

'You did?' says Chris. 'They're brilliant.'

He doesn't have to sound so bloody surprised. Clare attempts to cover the glass with her hand.

'Oh, no more,' she says feebly, 'I really can't be drunk in charge of a two-year-old.'

I want to slap her. You're not fit to be in charge of a goldfish, I scream in my head.

'You're not with him now,' I say calmly, removing her hand. 'I could take some photos of Ben if you like?'

Her reaction is perfect. She doesn't understand how I know her child's name.

'You're a good photographer,' she says, but I can see her mind working,

'She should be. It's her job,' laughs Tom.

'Really?' says Chris. 'Who do you work for?'

'Chris is a town planner. He's always taking photos of roads. You know, for road improvements,' says Clare, helping herself to a Melba toast. She seems unsteady on her feet.

'It's not quite the same,' says Chris.

He seems embarrassed. They're not used to professional people. They're out of their depth.

'I'm freelance,' I say. 'I take fashion photos. I design the sets for fashion shoots. I do a lot of work for *Vogue*, do you know it? I have a studio in their London offices.'

'But mostly she gets to work from home, the lucky woman,' says Tom, kissing me on the cheek. 'Town planning, that's interesting,' he adds, turning to Chris.

'These are excellent,' Clare slurs as she looks at the photos.

'It would be great to have a professional photo of Ben,' says Chris. 'Wouldn't it Clare?'

I knew he'd take the bait. He's weak.

'I'd be happy to take photos of him,' I smile. Chris will be like putty in my hand.

'What do you do Clare?' Tom asks as he uncorks another bottle of champagne.

'I'm a school teacher. I only do two days a week now.'

'She helps at the local nursery too,' adds Chris.

'That must be great for Ben,' I say, trying to keep my voice flat. I don't want the sarcasm to show.

'We like to get involved,' says Chris. 'We're key holders too, so should there ever be a problem we're the first on the list.'

Tom likes Chris, I can tell. God knows why. The guy is an idiot. Poor Tom, if only he knew.

'Lucky you,' says Tom, clinking Clare's glass. 'I feel like I do eight days a week.'

'Tom's a barrister, so it never really stops,' I say.

'That must be really interesting,' says Chris.

I sip my champagne. I mustn't drink too much. I need to stay in control. If she asks for the vase I'll tell her it's in our bedroom. I'll apologise profusely and promise to give it back in the morning. I'll have to tell Tom I lost it. It's not far from the truth after all.

'Clare is brilliant at interior design,' I lie.

'No, I'm not really,' she protests.

I tend to agree with her but don't let it show on my face.

'You're too modest,' I laugh.

'I'll get some beers,' Tom says.

'I'll get them,' I say and grab Clare by the arm. 'I want to show Clare the kitchen.'

She looks surprised at the mess. I pull a tray of tartlets from the Aga while she looks around.

'The kitchen's a bit of a tip, I know. I thought I'd wallpaper, what do you think? I really value your opinion.'

Like hell I do.

'I think wallpaper would be nice,' she says nervously.

'I'm not sure. Paint is so much easier,' I say, deliberately confusing her.

'Yes, our kitchen is painted.'

'Do you want a beer?' I offer.

She shakes her head. I take a breath and say,

'Perhaps we could go to Liberty's together. How about Monday? You don't work Mondays do you?' I attempt to sound excited but I'm not sure it works.

'How do you know I don't work Mondays?' she asks sharply.

My first mistake but never mind. It has unsettled her so perhaps it was not so bad a mistake after all. I pause for a second to think of a way to recover.

'It was Monday when we moved in. You were home. I just presumed you don't work on Mondays.'

'Oh, of course, I forgot.'

'We could do lunch too,' I suggest. This would give me more time with him.

'I'll have Ben,' she says.

As if I needed reminding.

'That's okay. It'll be great to take Ben out. I can take some photos of him. Kill two birds with one stone.'

'Well ...'

I pour more champagne into her glass.

'Let's get these beers to the guys,' I say ushering her back into the lounge.

After two hours Clare is so tipsy that she can't even find her phone in her handbag. We all respectfully look away as she pulls lots of rubbish from the oversized tote in an attempt to find it. She's worried about the sitter. She has no need to be. Kathryn is perfect. I'd checked her out thoroughly.

'Can I use your loo?' she asks.

'Sure,' I say. 'It's upstairs first on the left.'

'You've dropped something,' says Chris.

She fumbles around the floor picking things up. I manage to

kick the keys behind my handbag before she sees them. I watch her stumble up the stairs.

'There's no light bulb,' I call. 'Turn the lamp on.'

She doesn't hear me follow her up. She's looking at the lamp.

'I got it from John Lewis.'

She starts. Her cheeks are red from the alcohol and her eyes look bleary.

Call yourself a mother, I want to shout. *Look at yourself. I'd never allow myself to get in this state,* but instead I say,

'Sorry, did I scare you?'

'It's okay,' she says shakily, and grabs the bannister for support.

'I hope you don't mind,' I say pointing to the lamp. 'I love it so much. I thought I'd put it up here.'

'I'm flattered,' she smiles.

'You girls okay up there? I'm making coffee,' calls Tom.

'Clare just saw our new lamp,' I smile.

'You shouldn't have such good taste Clare,' says Tom. 'Do you want a coffee?'

'We should be going,' she says.

I'm relieved. It's been a strain having them here but things couldn't have gone better.

'I'll see you Monday,' I say, forcing myself to give her a hug.

'You must come to us next time,' says Chris. 'Come for dinner.'

We watch them walk down the drive and finally Tom closes the door.

'That went well didn't it?' he says yawning. 'You seem to get on well with her. I can't think what you've got in common though.'

'I'll clear up,' I say. I don't want Tom to find the keys.

'Chris is an okay guy. I'll see if he wants to play badminton one evening.'

I should tell him. I open my mouth to speak and then stop myself. I can't face his recriminations and the look of disbelief on his face. He'll be disappointed, let down.

'Just when I thought it was all over,' he'll say. But he doesn't realise that it will never be all over for me.

'I'll load the dishwasher,' he says.

The keys are still beside my handbag. They're labelled, *NURSERY KEYS*. I drop them into my bag and then clear the table.

Chapter Thirty-Two

I need to work fast. The woman is already neurotic. It won't take long to push her over the edge. I make the most of my time with Ben. He loves the camera and I take lots of photos. Her ideas for the house are useless but I pretend otherwise and wander around Liberty's with her pointing out things that I would never have in my house.

'Shall we get a coffee?' I ask.

'Sounds good,' she agrees.

I stay silent. I want her to offer.

'I'll get them,' she says. 'You bought lunch.'

She throws the tote over her shoulder.

'Okay to leave everything with you?' she asks.

I smile.

'Sure. I must get some flowers before we go home,' I say pretending to look at a shopping list. She hesitates. It's killing her. She wants to ask about the vase, I can read her like a book. She doesn't know how to bring it up. She's clearly intimidated by me. I smile and wait for her to speak but she doesn't.

'A cappuccino for me,' I say.

She nods and walks to the counter. There is a long queue. I

wait until she can't see me and then I buckle Ben up and hook our bags over the stroller.

'Are you leaving?' asks a guy approaching with his girlfriend.

'Yes, we are,' I say, standing up.

I push the stroller to the other side of the room and sit at a table behind a pillar. I watch as Clare looks frantically around for us. Confident that she can't see me, I open the pharmacy bag and look inside. I carefully remove ten diazepam tablets and slip them into my purse. I smile at Ben and adjust his blanket.

'Okay gorgeous?' I ask pulling out my phone.

We're by the window. I text and move my chair so I can be seen from the counter.

Clare spots us and I wave casually from behind the pillar. She looks about to collapse and I almost pity her, but only almost.

'You look really hot,' I say when she reaches us.

'It's stuffy in here,' she says in a trembling voice.

'We had to move,' I lie. 'The draught there was awful. I didn't think it was good for Ben.'

'I wondered where you'd both gone.'

She's struggling to keep her voice even. I wonder how many diazepam she has already taken.

'Ooh muffins,' I say.

'I didn't know what you liked so I got blueberry.'

'Chocolate's my favourite,' I say to add a feeling of disapproval to her anxiety.

Her face drops.

'But blueberry is nice too,' I add.

I wait a while and then suggest she and Chris come for Christmas. I'd discussed it with Tom. He was surprised at my suggestion. It would be nice to have a child at Christmas I had begun and argued that we would only be on our own anyway and that it would make me happy to have a child around at Christmas. Tom had agreed, but only after he had cross-examined me, checking that I could cope.

'I'll ask Chris,' Clare says.

'Great,' I say but she doesn't hear me. A friend from school approaches her and I leave them chatting. I make my escape and walk around the food hall for a while. It's a relief to be free from Clare.

Chapter Thirty-Three

'Jesus,' mumbles Tom. 'What's wrong with that child?'

'He's been screaming for ages,' I say.

'Where are those earplugs?'

He flicks on the bedside lamp and I squint at the intrusion.

'I've got a lot on tomorrow,' he grumbles, rummaging in a drawer.

I can't bear listening to Ben's screams. It's all I can do to stop myself from marching to their door and bringing him back here where he'll be safe and loved.

'I can't imagine what it's like for them,' he mumbles before pulling the duvet over his head.

I think about what I'm going to say to Rachel. Will she talk about Nathan? I close my eyes and picture her face. Tom begins to snore and I quietly climb from the bed and go to my office. I open the wardrobe and lift the photo albums from the top shelf. I have to search to find it but when I do the feelings of loss envelope me like a black shroud and I feel like I'm suffocating. Rachel is smiling, her thick hair flying behind her. The sky is a clear blue and Nathan's face is visible under Rachel's cotton kaftan.

I close my eyes and allow myself to travel back to happier times.

'He's going to be the most photographed baby in the world,' laughed Rachel.

I composed the picture through the viewfinder and clicked the shutter. We laid Nathan on the blanket and stretched ourselves out on the warm sand. The sun burnt our faces. I felt happy and complete.

'This is the life,' Rachel said. 'Shame I have to go back to work on Monday. It's been a fab week. I've got some great sketches.'

Our feet sunk into the sand as we wandered down to the lake.

'We need to make lots of memories,' I said as I clicked the shutter.

'I'm going for a paddle,' Rachel said.

I checked Nathan was protected from the sun and followed her to the water's edge. I took more pictures of a smiling Rachel, with the blue water behind her.

'When we're old, Nathan can look back at these photos and see how young and carefree we were,' laughed Rachel.

'He's going to be very clever, aren't you darling,' I said. 'Tom and I have decided he will go to Oxford.'

'Blimey, no pressure then.'

I took photos of Nathan's tiny feet. The milky smell of him soothed me and I changed lens and took shots of people enjoying the sunshine. We had coffee in the little teashop near the beach and bought fish and chips to have later. It was that day Tom won. The day I wondered how much longer we could stay in the Lake District.

'We won! I'm bringing bubbly home. Can you have just a little drop?'

'Congratulations, I'm so pleased for you. You deserved to win.'

I knew it was only a matter of time before he got an offer from a practice in London.

'If only these times could last forever,' Rachel said.

'Nothing lasts forever,' I said.

It was an unsettled calm but of course I didn't know that then. The crying becomes fainter and I picture Clare taking Ben downstairs.

I go back to bed and try to imagine her reaction when they phone from the nursery tomorrow. What if she has someone else who could look after him? No, it's not possible. I'd covered all avenues. She would only ask Kathryn or Helen. Kathryn will be at college and Helen at school. She will have to ask me. There is no one else. It's her appraisal and she won't want to miss that. I'd overheard her talking to Helen about it. She's anxious about losing her job. She needs the money. She won't miss it. I am certain of that.

Disrupting Clare's life had been easier than I imagined. The nursery had closed at seven. I'd told Tom I had to go into the studio to sort out a problem with the Chanel shoot. He had a meeting with a client, so it didn't matter to him that dinner would be late.

It was dark but I'd spent some time looking around the nursery with the light from my phone. It's a good nursery. I'd be happy for a child of mine to go there, not that I would ever need to send my child to a nursery. I'd be at home with my child, all day, every day.

It took just a few minutes to block the sink and turn on the taps. I remembered exactly where the toilets were. Hopefully the place would be out of action for a couple of days. A shame for the other parents but I had to think of Ben. I closed the toilet doors and found my way to the exit and let myself out. It had been that easy.

I strain my ears to hear the cries but everything is quiet now. I close my eyes and try to sleep.

I take my time opening the door. I don't want her to guess I was expecting her. She looks harassed.

'Clare, is everything okay?' I ask, feigning concern.

'I'm really sorry,' she says fighting back tears. 'The nursery phoned and they've had to close for the day. I've got an appraisal at eleven and ...'

'You've got no one to have Ben,' I say.

'I'm so sorry to ask but ...'

'Of course I can have him,' I say, taking the bags from her. I fight the urge to grab Ben and wait until she is inside the house before taking him out of her arms. He feels warm and cosy. I inhale the scent of him and sigh with contentment. I see her looking at me.

'You look terrible,' I say. 'Are you okay?'

Like I actually give a damn if she's okay or not. If she were to fall at my feet gasping for breath I wouldn't help her. She mumbles something about not getting enough sleep. That's all she does. Complain, complain.

'We'll be okay, won't we Sweet Pea?' I say, unbuttoning his jacket. I just wish she'd go and leave us alone. Then she has the nerve to hand me a screwed up piece of paper with instructions on it.

'It's all on here. His nap times and what time he has his lunch and ...'

'Great,' I smile. 'We'll be fine.'

'That bag has his training pants and ...'

'We'll be fine,' I say sharply.

'Are you sure?' she asks stupidly. 'I can take him in with me.'

I fight back a sigh.

'That won't look very professional will it?' I say and smile at her condescendingly.

'No,' she says.

I make a point of looking at the clock in the hallway.

'You'll be late.'

She doesn't want to leave him. She's nervous because she doesn't know me well.

'You can call my mobile as many times as you like,' I say encouragingly.

'Thanks,' she says finally and turns to the door.

'I'll phone you later,' she says kissing Ben on the cheek.

As soon as she's out of the door I close it. I can't stand to look at her face for one minute longer. I'm so taken up with my darling child that I completely forget about her key. I hurriedly open the door and call out to her.

'Do you have a spare key to your house?'

'A key?' she asks suspiciously.

'Just in case, for toys, and the stroller, so we can go for a walk.'

She seems uncertain for a second and then hands me her key.

'The stroller is in the porch. His toys are in a box in the lounge. Oh, and his playpen is in the bedroom. I'd better go.'

With the key clasped tightly in my hand I turn back into the house and close the door.

'Just you and me darling,' I whisper into his little ears. 'We're going to have a lovely day aren't we?'

Not long now and we're going to have lots of lovely days. My thoughts turn to Tom and the familiar churning returns to my stomach. How am I going to explain this to him? Do I even want to explain it to him? I force my thoughts away from Tom and take Ben upstairs.

'Shall we take some photos?' I say, grabbing my camera.

I can't believe I've got a whole day with him. I'll puree vegetables for his lunch. She's too full of herself to ever think about doing that. I can't stand the thought of him eating all that processed baby food.

The morning flies by. I decide to unsettle Clare by sending her a text asking if Ben has any allergies. As expected she goes into a panic. She not only texts a reply but then phones me. No doubt she popped a couple of her tranquilliser pills in the meantime. I wrap Ben up and walk to Clare's house to get the stroller. The woman across the road is sitting at her window again and I wave. She doesn't wave back. I'm glad I put the vase in a carrier bag. The last thing I need is a witness seeing me taking it in. The living room is a mess. A pillow and blanket are strewn on the couch. A half-eaten bowl of porridge lies on the coffee table alongside a cold cup of tea. Ben's toys are strewn all over the floor. I tut in annoyance and make my way upstairs for Ben's playpen. Not that I'll need it. No child of mine would ever be put inside a cage. I would watch him properly. The diazepam is in the bathroom and I take five yellow pills and slip them into my jacket pocket. The bedroom is tidy and I take a photo. Ben plays happily on the bed while I slowly look around and check labels.

'Come on Sweet Pea,' I say. 'Let's go shopping and get a copy of the key cut.'

I drop the nursery keys on to the floor as we leave and kick them under the couch. I place the vase at the back of the cupboard under the sink, and hide it behind some cleaning bottles and dusters.

The duvet cover is easy to find. The lamps are out of stock so I order them to collect the next day. Waterstones is quiet and I have a coffee while Ben cuddles his new rabbit.

'Do you have *The Lovely Bones*?' I ask the assistant. 'I can't remember the author.'

'Yes we do,' she smiles.

'We're doing well aren't we,' I say to Ben. 'Let's get you some building blocks and some nice dungarees.'

He claps his little hands in excitement. I decide to get some reins so that next time we come out he can toddle around while I have a coffee. The bedside cabinets are in stock and I arrange for them to be delivered tomorrow as well. We stroll around Marks and Spencer where I buy Ben some new clothes.

'He's adorable,' says the assistant. 'How old is he?'

'Just over two.'

'What's his name?' she asks, pinching his cheek.

'Nathan, his name is Nathan,' I say.

'Hello Nathan. You must be so proud,' she smiles.

'We are,' I say smiling back.

And Tom would be, if only he understood. The day goes much too quickly and I find myself hoping that Clare gets held up at the school. When Chris phones I feel my hopes rise.

'I can't get hold of Clare. Everything's okay with Ben isn't it?'

'He's fine. He's having a nap. I should wake him actually. I got carried away with work.'

The truth was I'd got carried away with printing the photos of Ben. I hadn't done any work.

'I'm sorry to have bothered you.'

'Don't be silly. I'd be phoning every two minutes if I'd left my child with someone.'

'Oh, we're not like that,' he says. 'Has Clare been in touch?'

'Yes, earlier today.'

'Great, well, I'd better get back to work. Thanks for having Ben at such short notice.'

I check the time and slowly remove the new dungarees. I'm ready for when she arrives. She's taken aback by the perfume I'm wearing and recognises it as *Grapefruit* right away. I want to take everything from her, bit by bit, until she knows what it feels like to have her life stolen from her. How it feels to hang on to reality by a thread. Then she checks Ben's forehead. I fight back a comment and wait for her to see the photos, just the ones I want her to see. The best ones are upstairs. She's pleased with them. Excitement and pleasure are written all over her simple face. She tells me the appraisal went well and then hesitates before revealing she has been offered more hours. This is my chance and I grab it with both hands.

'You know if ... well, I don't mind having him if you didn't want to pay out to the nursery. It would be a shame if all the extra money you earn goes to pay the nursery fees. I'm home and he's no trouble.' I try to sound nonchalant and shuffle the photos.

'Oh, I couldn't ask you to do that,' she says, but I can see her brain working. She's thinking about it.

'It's really not a problem to me,' I say. 'Have a chat with Chris about it.'

She nods. Chris will say yes if he thinks he can save a few pennies. It's all I can do to hide my excitement.

Chapter Thirty-Four

'So, we'd love you to have Ben if the offer still stands.'

'It would be a pleasure to have him,' I say, giving Ben a loving look.

'We'll pay you of course,' she says earnestly.

'I'd be insulted if you paid me. After all, isn't that what friends are for? Besides the idea was so that you didn't spend your extra earnings on childcare.'

She looks relieved. They're saving a packet by not paying nursery fees. What kind of mother would give her child to someone she barely knows just to save money? Clare and Chris Ryan, that's who.

Tom is playing badminton with Chris at lunchtime. I don't know what it is about Chris that Tom likes. No doubt Chris looks up to him. Tom has always liked that, he feels flattered. I'm anxious for her to leave. The bedside cabinets are being delivered today and I really don't want her to be here when they arrive.

'I'd better get on,' I say.

'Oh yes me too. I'm off to Ikea with Helen.'

She hesitates a bit longer and then says,

'I'll see you Thursday then.'

I watch as she trots down the drive with the stroller and then close the door. I'd already stripped the bed. By the time I change the bed linen and vacuum the carpet the cabinets should have arrived. The new lamps are in their boxes under the window. Tom had really liked them which had been fortunate. He's so bogged down with his latest case that I don't think he's noticing anything. I wish I could go back to the cottage. I so hate London, but I can't. I can't go back until everything is done. I check the time. The delivery is for eleven-thirty and my hair appointment is for two. I've got plenty of time.

The sound of a door slamming makes me jump.

'It's only me Mrs Larson.'

I look over the bannister to see Jack.

'You found the key okay?'

'Yes, should I have knocked?'

'No, that's fine. I'll be working on the bedroom today so you just carry on. I've cleared the kitchen for you.'

At some point she will come in. At some point I will guide her to the bedroom. Soon she will realise what it feels like to have your life stolen from you and that's a moment I will treasure.

Maria looks back at me through the mirror.

'It's a lot to take off,' she says.

Her own hair is immaculately styled and she tucks her streaked locks behind her ears.

'That's what I'd like,' I say, stepping into the overall.

Trudi, the junior, sprinkles water over my head and begins massaging in shampoo.

'Are you at home for Christmas?' she asks, rubbing in coconut conditioner.

I give a small nod. I'm not in the mood for small talk and close my eyes as the warm water runs down my neck. I'm led back to Maria where a cup of strong coffee awaits. Maria snips and I watch my hair fall on to my shoulders. The loud buzz of the hairdryer drowns out the radio in the background. I flex my neck and ignore the thumping of my head. Fifteen minutes later and I'm all done. I glance at my reflection and smile.

'What do you think?' Maria asks.

I much preferred it the way it was but it will soon grow out.

'It's terrific,' I say.

I leave the hairdressers and catch a taxi to Harley Street. I stand outside Dr Grant's clinic and look at the brass plaque outside. I'm too nervous to go in, so I jump on a bus to Oxford Street. I occasionally catch my reflection in a shop window. It's like looking at a stranger. The thick-rimmed glasses make me look so plain. Maybe I should get more appealing frames. I think better of it and catch another bus back to Harley Street where this time I go into the clinic and make an appointment with the receptionist and then make my way back home.

It happens sooner than I imagined. I'm thrilled to see Ben again but I'm not prepared for her and I'm afraid the surprise shows on my face.

'Oh hi,' I say.

She stares at me.

'Your hair looks different,' she says.

She has caught me off guard. I didn't expect to see her again today.

'Do you like it? I thought your style was so tidy. Mine was such a wreck.'

'Hello Sweet Pea.' I can't resist him and lean down to touch his cheek.

'I liked your hair as it was,' she says.

'Ditto, do you want to come in for a coffee?' I laugh.

'I went to Ikea with Helen. Both Ben and I are knackered.'

'God, you're brave. I never go to Ikea,' I lie.

She looks behind me. She can smell the paint.

'I've been painting the kitchen. I know we looked at that great wallpaper but ... Anyway come and have a look and tell me what you think.'

She takes Ben out of the stroller and follows me to the kitchen. She's surprised to see the painter. Her eyes widen when she sees the colour.

'Sorry, did you think I was doing it? I'm giving out the orders. This is Jack. If you ever need a painter I can recommend him, he's the best. Are you sure you don't want a coffee? I'm just about to make one.'

'I'm fine, really. You've gone for the same colour as ...'

'Yes, your kitchen is so lovely, I had to copy you,' I say casually.

Ben reaches his arms out to me. I can barely hide my elation.

'Is it okay?' I ask.

Before she can answer I've taken him into my arms where he belongs.

'Hello darling.'

She can't find her keys in that awful muddled handbag of hers. I could offer my set but of course I don't.

'Everything okay?' I ask, while not caring if it was or wasn't.

'This damn handbag, I can never find anything in it. I can't find my keys now.'

She walks straight into my traps. She's forever making things easy for me.

'I'm sure they're there. But you know if you ever do get shut out you can always come in here. There's a spare key under an old paint tin in the garden. That's how Jack gets in if I'm not around.'

I'm not sure if she's heard me as she makes no comment. She asks to use the loo. I try to remember if I'd left the bedroom door ajar. I do hope so. She goes upstairs and I take Ben into the lounge. I don't want Jack to see me with him. I can't help wondering why Clare has come. Was she going to ask for the vase? I hear her footsteps on the stairs and I step into the hall with Ben. Her face is ashen. She's trying to hide it but she's clearly shaken. Her hand grips the bannister. I know she has seen the bedroom. I try to hide my smugness but I'm sure it shows.

Chapter Thirty-Five

'I preferred your hair the way it was,' Tom says, pulling off his shirt.

'It was unmanageable.'

He shrugs.

'In fact, I preferred how you had it a few years back and ...'

'Tom,' I say sharply.

'Okay, I'm just saying,' he finishes lamely.

I pull a brush through my hair and say cheerily,

'I'm enjoying having Ben.'

He stops fiddling with his tie and looks at me.

'You're not finding it a strain? I don't mind you doing it but if it becomes too much ...'

I sigh.

'No I'm not finding it too much at all. In fact ...'

His phone bleeps and he looks down at it.

'Oh Christ, I'd better phone James.'

'It's Saturday,' I groan. 'We're expected at Clare's in ten minutes.'

'It won't take long. It'll take you another fifteen minutes to do your make-up and whatnot.'

He wraps his arms around me and buries his head in my breasts.

'I wish we didn't have to go,' he mumbles. 'I'd much rather stay here with you.'

'She's gone to a lot of trouble,' I say stroking his head. 'I really should get my dress on.'

'Okay. I'll see you downstairs. Wear your contacts tonight. You look far better with them.'

'I don't want sore eyes,' I lie.

He nods absently, his mind is on the call he's about to make.

'Thanks for inviting us,' says Tom, handing Clare the bunch of flowers I had bought from the garage. She has the photos I took of Ben on display and a pain shoots through my heart. I turn away and smile at Clare's friend, Helen.

'Hello,' I say. 'I think we met in Marks.'

'Good memory,' says Helen. 'I've been admiring your photos of Ben.'

I'm forced to look back at the photos. I keep a smile pasted on my face.

'If you'll excuse me,' says Clare.

She looks harassed and anxious. A few seconds later I hear her footsteps on the stairs. I wonder if she's yet noticed how fast her diazepam is going down. She's made a big effort with the food. I'm not so sure the Melba toasts were a good idea but Helen seems to like them.

'Clare made them. I think it's the first time she has,' Chris says, offering a tray around.

'We were just complimenting you on the toasts,' says Tom when she returns.

'I had a bit of time to spare,' she says looking embarrassed.

'I hear you're going to be looking after Ben when Clare's at school,' says Helen.

Helen doesn't like me, I can tell. She's more suspicious of me than Clare.

'I'm looking forward to it,' I reply.

'So, you don't work full-time as a photographer then?' asks Helen.

Right from the beginning I had a feeling Helen might be a problem. She's no fool. I sip from my glass.

'I work from home,' I say. 'Ben is no trouble.'

'It's very good of you. I said to Clare, not many women would have another woman's child free of charge.'

'What are friends for but to help?' I smile.

I must keep calm. To lose it now would spoil everything. I keep the smile pasted on my face and feel my jaw ache from the effort.

'As long as you don't take on too much,' Tom says, kissing me.

God, does he have to make me sound like a bloody fragile doll. I brush him off gently. Helen raises her eyebrows but says nothing. I can see I'm going to have to work on her.

Just when I was beginning to think the evening was a total waste of time Helen starts banging on about the flowers and how Clare should put them in some water. She winks at Clare and I know that Clare has mentioned the vase to her. I purposefully give Clare a questioning look which does the trick and she seems unnerved.

'Let me help,' I say, adding to her agitation.

'It's okay, you relax.'

There's a murmur from the baby monitor and Clare rushes upstairs. Helen follows her and I smile to myself.

'Thanks for a lovely evening,' I say to Chris.

'Thanks for coming. It's the least we could do to thank you for everything.'

He hasn't noticed my hair is in the same style as his wife's. I wonder if he notices much at all. Tom had commented on the similarity. I know he doesn't like it. I want to tell him it won't be forever. Soon everything will be the same, exactly the same. If he was more open I could tell him, but I know he will drag me back to those stupid doctors and we'll be back where we started. I can't have that. Not now, not now I'm so close.

Clare marches back into the room and we all turn to look at her.

'I'll put the flowers in water, can you get a vase Chris?' she says and pointedly nods towards me. I feel a tingle of anticipation run down my spine.

Chris turns to me and says,

'Ah, Sharni, now you and Tom have the house a bit straight would it be okay to have our vase back, or do you still need it?'

Helen has followed Clare into the room and is watching us all expectantly.

'I gave Clare the vase,' I say triumphantly.

I look Clare straight in the eyes. She turns away. She feels uncomfortable.

'Oh, well there you go then,' says Helen. 'Why don't you put the flowers in that?'

'I don't think you did Sharni,' Clare says. 'I'd have remembered. It's a special vase.'

'Well, someone's got it wrong,' says Helen.

Tom taps me on the arm but I'm not stopping now. I'm going to enjoy making a fool of her.

'I came round with it Clare, don't you remember? I was a bit late bringing it back. I apologised for that. You were having trouble with your washing machine.'

She struggles to remember. Her face shows recognition but of course she doesn't recall having the vase. I decide to kick her while she's down.

'The postman knocked but you didn't hear him,' I smile at Chris.

'I remember you brought a package,' she says reluctantly.

'I gave you the vase and you put it under the sink.'

'Well, let's get it then,' says Helen as she marches to the kitchen. I could have kissed her. We all watch as Clare argues with Chris.

'I wouldn't have put it in the cupboard under the sink,' she hisses.

'Perhaps you were in a rush,' he says.

'You don't believe me?'

I want to ask her how it feels. How it feels not to be believed. Helen rummages in the cupboard while Clare stands over her sipping a glass of wine. She's nervous, edgy even. She's starting to wonder if she did forget.

'I wouldn't bother Helen, it isn't ...' she begins as Helen pulls out the vase.

'Is this it?' she asks, her cheeks red.

'But ...' Clare begins.

Helen retreats to the garden for a smoke. I keep silent. I'm enjoying Clare's discomfort. Tom joins Helen and I continue to look at Clare. She seems to shiver under my stare and turns to look at Helen and Tom from the kitchen window.

'I didn't know Tom smoked,' she says finally.

'I think I'll join the smokers. I could do with some air,' says Chris.

God forbid he should have to face a confrontation.

I sip my wine and say, 'Tom and I had a bit of an upset some years back. We almost broke up in fact. We found different ways to cope. Tom took up smoking and I gave myself the luxury of a breakdown.'

I'm not sure why I'm telling her this. The last thing I want is to make things easier for her, but I want to stay the vulnerable one. I need her to like me for a bit longer.

'I'm so sorry,' she says.

I shrug.

'It's past.'

I look at the vase, that hideous awful vase.

'I'm sorry about the vase. I don't know why you don't remember.'

'I get anxious,' she says. 'I ... I lost a child and ever since ...'

Tears fill her eyes. My heart hardens but I manage to say, 'I'm sorry Clare, when did that happen?'

She doesn't answer but instead kicks me in the stomach by saying, 'Anyway, I have Ben now.'

'Yes, you do,' I say and this time I'm unable to hide my feelings. I make an effort to put it right by draping a comforting arm around her shoulders but it's so forced I feel sure she can tell. Thankfully the others are at the door.

'They're coming back, why don't you go upstairs and freshen up. I'll make coffee,' I say removing my arm.

'Everything okay?' Tom whispers.

'Yes, but I think Clare is tired. We should go after coffee.'

'Sure,' he smiles.

I pick up *The Lovely Bones* and then put it down again. Tom taps on his Apple Mac.

'How did you find tonight?' I ask.

'Yeah, okay. Chris is alright. She's a bit intense for me. I don't know why you like her.'

I slide down under the covers. I twiddle my toes and say, 'Are you happy with the kitchen?'

'Sure.'

'Do you think she's a good mother?'

'Who?'

'Clare,' I snap.

He groans.

'I don't know Sharni.'

I fight back a sigh. I really thought I could talk to him. Maybe tell him how I've been feeling. Open everything up with him but I can see that I'm not going to be able to do that.

'I wish you'd stop smoking,' I say.

'I'll try again,' he says, but I know he isn't really listening to me.

'I'm going to sleep,' I say, turning over.

'I'll only be ten minutes,' he says, kissing me on the cheek.

Twenty minutes later I can still hear the tapping of his keyboard. I think of my time with Ben next week and drift into sleep.

Chapter Thirty-Six

I look up at the office building. I'd been here before, many times. I'd stood outside looking up at the windows knowing that he worked here. I'd watched him leave the building often, sometimes he was alone and sometimes he was with work colleagues. I probably hate him more than I hate her. How can he stand by and watch it happen? What's wrong with him? She's an evil woman and an even more evil mother. I'm almost glad she lost her baby to a cot death. She thinks I don't know about that. There's nothing I don't know about Clare Ryan. I probably know her better than she knows herself. I can't let the same thing happen to Ben. I can't and I won't.

I confidently stroll into the foyer and make my way to the reception desk. The receptionist smiles warmly at me.

'I'd like to see Chris Ryan,' I say.

She clicks her mouse and studies the computer screen.

'Ah, I don't have an appointment though,' I say with an apologetic shrug.

'Oh,' she says, lifting her eyes.

'I'm his neighbour, Sharni. I just wanted to ask him a quick question.'

She seems to size me up and then says, 'Yes, he's free. He's having lunch. He has a meeting in ten minutes though. Go in.'

I open the door and am hit by a scrunched up ball of paper.

'Oh,' I say. 'Was that a reject?'

He's surprised to see me. He's wondering how I know where he works. I'd covered myself by checking with Tom first.

'I hope it's okay for me to call in. The girl at reception said it was your lunch break,' I say coyly.

'How did you know where I worked?' he asked.

'Tom mentioned it.'

'Oh right.'

He's handsome if you like that kind of man, the boyish helpless looking type. He's the kind of man Clare would go for. His brown hair is cut in the newest style. It makes him look innocent. His heavy-lidded eyes look curiously at me. He's weak. He doesn't think things through. Everything is superficial for him. I show him a copy of *Vogue* that features the Chanel shoot. He's impressed as I knew he would be. Success appeals to him.

'Clare will be pleased to see a copy,' he says.

'She said it was your anniversary in a few weeks. Seven years together,' I lie.

He won't question it and if he does she'll say she thought he'd told me, and then she'll doubt herself, find herself wondering if she told me after all.

'Yeah, a whole seven years,' he smiles. 'I would have got less for murder.'

'You know what they say about seven years,' I say with a wink and nudge his arm. I then mention the photographs. I'm confident and bold. I make it all sound perfectly innocent and he believes me.

'That sounds great, thanks Sharni.'

'Give me a text tomorrow when I've got my diary in front of

me and we'll fix a time,' I say handing him my card. I could fix a date now but I want him to have my contact number in his phone.

It was that easy. Helen was going to be a bit harder. I'll work on her next. Most importantly though, I need to change Ben's doctor's appointment as there is no way she is going to take him for his vaccinations. God knows, she'll most likely mess that up too just like she messes everything else up.

My time with Ben is one of the happiest of my life and they are for him too. I've finally got him off that stupid blanket and he now loves his cuddly rabbit. I knew he would. He's getting decent food inside him instead of that ghastly processed rubbish and now he has a mummy who loves him with every part of her being, just as a mummy should. All I have to do now is get rid of this imposter, who calls herself mummy, and everyone can be happy again. I know it will take time and I'm prepared for that. I'm scared to attend my appointment with Dr Grant. Every time I think about it my stomach churns and I feel I'm going to throw up. What if I'm wrong? What if I have everything wrong? No, it isn't possible. The camera never lies. I'm not wrong.

I hear Tom turn his key in the lock and check the dinner.

'Hi,' he says throwing his case on to the couch and kissing me. He spots the *Vogue* magazines on the coffee table and raises his eyebrows.

'Happy with them?' he asks, flicking through the pages.

'Yep, it was a good shoot. I think it shows. How was your day?'

'Tough, we're facing a pretty strong prosecution but still ...'

He pours wine into glasses and I take mine gratefully.

'It's Clare and Chris's anniversary in a few weeks. I thought it would be nice to take them for dinner. There's that nice French place.'

He dips a spoon into the curry sauce that bubbles on the hob.

'Won't they want to spend it alone? I know I would.'

'Maybe,' I say.

He shrugs. I decide not to say that I'd booked a table.

'I guess it's up to them. Look Sharn, I've been thinking about this Ben thing. I don't want you ...'

'I'm fine,' I say, pulling down plates and clattering them on the kitchen counter.

'It's just I'm not sure you're strong enough ...'

I wipe my hands on a tea towel and look at him.

'It's doing me the world of good Tom,' I say.

He nods.

'I know that, it's just I don't want you to forget that Ben is Clare and Chris's child.'

I wince at his words.

'It's okay Tom,' I say.

'Well, you know, I just don't want ...' he trails off. I nod and turn back to the curry.

'Do you like the bedroom?' I ask, changing the subject. 'I thought we could get some paintings.'

His face lights up.

'There's an exhibition at the Tate Modern. I really want to see it. Fancy it?'

'Sure,' I say, relieved to get things back the way they were.

'We could go to Nick's new wine bar afterwards.'

I lay the plates on the table. Tom senses my hesitation.

'You have to get back into the swing of things again, Sharn. Just being friends with a neighbour isn't enough. I can't keep seeing Nick and Rachel and all the old guys on my own.'

'I know. It sounds good. It'll be nice to see Rachel. Just Nick and Rachel though Tom, okay?'

He smiles.

'Great, let's have dinner.'

I try to picture Rachel's face the last time I had seen her. Her look of sympathy and bewilderment was too much to bear. I block out the memory and pour more wine into my glass. It will be okay. Everything will be okay soon.

Chapter Thirty-Seven

'Rachel, hi, it's Sharni.'

I can't believe how my breathing has quickened. Her voice sends memories flooding through my brain and I have to grasp a chair for support.

'Sharn?'

There's disbelief in her voice.

'Yeah, it's me.'

'I've been leaving messages on your voicemail.'

She isn't accusing. She's simply stating a fact.

'Yes, I know, I'm sorry. I ... I don't feel ready yet Rachel.'

There's silence and I have no idea how to break it. I'm very close to hanging up when Rachel says.

'I've missed you.'

I fight back the tears.

'I'm not the same.'

'That doesn't matter.'

I wipe the tears from my cheek.

'Tom and I thought we'd pop into the wine bar one night ...'

'That would be wonderful,' she says excitedly.

'Great, I'll text you when. Tom's at badminton at the mo, so I can't ask him. Anyway, I'd better run, millions to do.'

I hang up before she has time to say goodbye. The tears flow and I allow them free rein. I've held them back for too long.

'Let it all out,' Rachel had once said.

'Let it out Sharn, you'll be all the better for it,' said Rachel.

'It can't be true,' I said. 'Tell me I'm dreaming.'

Her face had been kind, sympathetic as always. I wanted to hear her say that we'd go walking along the beach when I was better. She could sketch while I took photographs. But she didn't.

'I wish it was a dream Sharn, I really do,' she sobbed.

I looked down. Her hand was clasped in mine. Hers was pink and warm, mine blue from where the catheter had bruised me.

'I can't remember properly.'

'You will, the doctor said you're in shock.'

I looked beyond her to my mother. She looked tired, washed out. Her eyes met mine and I knew it was true. Nathan had gone. Why couldn't I remember?

'No,' I said.

'Darling,' said Mum.

She'd lost a lot of weight. I hadn't noticed it before. I'd been so preoccupied with my precious baby that I hadn't even noticed my mother deteriorating in front of my eyes. And now all that was precious had gone.

'No,' I screamed.

Mum wavered in front of me and Rachel's hand tightened on mine. Tom stood on the other side of the bed, his grief stricken face leaned over me.

'It's okay, Sharn, it's okay.'

But it wasn't okay at all. It would never be okay again.

I look around the kitchen. The fresh paint is irritating my throat. I wonder what Clare is doing. She'll be wondering what I'm doing. I note that she hasn't invited me round while the men play badminton. I check the time and grab my coat. I check upstairs to make sure everything I want her to see is easily accessible. She may not come in but if she does then I want her to be unsettled. My tears have dried and I force my lips into a smile before leaving the house.

I arrive home to find her in the back garden. She looks sheepish and makes some excuse about looking for a broom. I pretend to believe her and invite her in for coffee. She's flushed and nervous and backs away claiming she's meeting Helen. I smile and go back into the house. Everything was going according to plan.

I decide to make a nut roast for dinner. Tom's into a healthy eating regime.

'Smells good,' he says, coming in from the garden. 'I've just seen Chris. Clare's out so I told him to pop round for a drink. That's okay isn't it?'

'Yes, of course.'

The doorbell sounds and a sheepish Chris wanders in.

'I hope it's okay,' he says uncertainly.

'Who cleans out their shed on a Sunday afternoon,' laughs Tom, 'when your neighbour has the rugby on and a beer in the fridge? Come into the lounge.'

I pretend to make a tutting sound.

'A man needs to relax,' he argues.

I leave them to it and spend the rest of the afternoon making gingerbread men for Ben and printing the photos I have taken of him. I lose track of time, as does Tom and Chris. I'm in the middle of preparing a salad to go with the nut roast when there is a loud rapping on the door. I know it is Clare. I try to warn Tom but he gets to the door before I can.

'Hi Clare we ...' I hear him say.

'Chris isn't back and I was just wondering what time you two finished?' her voice echoes in the hallway.

'Chris is here,' he interrupts.

Her eyes widen in surprise.

'What?'

'Come in.'

He steps to one side as Chris enters the hallway.

'Clare,' Chris smiles.

Clare's lips tighten and she glares at him.

'I sent you a text,' she says angrily. 'And I just tried to phone you.'

Tom looks uncomfortable.

'I've got no signal,' Chris says calmly.

Ben is screaming and all I want to do is grab her by the hair and throw her out of my house. I pop my head around the kitchen door and give a little wave.

'Hi,' I say, trying to ease the tense atmosphere. She ignores me and pushes past Tom.

'Here,' she says, thrusting Ben on to Chris. 'He's been like this all day and I've got a splitting headache. He's all yours.'

I clench my fists until my fingernails bite into my flesh.

'Can we ...?' begins Tom.

'No, you can't,' she says rudely and strides to the door. 'I'll see you back in *our* house,' she says to Chris before marching down the drive. Chris shushes Ben and smiles nervously at us.

'I'm sorry about that,' he says.

'Not a problem,' Tom assures him.

'I should go.'

'Yeah, well, thanks for coming over,' Tom says as he opens the door.

He closes it and I sigh.

'That was a bit extreme,' he says, shaking his head.

'Yes,' I agree and go back into the kitchen.

'I feel sorry for that poor guy. She's bloody neurotic if you ask me.'

Chapter Thirty-Eight

'We're going out,' I say to Ben, handing him a gingerbread man. 'This is a special treat and when we get back from the doctors you can have another one.'

He hugs me tightly and I'm overwhelmed with love for him. We have forty-five minutes before we leave for the doctors and I use the time to take photographs. I'm just in the middle of setting the timer when my mobile trills. It's Chris.

'Hi, how's it going with Ben?'

'Great,' I say hesitantly.

'I'm really sorry to hassle you but I'm not sure what to do.'

My heart jumps into my mouth. He's not taking him away from me if that's what he thinks.

'The doctors phoned. Apparently Ben has an appointment today for his vaccinations. I'm not sure why Clare forgot. It was for eleven, but they've had to push it back to eleven-thirty. The nurse has been taken ill. I know it's a cheek but would you mind taking him? It's fine if you'd prefer not to. It's just I don't think Clare will check her phone until lunchtime. I'm not sure why she made it for a Tuesday to be honest.'

'Of course I will,' I say. I was going to anyway. There was no way I was leaving an important doctor's appointment to her.

'Oh that's great, thanks Sharni. It saves changing the appointment. Do you know the surgery?'

'No worries. Actually, it'll give me a push to get the forms so Tom and I can join.'

'Great, thanks.' He hangs up, relieved that he's passed the responsibility on to someone else.

'Hello, I've brought Ben for his vaccinations. Mrs Ryan couldn't make it.'

The receptionist gives us a warm welcoming smile.

'Ah yes, we have left a message for her. Are you Sharni?'

I nod.

'Mr Ryan said you would be bringing Ben.'

'It's the least I could do. I was surprised though that Clare had made the appointment for a Tuesday as that's a day she works.'

She studies her computer screen.

'Well, Mrs Ryan changed the appointment herself.'

I sigh tiredly.

'She did? Oh dear, I think she's overworking. She gets very confused about dates these days.'

The receptionist smiles kindly. She'll never repeat this to Clare. It's more than her job is worth. But I've planted the seed and that's all that matters. Clare is a bad mother and I want the whole world to know.

'At least he is here,' she smiles.

'Is there anything I should know? I'll be having him all day you see,' I say.

'I'm sure the nurse would be happy to advise you.'

I'll ask a few other questions while I'm with her. After all, as the person who cares for him most of the week, I should be informed of issues regarding his health.

'Are you his nanny?' the nurse asks when I take him into the treatment room.

'I'm a neighbour,' I say. 'I look after Ben while Mrs Ryan works.'

'Sorry about the appointment change. I'm glad you could bring him.'

Ben hugs his rabbit and I tell him all that we're going to do after the doctors. He doesn't even cry and I am so proud of him.

'There, all done,' says the nurse. 'There shouldn't be a reaction.

'That's good to know, thank you. I'm sorry Clare couldn't bring him but she's very busy at work.'

The nurse frowns but doesn't say anything. I leave the treatment room with Ben and thank the reception staff.

'Let's go shopping and buy you something very special for being such a brave boy.'

Ben claps his hands.

I hear his car pull up and hurriedly pile Ben's toys into a box. I tip out the toys Clare had left with me. Ben ignores them and continues playing with his new building blocks. I hurry to the door and open it before he knocks.

'Hi, sorry I'm a bit late,' he says apologetically.

'I didn't notice the time,' I say. The truth is I hadn't taken my eye off the clock and had been busy preparing for this visit since we returned from the doctors.

'I have to be back at four,' he says.

He's been drinking. I can smell it on his breath. Tom would

never drink during work hours, not even at lunchtime and most certainly not if he was driving.

'No worries, it won't take long.'

Edna, across the road is looking out of her window. I couldn't have planned it better if I'd tried.

'She clocks everything doesn't she,' I say, nodding in her direction.

He raises his eyebrows. A worry frown creases his forehead. He's anxious the old girl might tell Clare that he came here. It doesn't look good. Clare and Tom are at work and here I am letting Clare's husband into the house. He steps nervously into the living room and kisses Ben on the forehead and I have to fight the urge to pull him away.

'I was going to make a coffee, do you want one before we start?' I ask.

'Great thanks.'

I see him looking at the photographs I'd been working on.

'Ignore the muddle. I'm working on a fashion shoot for L'Oréal.'

'Wow, that's impressive,' he says.

He's easily impressed.

'Not really, it sounds more impressive than it is.'

I reluctantly hand him Ben and make the coffee.

'Thanks for earlier. I don't know why Clare forgot.'

'It happens to the best of us.' I smile but it would never have happened to me.

'She's normally on the ball.'

'Is that right?' I hear myself say. He looks at me sharply but simply says, 'Has he been all right since the jabs?'

'We've had lots of cuddles, haven't we Ben?'

My beautiful darling holds out his hands to me.

'You're certainly a hit,' says Chris.

'You hang on to him. I'll get the camera.'

I want to get this over with. I've no intention of taking portraits of my beautiful boy for them.

'Naked photos are best,' I say, setting up the backdrop. I ignore his surprised look.

'Naked?' he repeats.

'Just your shirt off,' I say, taking Ben from him. I'm not interested in your puny little body, I want to snap. I remove Ben's top to encourage him. He looks at the window. He's worried about Edna.

'Right,' he says pulling off his shirt. 'Clare will love these.'

I don't respond. If he thinks I'm giving her a cosy family photo he's mistaken. There's only one photo I want her to see.

'I've found a great restaurant,' I say. 'It's French, in the West End.'

He nods. He has no idea why I'm telling him this.

'I've booked a table for your anniversary. Tom and I would like to take you out. I thought eight would be a good time. I'll surprise Clare with the photos.'

He's struggling not to look surprised.

'Ah, right,' he says finally. 'That's great, I'll tell her. We'll need to get a sitter.'

I position him and begin to take photos. I focus on his torso and tell him how to stand. He'd make a good model.

'I'll do a few of you first to get the light right. I don't want to be fiddling around when I take Ben's photos or he'll get agitated.'

He's uncomfortable but does it anyway. I do them as quickly as I can. I don't want him in the house longer than necessary.

'Thanks for that,' he says. He kisses Ben on the forehead and turns to the door.

'Thanks for taking those, and for taking Ben to the doctors.'

'My pleasure,' I smile.

My jaw aches from so much forced smiling. Finally he's gone and I breathe a sigh of relief.

Clare barely talks when she collects Ben. She's slightly early so we're not quite ready. I hand over his comfort blanket and the carrier bag of her usual stuff and smile.

'He's been very good,' I say, 'especially at the doctors.'

'Good,' she says, forcing a smile. I can tell I'm getting to her.

'Have a nice evening,' I say before closing the door.

That evening we hear them arguing again.

Chapter Thirty-Nine

'I love this,' Tom says. 'This would be perfect in the bedroom. Shall we get a print?'

I look at the painting. I don't really understand it. I've never understood modern art.

'It's nice,' I say.

'Are you okay?' he says turning to me.

I smile. I can't say that all I really want is to be with Nathan. He'll think that I've gone off track and demand I go for more counselling. He'll also stop Clare bringing him to me.

'I'm thinking about our meeting with Rachel and Nick later.'

'It'll be fine,' he says, draping his arm around my shoulder. 'Let's get the print.'

'Okay.'

I wander around the gift shop, idly leafing through books while Tom examines the print. I see my reflection in the window and wonder how Rachel will view me. It will be a shock to see me I imagine. I'm wearing a black dress from *All Saints* and a white cashmere cardigan but I still didn't look like the old me. I'm much thinner in the face than when she last saw me. I plump up my hair with my hands. God, I so wish we didn't have to go to the wine bar.

'Ready?' says Tom.

The wine bar is heaving, just as I expected it would be. I hadn't expected there to be so many people. It's been almost three years since I've been somewhere like this. I spot Rachel. She can't hide the shock from her face and it takes her a while to recover, but she's managed to do so by the time we reach them.

'Hey,' says Nick, hugging me.

'God, it's amazing to see you,' Rachel says.

I hug her and smell her Rive Gauche perfume. It's comforting and evokes wonderful memories.

'I'll bring over a bottle,' says Nick. 'I've kept the table in the corner for us.'

'Let's go to the ladies,' says Rachel, pulling me through the throng and into a messy loo.

'God, you look so different. What have you done to your hair?'

I look at myself in the mirror and pull a brush from my bag.

'I needed a change.'

'I don't ever remember seeing you with your glasses. You look kind of clever,' she laughs. 'Oh God, Sharn, I've missed you. I've missed the fun we had.'

'I've not felt much like fun,' I say.

She bows her head and fumbles in her handbag.

'I've got the most divine red lipstick; Chanel. I saw the photos you did in *Vogue* for the ad last year.'

She hands the lipstick to me and I apply it carefully.

'That's better. You look more like the old you,' she smiles.

'I don't feel like the old me,' I say, studying my face.

'Let's get a drink. I reckon we both need one. It's been a bit emotional seeing you after all this time.'

We make our way back to the table where Tom is showing Nick his print.

'I said Nick and Rachel should come to the house, see what we've done.'

'We've not done much,' I say.

'Do you still have the cottage?' Rachel asks softly.

I nod.

'We didn't want to give it up.'

The effects of the wine are beginning to work and I feel myself relax.

'I miss that place,' she says wistfully.

I'd worried needlessly about Rachel. I should have known it would be okay.

'Come downstairs and see my special wines,' Nick says to Tom, leaving Rachel and I alone.

'I should have made contact,' I say, topping up my glass.

'It's okay. I thought you needed some time. I just hadn't figured it would be so long.'

'The wine bar is fabulous,' I say looking around.

'Yeah, well you know us. London and wine, we can't be without either.'

'Are you still painting?' I ask.

Her eyes sparkle.

'I've sold a couple,' she smiles.

'That's wonderful.'

We look at each other.

'I miss the cottage too,' I say.

'Why don't you go back?' she says as she lays her hand over mine.

I shake my head.

'I can't, not yet, and Tom's doing really well and he wants to set up his own firm. Maybe then I'll be ready.'

I find myself topping up my glass again.

'You know, that time ... I didn't mean to ... I just didn't know what to think,' says Rachel.

'It's okay.'

'You were saying some crazy stuff and ...'

'It's okay,' I say again.

She nods, relief relaxing her face. I can see Tom and Nick weaving their way through the crowd back to us.

'We're going on to that new Indian place up the road. Nick says it's outstanding,' Tom says excitedly. I can't say I don't feel like Indian food, or any food, come to that, so I just nod.

'Great,' says Rachel, hooking her arm through mine. 'It seems like forever since we all had dinner together.'

I reluctantly allow myself to be led outside.

Chapter Forty

I don't believe Clare went to the school Christmas party without asking me to babysit. How dare she ask Kathryn when I was right next door? Just the thought of seeing her this morning makes me tremble with anger. I couldn't believe she had asked Kathryn to look after Ben when I would have been here the whole evening. I could have sat with him in their house if that's what the bitch preferred. What the hell is wrong with her? If Tom and I hadn't popped out to the library we would never have known. She looked bloody ridiculous in that stupid red velvet dress. I could tell she was embarrassed to see me. I had to tell her she looked nice even though she looked bloody awful. I'm sure my annoyance showed. A whole evening with Ben and she'd taken it away from me.

I check the time. She's late. This is bloody madness. I should just go over there and take him. That would be the right thing to do. I'm just about to get my coat from the hallway when she knocks at the door.

'You're late,' I snap. I should have calmed down before she came. Damn it.

'We overslept,' she says. She lifts Ben from the stroller and I take him from her.

'Sharni, about the anniversary dinner you've arranged,' she begins.

'Is the restaurant okay?' I say, attempting my friendly voice, my 'I like you' voice.

'It's just I really wanted to spend that evening with Chris, just the two of us.'

'Oh, of course. I should have realised. I'll cancel it.'

She's so nervous her lips are quivering.

'It was nice of you to ...' she says but trails off.

'Not a problem. Maybe we could all do something on the Saturday. I obviously misunderstood Chris. I thought it was all okay.'

'Misunderstood?' she asks, raising her eyebrows. I've got her again.

'When I saw Chris at his office the other day we were joking about the seven year itch and all that, so maybe I just misunderstood what he said. I thought he was keen but I must have got that wrong.'

She tries not to show her distress but I've thrown her. Serves you right you evil little bitch. I don't give her a chance to come back and quickly add, 'He said he would tell you.'

'He did tell me,' she says stiffly.

I shrug. Not that I ever want to go out with her. It'll never happen but winding her up is good.

'I'll check with Chris,' she says.

'Well, not to worry. Did you have a nice time on Saturday?' I ask, trying to hide the bitterness in my voice. Ben clutches her necklace and I pull him back sharply so that the chain breaks.

'Oh no,' I say. 'Leave it with us and we'll get it repaired.'

'It's okay,' she says.

'It's the least I can do,' I say, taking it out of her hand. 'I know a jeweller who can do it. We'll see you later then,' I say dismissively.

She doesn't seem to hear what I'm saying. She's probably wondering when the hell I was in her husband's office and what the hell I was doing there. I close the door before she has reached her car. I look at the necklace and feel a cold chill run down my spine. Ben reaches out for it.

'Not this one darling. This one is no good.'

I put the comfort blanket away and then pull out his box of toys. He whoops with delight at the sight of them.

'Why don't you make some bunny rabbits while I check my emails and then we can go out?'

I sit him at the table with his crayons and paper. I quickly scroll through my messages, checking there is nothing urgent and then send an attachment with the L'Oréal prints for Michael, the fashion editor, to check over. An email from 'Helen' catches my eye as I scan my inbox. I click into it. It is from Clare's friend.

Hi Sharni, I've got a terrible nerve I know. But the photographer we hired for the school Christmas photos has let us down at the last minute. Would you be able to help us out? Or do you know anyone who could? We'd be so grateful. You can get me on my mobile. Love Helen.

Her mobile number is at the bottom of the email. I grab my phone and call her. She answers right away.

'Hi, Helen, it's Sharni. I just got your email.'

'Oh, thanks for phoning. I hope you don't think I've got a cheek?'

'I'd love to help. I can take the photos for you.'

'Oh wow, I didn't really expect you to do it. I thought you might be able to recommend someone.'

'I'd love to do it. I can do it at cost price too. I know someone that can print the photos with frames at a discount. I would love to support the school in any way that I can.'

'Wow, that's brilliant. Thanks so much.'

'No worries. When can I come?'

'We had everything arranged for tomorrow. Is that okay? I realise it's very short notice.'

'Not a problem, I'll be there,' I say, and hang up.

'We're going to have a really lovely day today,' I say, lifting Ben into my arms and kissing him.

Chapter Forty-One

I feel like I'm walking on air as we leave Dr Grant's office. I've done it. There's no going back now.

'You were such a good boy,' I tell Ben. 'A really good boy.'

I push the stroller into John Lewis and take the lift to the toy department. I nearly cancelled the appointment. What if I'd made a mistake? How would I explain it to Tom? No, I can't tell Tom, not yet. My stomach churns when I think that I could be wrong.

'Let's go,' I say to Ben, feeling like I've been reborn. The shadow that had weighed over me for so long has lifted. Everything around me seems clearer and brighter. I've done the right thing. It will be proved that I've done the right thing. Ben points to Santa's grotto and I smile. We sit and wait by the Christmas tree with its glittering baubles and prettily wrapped packages. Ben's eyes are fixed on Santa's grotto, his little face alert and curious. We wait for twenty minutes but when the time comes, the look of wonderment on Ben's face makes it all worthwhile.

'And what's your name?' Santa asks.

'Nathan,' I reply.

'Mama,' he says, grasping my hand uncertainly.

'Say hello to Santa darling. You'll get a present.'

I pull my Nikon from my bag and take a photo. I need to make lots of memories.

After collecting the necklace from the jeweller I take Ben to Winter Wonderland. The smell of roasting chestnuts greets us and I decide to look around the Christmas market when we have finished. I pull my phone from my bag and switch it off.

'Just you and me,' I tell Ben. It's getting colder and I put his mittens on. I know he'll pull them off but it's a fun battle. He giggles at the sight of another Santa and points until I agree to take him again. We play on the swings and then watch *The Gruffalo* on a large screen. He clutches his rabbit close to him the whole time. We mingle with other parents and their children, all celebrating Christmas like we are.

Ben naps in the stroller as I wander around the market and by the time we've finished it's almost five. I picture Clare's panic-stricken face when she finds she can't get hold of us. She'll be home by now and frantically knocking on my door. Or has she gone into the house? Will she phone Chris in her panic? Has she accused him of having an affair with me yet? She must be wondering what I was doing at his office. It will be driving her insane. I hope she knows what it feels like to be isolated, to feel totally helpless and to have no one supporting you. I hope she's experiencing that horrible feeling of being alone, right now.

'Let's get a drink,' I say as I open the door to the café.

I take the stroller from the bus driver and thank him. Once I have settled Ben, I take my phone from my bag and turn it on. It bleeps immediately. There are five missed calls and three text messages from Clare.

Running late, school concert rehearsal going over time, I hope all is okay.

I tap in her number. She answers on the first ring.

'Hi Clare, it's me. I've had no signal. I had to pop into the office. They had a crisis, and I had to help out. We were in the basement. Ben's great. He's had loads of attention and loads of new toys. Ooh and I got your necklace repaired. I'm really sorry we're late. I've given Ben his tea and ...'

I can hear her breathing heavily at the other end of the phone.

'When will you be back?' she interrupts.

As if she has got any right to make demands. I almost tell her so but I bite my tongue.

'In twenty minutes but traffic is really bad,' I lie. I'm literally just around the corner.

'Okay,' she says meekly.

'See you soon,' I say cheerily.

I click off my phone and walk slowly home.

Clare opens the door. She looks terrible. Her hair is a mess and her face is blotchy. She's clearly been crying. I try to feel sympathy for her.

'Sorry we're late,' I say. 'The traffic was crazy. He's great though and here's your necklace.'

She takes the necklace and mumbles a thank you.

'Is Chris not home?' I ask.

'He's going to be late.'

It must feel like everything is getting on top of her. What a shame.

'You look knackered,' I say.

'It's been a long day.'

'I'll leave you to it then. Bye bye Sweet Pea.' I lean forward to kiss Ben but she pulls him away. He struggles to get to me but she holds him back. I hate her in that moment more than I've ever hated anyone.

'Mama,' he says, reaching out to me. She wants to kill me. I can see it in her eyes.

'Bless him,' I say before turning and walking down the driveway.

'Aw, bless him,' said Rachel. 'He smiled when his daddy knocked down all the pins.'

I laughed.

'Here's to the top legal brain in the country,' toasted Nick.

'Oh sod off,' laughed Tom.

'It was a big one, well done on winning,' said Rachel.

'You'll be off to London next and won't want to know us,' smiled Nick.

'Not too soon I hope,' I said as I clinked my glass of orange juice against Tom's champagne flute. 'Well done darling.'

'If we'd have known you were going to have such good news we'd have chosen a more upmarket venue,' said Rachel. 'Not the bloody bowling alley.'

'I love bowling,' laughed Tom 'We've got the champagne and the best company ever. That's what counts. The thing is though, I'm at a disadvantage. My partner is injured.'

'Objection your honour,' I said, jabbing him in the ribs. 'I've just had a baby. I'm not injured, I'm exhausted.'

'Sustained,' said Nick, slapping Tom on the back. Rachel leaned over her to peek at Nathan.

'He's so adorable. I just want to keep on holding him.'

'He's handsome just like Tom,' laughed Nick.

I hand him over, feeling suddenly empty without Nathan in my arms.

'He's like Sharni. He's got her fair hair and blue eyes,' argued Rachel.

I sat contentedly and watched the others play, my camera recording Tom's shouts of joy and Rachel's perfect bowling. Nathan slept soundly throughout and I was so grateful for such a good baby. Tom looked at us often, sending kisses or cheeky winks. My heart overflowed with love for him. It was the happiest time of my life.

Chapter Forty-Two

'I can't stand it,' I say. 'I'll have to go round.'

'It's not our place, Sharn.'

'But he's screaming. He's really distressed. She needs to give him the bunny rabbit.'

'I agree her screams aren't helping the poor little mite. She's got a bit of a temper by the sound of her,' Tom says as Clare's shouts penetrate the walls.

'I'm going round Tom,' I say.

He puts out a hand to restrain me but I ignore it.

'Sharni, it really isn't your place ...'

I go downstairs and open the front door and come face to face with Chris.

'Sharni, will you just wait a minute?' Tom calls, following me down the stairs. He stops at the sight of Chris.

'Christ mate, what's up with Ben?' he asks.

Chris looks haggard and embarrassed and turns to me.

'He doesn't have his comfort blanket. Do you know where it is?'

I deliberately hesitate.

'Sharn?' asks Tom.

'I gave it to Clare when I brought everything around,' I lie. 'She seems to keep forgetting and ...'

'I don't know why she keeps forgetting things,' Chris sighs.

'It could be the diazepam,' I say.

Chris's head snaps up.

'How do you know about those?' he asks.

I look at Tom.

'Sharni saw her diazepam diary in the kitchen when we were round at yours,' Tom explains.

Chris shakes his head miserably.

'I don't know what to do. She's getting anxious at the smallest thing. I'm sure Ben's picking up on it.'

'It's not good for him,' I agree.

'If we can help,' begins Tom.

'Do you want me to come back with you? I can help look for the comfort blanket,' I say.

'If you're sure you don't mind,' Chris says uncertainly.

I somehow think the sight of me will rile her even further but I don't say that.

'I'm happy to help,' I smile.

Ben is still screaming and I can hardly bear it. Clare looks at me wildly and then to Chris, her eyes questioning.

'Sharni doesn't have it,' says Chris simply.

'I gave it to you,' I say, 'when you picked Ben up. I gave you everything.'

She's about to disagree with me and then she looks at Chris and seems to stop herself.

'Try his rabbit,' I say. 'He loves it. He's been cuddling it all afternoon.'

'That won't work,' she snaps.

Chris gives me an apologetic look. I ignore Clare and go to Ben. He looks up at me, and hiccups. His crumpled face breaks into a smile.

'Here you are Sweet Pea,' I say gently, handing him the bunny rabbit. 'Shall we sing to it?'

I gently wipe away his tears and take his little hand in mine. He calms down immediately and cuddles his rabbit.

'I think you should move in,' jokes Chris.

'And I'll move out,' Clare says angrily.

Making her out to be a terrible mother has been easier than I imagined it would be. I stroke Ben's head and whisper, 'Not much longer, darling, not much longer.'

I want to make it as easy as possible for him. He's all that counts.

'I didn't mean ...' I say, turning to Chris, but before I can finish Clare has grabbed Ben and marched upstairs with him.

'I'm so sorry,' says Chris, avoiding my eyes.

'Well, at least he is calm now,' I say, turning to the door.

I fight the urge to march upstairs after her. It would take just a few seconds to grab Ben from her arms and hurry to my car. But it's not time yet. I need to be patient. I don't want the police on my doorstep, not yet.

Tom looks at the bedside clock. We're silent as we listen to the muffled sound of Clare's voice through the bedroom wall. Tom turns the light on and says, 'What is she on about Sharni?'

I feel myself blush. I sigh. Clare has been accusing Chris of having an affair with me for the last ten minutes.

'I went to Chris's office to ask him if he wanted me to take some portrait photos of him with Ben. I was going to give them to Clare at their anniversary dinner. You remember I told you about that?'

He looks thoughtful.

'I vaguely remember. That was not very sensible was it?'

'What do you mean?'

I want to shake him. Is he really that blind?

'She's obviously got issues,' he says, yawning. 'And it's no fun hearing her scream all kinds of abuse about you.'

'She's clearly got the wrong end of the stick,' I say. 'It was supposed to be a nice gesture.'

'The woman is unhinged,' he says, looking at the time. 'You should probably steer clear of her. I think you should tell her you can't have Ben any more.'

I clasp the bedcovers tightly.

'That would be really unfair on him don't you think. It's not his fault his mother is neurotic. Anyway, we don't want to make things worse. They are our neighbours after all.'

He fumbles in the drawer for earplugs.

'This is getting ridiculous, that's all I know. I can't put up with this too often and I don't want to listen to her ranting about you in that slanderous way. It's unacceptable. She needs to get off those bloody pills if you ask me. A good glass of wine wouldn't do her any harm and would be far better for her than Valium.'

I snuggle close to him.

'I'm sure everything will be okay,' I say.

He grunts and clicks off the light.

'Well, I don't want her here for bloody Christmas, that much I do know.'

Chapter Forty-Three

I'm worried that Clare is looking at nurseries. I've pushed her too hard. I may have to put my plan into action sooner than I'd wanted. But I'm not ready yet. There are still things I need to do.

'I think it would be better for you to pull back from them,' Tom says, putting on his jacket. 'You're not that strong yourself. If she finds a nursery, all well and good, if you ask me.'

I'm stronger than you think but I don't tell him that.

'You probably shouldn't have gone round there,' I say crossly. 'You've just made things worse. It takes her ages to get over things it seems.'

'I couldn't let it go, Sharn. She was way out of order.'

I sigh.

'I've got the school photo shoot today,' I say.

'Great, enjoy it. Drive carefully; it's blowing a gale out there today.'

His words echo through my head. The front door slams and I sit on the stairs as the memories assail me.

. . .

'What are you doing Sharn?' Tom demanded as he hurried into the bedroom.

'I wanted to move the crib nearer the window,' I smiled.

'You've just had a baby.'

'It's not that heavy.'

I exhaled and wiped my forehead. The humid weather seemed never ending. I placed my hand on my lower back and looked admiringly around the room.

'It's looking nice isn't it?' I said taking Tom's hand.

'He won't be using this room for another two years,' grimaced Tom. 'I really don't know why I had to give up my office. I've got a feeling I'm going to be in competition with this little guy for some time.'

'You'll always be my main man,' I said, happily wrapping my arms around him. The sun shone in through the window and cast a halo over us.

'Have a good time, drive carefully,' Tom said, kissing me passionately on the lips. 'Take good care of my boy.'

'I always drive carefully,' I smiled, slipping in my contact lens.

'Give your parents my love.'

I followed Tom out into the sunshine and placed Nathan carefully into the baby carrier in the front seat.

'I wish you could come with us,' I said, kissing Tom.

'Some of us have to work.'

I kissed him again and he stroked my bottom.

'How are things?' he asked nodding. 'Are you up to having me tonight?'

'I might be,' I smiled. 'Let's see shall we?'

I pulled the blanket from my holdall. I'd crocheted it myself, especially for Nathan. I laid it over him and kissed him on the cheek.

It was hot in the car and the air conditioning was not

working properly. There had been talk of storms for days but nothing had materialised. I felt myself perspiring and was grateful I'd brought along a change of clothes. Nathan slept the whole journey. By the time I arrived my dress was clinging to me. Mum hurried out of the farmhouse and lifted Nathan from the car.

'It's so hot,' I said.

'I've made lemonade and your aunt Wendy is here. She can't wait to see Nathan.'

It was another perfect day. I lazed in the garden while my parents doted on Nathan. The home-made lemonade was refreshing and Mum's fruit cake, as always, was delicious.

'He's a real credit to you,' said Aunt Wendy. 'You need to make the most of him. I only had one too. Just make sure you don't spoil him.'

'Try telling Tom that,' I laughed, taking Nathan from her and putting him on my breast. The storm began brewing early in the afternoon but it was only light showers and everyone complained how it hadn't eased the mugginess. I phoned Tom and said I had decided to stay for supper. I was enjoying the attention everyone was giving Nathan. When the time came to leave I was disappointed to see that the earlier light rain had now turned into a torrent. A strong wind had come up and Mum looked out of the window, concern etched on her face.

'Maybe you should stay the night,' she said worriedly.

'I haven't got far to go,' I said. 'I'll drive slowly.'

I'd only gone a mile when the wind picked up. The road was busy making it difficult to see through the spray that lashed at the windscreen. I turned on to a minor road only to find it flooded. The car shuddered beneath me as I made my way slowly through the water.

'Shit,' I muttered. The storm had blackened the sky and everywhere was eerily dark. Rain beat at the windscreen and

even with my full headlights on, all I could see was a curtain of mist ahead. My eyes flickered to the rear-view mirror and then to Nathan lying beside me.

'Damn,' I mumbled. I was cross with myself. Why hadn't I left earlier? It was hard enough navigating the roads in the dark but the addition of the heavy rain made me anxious. My dress felt damp beneath my breasts. Nathan would need feeding soon and I was still a long way from home. Oncoming headlights blinded me and I shielded my eyes. Nathan had started crying, no doubt picking up on my anxiety. The dashboard clock said almost nine. I was so late.

My head had started to pound and no amount of neck flexing seemed to help. Nathan's cries were getting louder and I could feel myself tense with each breath. The road cut through a wood and we were now in pitch blackness. I knew the turning should be coming up but everything looked different. Thunder cracked through the night, making me jump. My head was pounding as though someone were thumping at me with a hammer. I prayed for the turning and finally saw it ahead. I sighed with relief. Not much further and I'd be home. I glanced at Nathan and shushed him comfortingly. I had barely taken my eyes off the road. It was just a second, a moment in time that I forever wish I could go back to.

The road descended and turned sharply on to the old bridge. It narrowed at this point and I braked sharply as an oncoming car turned the corner, its headlamps flashing. For a brief moment I was blinded. I was going too fast. I screwed my eyes up against the blinding light, struggling to see. My foot reached for the brake and then I saw it. A deer had run out of the woods. In the sharp glare of my headlights was its terrified eyes reflected back at mine.

'Oh God,' I'd screamed, my hands instinctively tightened on the steering wheel and turned it frantically. I braced myself for

the thud as the car hit the animal and reached my hand out to cover my baby. I rammed my foot down hard on the brake. There was nothing, except silence and then I saw the bridge gliding towards me as if in slow motion. The world seemed to spin around as tree branches crashed and scraped against the side of the car.

'Oh God, help us,' I screamed.

It felt like there was grit in my eyes and I struggled to see the baby beside me. It comforted me that I could feel his warm body under my hand and hear his angry cries. The nose of the Golf lurched on to the bridge with a thud. My hand slid from Nathan as I was thrown forward. The windscreen came up to meet me and everything went black.

Chapter Forty-Four

Clare never seemed happy when she finished work but I can't understand why. The children are really nice and polite. They are perfect little models too. The teachers seem delighted with my Christmas backdrop.

'Can I stand by the elves?' asks a rosy-cheeked child.

'Of course, would you like your friends to stand with you? It's important that we get the tallest at the back isn't it?'

'Oh yes,' she says.

'Hands up if you're the tallest?' I ask the group of kids in front of me.

Helen smiles and pushes some of the children forward. She's changing her opinion of me, I can tell.

'How about if I take a teacher group photo?' I call to Helen, who laughs excitedly.

'Ooh, one of us. That makes a change.'

'It's not normally what we do,' says the head, uncertainly. 'But I agree it's a good idea. We don't have all the staff in today though.'

'We could phone around,' says Helen. 'We're only three down. Do you want to call Clare?'

I frown.

'I'll leave that to you,' I reply with a smile.

The other teachers laughed amongst themselves.

'I don't imagine we'll be able to do it until after the kids finish at three,' says Geoff.

'That's fine,' I say, 'I'm enjoying it.'

'I'll take Sharni for lunch shall I?' asks Helen.

What a turnaround. I never imagined Helen would be keen to take me out to lunch.

Helen turned out to be okay. Clare had obviously made her suspicious of me. She took me to a little place just around the corner from the school.

'God, you've got some patience,' she says, offering me a cigarette. I shake my head and she shrugs before lighting up.

'I love kids,' I say.

'That's more than I bloody do.'

'But you're a teacher.'

'Doesn't mean I have to like the little darlings. Here we are.'

The café is small but quaint. Helen knows her way around and leads me to a table in the corner.

'So, what's happened between you and Clare?' she asks, her directness taking me by surprise. I wonder if Clare has shared her suspicions to Helen about Chris and I having an affair.

'Has Clare said something?' I ask.

'I had a text this morning. She seemed upset. I said I'd give her a ring at lunchtime but I don't want to be all excited about you taking a teacher photo and stuff if things are not good between the two of you.'

This is my opportunity to isolate Clare completely. I almost feel bad doing it, but not for long. I want her to know exactly what it feels like to be totally alone, to not have anyone believe you. To feel like no one is on your side.

'I'm not really sure what I've done but she's got it in her head that I'm having an affair with Chris. It's my fault. I should have known she was insecure. I thought I'd give her a portrait photo of Chris and Ben for her anniversary. Tom told me where Chris's office was, and I popped in when I was passing one day to see what Chris thought of the idea. He said he'd text me when he could come round and have the photos taken.'

'Oops,' says Helen as she looked at the menu.

'I'm having a jacket potato, what about you?'

'The same for me,' I say, handing the menu to the waiter.

'That seems a bit over the top,' says Helen. 'Mind you, she does get very anxious, especially over Ben.'

'I think she was cross with me yesterday. I had to go in to work. I was a little late getting Ben back, the traffic was awful. I didn't text because I thought we'd be back in time, and Ben was fine.'

'She was pretty edgy. I tried to calm her,' says Helen.

So Helen has been seeing what a paranoid, anxiety-ridden wreck she is too.

'She takes a lot of medication doesn't she?' I say to add fuel to the fire. Helen's head snaps up. She clearly doesn't know about the diazepam.

'She said it was aspirin.'

'It's Valium,' I say. 'I don't think they're good for her.'

'Christ, she's always popping the things,' Helen says.

'I shouldn't really be saying this', I say, lowering my voice and leaning towards her, 'but last night Chris came round in a bit of state. Seemed Ben was screaming and Clare couldn't find his comfort blanket. But I'd given it to Clare earlier. Clare was in a terrible state, shouting and screaming. I'm sure half the neighbourhood could hear her.'

'Look,' said Helen. 'I've got to phone her. Let me see if I can talk her around. Maybe you two can talk after the photo session.'

'I don't think she'll come.'

'I think maybe those pills are affecting her. I'll be honest with you, and I am a bit outspoken, I thought you were a bit odd at the beginning. You know that stuff with the vase and ... anyway. I'm starting to think that maybe Clare's not well and probably needs our help. I'll call her now.'

I struggle to hide my smile.

As soon as I see Clare I know my time with Ben is over. She knows something. I'm not sure what she knows but she's wary of me. She won't be bringing Ben around, that's for sure but it doesn't matter now. Helen smiles at her but she doesn't smile back. Anger is written across her face. She thinks she's hiding it well. But she can't hide it from me.

I raise my eyebrows at her and then turn to the head.

'Thanks so much for this,' he is saying.

'I've enjoyed it,' I say and I have.

'Here's Clare,' calls one of the supply teachers.

'Oh she's brought Ben,' says someone. 'Isn't he gorgeous?'

They surround her and look admiringly at Ben. I stay in the background. There'll be plenty of time for me and Ben soon. Clare glares at me but I pretend not to see.

'Great you could come,' says Helen. 'We're just about to start.'

'Let's get the show on the road,' says Geoff, 'before some of us lose our nerve.'

'Sure,' I say turning to the other teachers. 'If you could all come up on the stage please, that would be great.'

Clare is uncomfortable. She constantly avoids my eyes. I wonder what nursery she will take him to.

'These are going to be really fabulous,' I say, pushing the shutter.

'Maybe we should do twelve individual ones,' laughs Helen. 'Make a school calendar, what do you think Geoff? Obviously we'll keep our clothes on.'

Everyone laughs and I deliberately look Clare in the eye but she quickly turns away. When we finish, Helen invites Clare to have a coffee with us. She shakes her head. It's completely thrown her that I'm friends with Helen.

'I have to get Ben back,' she says.

'Oh come on Clare, have a drink with me and Sharni.'

Geoff taps me on the arm and asks me to step on stage. He makes a little speech in front of the teachers, thanking me for stepping in at short notice and for supporting the school. The teachers clap enthusiastically. I watch Clare's face contort into an ugly grimace.

Helen smiles widely. She thinks everything will be sorted over coffee. I know it won't be. I can read Clare's face like a book. She feels alone, totally isolated. Her husband is wary of her and I've taken the one friend she could talk to. Even the school isn't her sanctuary any more. If she tries to tell any of these people what a scheming woman I am she knows that none of them will believe her. Best of all is that Ben is more comfortable with me than he is with her.

'Hi Sharni, come in,' says Chris as he opens the door.

'You're not eating are you?' I ask.

'No, we're finished.'

He leads me into the living room. There's no sign of Sweet Pea. I imagine she's put him down for the night.

'I've been meaning to congratulate you on your news. Tom said your company landed a big contract.'

He smiles proudly.

'Yes, it's in Amsterdam.'

'And you're going there in a few days?'

'Yeah, I've got to meet the contractors. I'm looking forward to it.'

He looks up to the ceiling.

'Clare's in the bath, do you want me to ...?

'Oh no, I just wanted to say I'm really sorry but the photos I took of you and Ben didn't come out. The memory card got corrupted. I'm so sorry ...'

'Oh, that's a shame,' he says, looking at the photos of Ben on the wall.

'I'm really sorry,' I repeat.

'It's okay, honestly,' Chris replies. 'It all went a bit pear-shaped in the end anyway. I'm not sure if Clare would want them now anyway.'

There's a creak on the stairs and we both look up. Clare stands barefoot, a white towel draped around her wet body. Her eyes meet mine. I find it hard to hide my feelings.

'I just thought I'd tell you both that the memory card must have got corrupted. The photos didn't come out. I'm really sorry.'

'That's a shame,' repeats Chris, looking up at Clare.

Clare doesn't speak. Her silence is disarming.

'Tom and I were wondering if you'd like to come over for a drink tomorrow night. Tom feels he said a few things he shouldn't have.'

'That's nice of you but we're going out tomorrow. It's our wedding anniversary,' says Chris.

'Oh, of course, I'd forgotten.'

I hadn't forgotten at all. I don't offer to babysit. There's little point.

'Thanks,' says Chris.

'I'll see Ben tomorrow,' I say.

'Yes,' says Chris.

Clare glares at him and then goes back upstairs. I follow her with my eyes and then turn to Chris.

'I hope she feels better soon,' I say and walk to the front door.

Clare doesn't bring Ben the next day. Chris sends an apologetic text saying he hopes we can work things out when he returns from Amsterdam. I see Kathryn arrive at their house. No doubt she has broken up for the Christmas holidays. I wave to her and she waves back. I spend the morning getting everything organised and then leave the house for my hair appointment.

I'll spend the afternoon getting everything ready. The day I had been waiting for is almost here. I don't want there to be any mistakes.

Chapter Forty-Five

I flick through an old copy of *OK!* My eyes scan the numerous photos of glamorous celebrities and royals.

'I think you're done,' says Maria, taking a peek under the foil.

I watch in wonderment as she blow-dries my hair. My skin seems to look smoother with the new colour.

'It really suits you,' says Maria. 'You should have had this colour before.'

'I used to be this colour,' I smile.

'It suits your complexion,' says Maria, holding up the mirror to show me the back. 'In fact, you look really different.'

I slip on my glasses and glance out of the window at the heavy rain.

'Are you driving?' Maria asks, slipping the black nylon overall off me.

I nod.

'I hate driving in the rain,' says Maria. 'Do you want another tea before you go?'

'No, I'm fine.'

'Watch out for floods won't you?'

My heart sinks at her words and when I stand up I'm surprised to feel my legs are weak. I grab Maria by the arm to stop myself falling.

'You need to drink more water with it,' Maria jokes.

My mind rushes back and for a few moments I can't move.

'I need to go back,' I said and struggled to get out of bed. My legs gave way and I had to grab the police officer to support myself.

'You're not going anywhere Sharni,' she said, helping me back into bed. 'Let me get the nurse.'

'I don't need the nurse,' I snapped. 'I want my baby.'

'I'm so sorry.'

Her name was Lucy. She kept saying how sorry she was. I wanted to tell her it was my fault not hers and she didn't have to keep saying sorry. They told me I had lost control of the car. It went over the bridge, they said. They think I crawled out of the car before it did, but ...

'Surely I would remember that?' I argued.

'You had a nasty knock on the head.'

'Then how did I crawl out?'

No one had an answer. I hadn't pulled Nathan out. The car had gone over the bridge and the lake was deep. The car had been submerged in water.

'I don't remember anything,' I mumbled.

'You will in time,' Lucy assured me.

But, how could I have dragged myself from the car but not taken Nathan with me? I wouldn't have done that. I wouldn't have left him behind. Nathan was my life. How did I get out of the car? I struggled to remember but nothing came.

Someone found me lying on the roadside. He rescued me. He

came to visit me in the hospital but I cross-examined him so much that he said he couldn't come again. He didn't see a baby, he'd said. The car was in the water when he'd found me. They'd lifted the car out of the lake five days later and I'd hoped that Nathan's body would be in it, but it wasn't. They had frogmen search the lake but couldn't find the body and this had given me hope. Perhaps it was a good sign. Perhaps someone had rescued him. Surely they would tell the police soon. But no one ever did.

Tom had packed everything away by the time I was discharged from hospital. It was as if we'd never had a child. Nathan's bedroom had changed back to Tom's office. I sat in the rocking chair looking into space. I put my camera away and turned down all the work that was offered. Rachel visited but I barely spoke to her. Every night I lay awake trying to remember. The doctor gave me tranquillisers but I avoided taking them. He suggested counselling but I shook my head. I tried to remember crawling out of the car but I had no memory of it. Mum came to stay and we went for long walks. She said I was trying too hard.

'Let it come naturally. You won't remember if you force it,' she'd said.

I didn't want a funeral. Lucy said I should, she said it would give me closure.

'Maybe someone rescued him,' I said.

'They would have reported it,' said Lucy.

I started to hate her. Every thread I hung on to she would snap with one of her common sense replies.

'She's right,' said Tom, 'we need to move on.'

The funeral didn't seem real. I listened to people talking about what a wonderful mother I was and how much Nathan would be missed. I thought how in a moment in time my life was destroyed.

Rachel tried to encourage me to go back to work. I reluctantly took my camera out of the cupboard. We went to the beach and it was there I began to remember. It came in dribs and drabs but I remembered fragments, flashbacks, and they weren't what the police had described.

Chapter Forty-Six

Clare didn't want to ruin the anniversary dinner but she couldn't stop thinking about those naked photos of Chris.

'I can't decide,' Chris says, studying the menu.

'Well, you never were good at decisions,' Clare says.

He looks up at Clare and closes the menu.

'What's wrong with you?' he asks, fighting back a sigh.

She closes her own menu and slaps it down on to the table.

'I saw the photos Sharni took of you,' she hisses.

Chris groans.

'I thought she said they never came out.'

Clare's head snaps up.

'You admit it then?'

He sighs.

'She took photos of me and Ben and ...'

'Ben wasn't in these ...'

'She said she wanted to set it up ...' he falters. 'I don't know. I wasn't comfortable about it. But she wanted to get the light and stuff right before bringing Ben in. How did you see them anyway? She said they never came out.'

'She must have lied again,' Clare scoffs. 'I saw them in the house.'

He stares at her.

'You surely don't still think I'm in the least interested in her?'

'I don't know what to think any more.'

He reaches for her hand across the table.

'I'm not having an affair with Sharni. I don't know why she lied about the photos.'

'She lies all the time,' Clare sighs. 'I'm sorry,' she says. 'It's just ... well you're going away and I feel a bit anxious.'

'I'm only away for four nights.'

'I know.'

'Anyway, I thought Sharni was the reason you were anxious. You've got Kathryn to have Ben this week haven't you?'

She nods and wonders how he could be so unaware. He sighs and tops up his glass with wine.

'Seems a shame to have to lay out money when ...'

'I don't want her.'

'Okay. Maybe you'll feel differently after the holiday.'

'Chris, I'm not going to.'

He holds his hand up.

'Okay. I'll ask Sharni why she said the photos hadn't come out. Maybe they didn't come out as she'd hoped and she didn't want to share them.'

Clare huffs.

'Not tonight Clare. Can't we have one night where you don't go on about your stupid imaginings?'

Clare takes a gulp of wine and forces herself to calm down.

'Are you still cutting back on the diazepam?' he asks.

She nods but avoids his eyes. The truth is she hadn't been. Every time Sharni had Ben, Clare found herself feeling edgy and needed to take one to keep calm. Although one didn't seem to be working as well as it did and she now often has to take two.

'If you'd only let me talk about what's worrying me,' she says, attempting to keep her voice soft.

The waiter approaches and Clare sighs. Typical, and just when she was getting somewhere.

'I'd like to spend one evening with you where we don't talk about Sharni,' Chris says, topping up his glass again.

Can't you see what she's doing? Clare wants to scream. Can't you see that she's trying to steal everything from me? And I have no idea why.

'Do you know what you're having?' he asks.

'The chicken.'

'We'll both have the garlic chicken with roast potatoes please.'

He lifts his glass.

'To us, and to a great Christmas,' he says, kissing her hand and in that moment she felt like everything would be okay. She won't think about who'll have Ben after the holidays. Maybe she could even get a teaching job somewhere else. Who knows what the New Year holds, and if the worst comes to the worst, there is the nursery in Knightsbridge.

'It's a nice house.'

Clare feels slightly bad at getting the house valued the first day Chris is away but it seemed the perfect time. School had broken up and it gave her time to clean.

She'd read in a magazine that the smell of coffee and freshly baked bread helps to sell a home. Although, the only thing Clare really cared about was getting the right price. She'd spent the morning polishing furniture and scrubbing floors. The house was spotless and smelt of coffee and Pledge.

'You've made it cosy,' says the estate agent, glancing at the back garden.

'Thank you.'

'Why are you moving?'

It's a reasonable question but she can't possibly say it's because her neighbour is a raving lunatic who's trying to steal her life.

'We want something bigger,' she lies.

He looks at Ben.

'Ah, a bigger family, yeah, I know the feeling.'

She nods but it feels like a knife has just stabbed her heart. It's such a flyaway comment. Just because she has a child it doesn't mean she can have more.

'The three of you at the moment, is it?'

'Yes.'

There's no need to mention that Chris is away and has no idea that she's putting the house on the market. Chris is still hoping she'll change her mind about Sharni. You'll feel better once the holiday is over he'd said, but all she wants is to get as far away from Sharni as possible.

'You'll get a good price,' says the estate agent as he measures the walls.

'Oh good,' says Clare.

'How soon do you want it to go on the market?'

'As soon as possible really, although we don't want any 'For Sale' signs outside.'

'Ah, that really does help a house get seen.'

'All the same, we'd prefer not to have one.'

'Not a problem. I'll send our valuation in the post and if you want to go ahead, let us know. You have another property to go to then?'

'No, not yet but we can always rent. It's important to us to get a buyer.'

'Great, I'll be in touch then.'

Clare lets out a sigh of relief. Surely Chris will agree it's for the best.

Chapter Forty-Seven

It's her first night without Chris and Clare feels edgy. Ben had settled quickly tonight. Clare feels sure being with Kathryn is much better for him. He doesn't get so unsettled after being with her. She takes one last look at him and then runs a bath. The warmth will relax her tense muscles. She's relieved it was the last day of school yesterday. At least now she doesn't have to worry about who will look after Ben for the next two weeks.

The teachers are meeting for Christmas drinks tonight.

'Do come,' Helen had pleaded.

Clare had excused herself by saying there was no one to watch Ben. The truth was she didn't want to go out drinking and she hadn't really forgiven Helen for siding with Sharni. Although the thought of some company, especially as Chris was away, was appealing.

She pours lavender oil into the steaming water and sniffs the calming scent. It is 7 p.m. – enough time to relax and read her book. She grabs her copy of *The Lovely Bones* and slips into the hot water. She'll give herself forty-five minutes of total relaxation. Surely that will help disperse the presentiment of doom she'd felt all day.

Clare jolts forward. She must have dozed off. She stiffens and strains her ears. Did Ben cry? Is that what disturbed her? *The Lovely Bones* sits on the side of the bath. There's only silence and she relaxes back into the warm bath water.

She strokes her hand gently over her belly and feels tears well up in her eyes. She again thinks of Ben and shakes her head. Poor Sharni, is she unable to have children, she wonders? But she shouldn't hate Clare just because she has a child. Has it turned her head? It's understandable. After all, hadn't Clare been there herself? She shakes her head to block the memories but they're determined to haunt her. She thinks of the diazepam in the cabinet and feels her heart flutter with anxiety. How can there only be twelve tablets left? She can't possibly ask Dr Rawlins for more, not this soon. She trembles at the thought of being without them. She'd been trying to cut back and felt sure she had been doing well, which doesn't explain why the number of pills has gone down so quickly. She can't discuss it with Chris. He'll only accuse her of taking more than she should. She climbs from the bath and reaches for the towel she had thrown over the sink and glances at the bathroom cabinet before opening the door. The bottle of diazepam beckons to her. She'll just take one to calm her down. A little hiccup sound comes from the baby monitor and Clare smiles. She reheats the bath water and steps back in allowing herself to relax as the diazepam takes effect.

Her mind drifts and memories of her baby overwhelm her. He was such a beautiful baby. The last two months of the pregnancy had been very difficult. The pre-eclampsia had made it almost impossible. But she'd done it. They'd done it.

'We would not recommend another pregnancy,' the doctor had advised. 'It would be a considerable risk for you'.

She thinks of the photos of her baby in the bedside cabinet drawer. She'd not been able to look at them. Maybe she will be able to once they've moved. She won't have to worry about Sharni. They'll buy a nice house where there is a good nursery. Perhaps she'll become a childminder. It would be lovely to have a house full of children. Yes, that's what she'll do. She'll speak to Chris about it when he gets home. It will be good for Ben to have other children around him every day. Clare feels sure Chris will see the sense in that.

There is another hiccup from the baby monitor and she leans over to turn the volume up. She decides to check on Ben to be on the safe side and wraps the towel around her again before padding barefoot along to the bedroom. Ben is curled up on his side, a small smile on his face. Satisfied, she returns to the bathroom and the luxury of her lavender scented bath. The counsellor had suggested lavender to help her sleep after the baby ... she struggled to find the words in my head.

'After he died,' she says loudly and feels the nausea rise up within her. It had been early in the morning. Chris had still been asleep. Clare had woken with cramp in her leg. She hadn't intended checking on the baby. She'd felt sure he was asleep. He looked so peaceful. She'd tucked his blanket around him and then her hand had brushed his tiny feet. He was ice cold. Clare had screamed until her throat was hoarse.

She shivers in the bath and forces herself to sniff the lavender. She craves another diazepam but makes herself think of something else. I must think of nice things, she tells herself. I have Ben. Everything is alright. Ben is alright. I just checked him. Nothing is going to happen. Chris will be back before I know it and then I'll explain to him why I'd be happier if we moved. He will surely understand.

Chapter Forty-Eight

Clare had been in the bath for ages. The water is getting cold and she shivers. It is quiet. There is no sound from the baby monitor. She towels her hair dry and then massages cream into her legs, the gentle coconut fragrance washing over her. Then she hears it, the click of the bedroom door. It came from the baby monitor. It was so faint that for a moment she wonders if she had imagined it. She grabs her bathrobe from the back of the door and silently puts it on. The only sound now is the soft purring of the radiator. Her breathing quickens and she tenses her shoulder muscles before putting her ear closer to the monitor, but all is quiet again. Clare swallows and tries to calm her trembling hands. Did she imagine it? There is no one else in the house. Her heart is hammering. Carefully, she turns the door handle as if about to leave the bathroom when the monitor crackles and a soft voice says,

'Hello Sweet Pea. Mummy's here.'

Clare can't breathe and fumbles in the bathroom cabinet for another diazepam. Oh God, what should she do? Her phone was in the bedroom so she had no way of calling for help. The bathroom suddenly feels stiflingly hot and perspiration runs down her back. She needs to get to Ben. She needs to get to her baby.

Quietly she creeps out on to the landing and sees that the bedroom door is wide open. She hesitates outside the bathroom. If she can get downstairs then she can call the police from the phone in the kitchen. She tiptoes towards the bedroom where she can hear Sharni's voice as she croons to Ben.

'Is that you Clare?' Sharni asks as Clare gets nearer.

Clare froze at the bedroom door. Her eyes fixed on Sharni. She looks different. The room is in semi-darkness and Clare can't make out what it is that is different about her. She's sitting on the edge of the bed. Clare strains to see Ben in the cot. Please God, let him be all right, she prays.

'Did you have a nice bath?' Sharni asks.

'How did you get in, Sharni?'

Clare tries to disguise the shake in her voice but feels sure she doesn't succeed.

'Oh, I have a key. Did you forget that?'

'I never gave you a key.'

Clare stares longingly at the phone on the bedside table.

'But you gave me yours. I couldn't resist getting a copy.'

Ben moves in his cot and Sharni turns to look at him.

Clare feels her stomach contract.

'He's a good sleeper isn't he?' smiles Sharni. 'I love watching him sleep. I always did.'

Something flashes in her hand as she moves and Clare fights back a gasp.

'I'm going to call the police,' she says dramatically.

Sharni looks down at the pointed scissors in her hand.

'Oh, have I frightened you?'

Clare grabs the bannister for support and shivers even though the heating is on high.

'Sharni, what are you doing?' she squeaks. 'You shouldn't be here.'

'I brought the comfort blanket,' she says as she lifts up the colourful blanket. 'You keep asking for it, don't you?'

Her smile turns to a grimace as she cuts through it roughly with the scissors. Clare takes a step back.

'He doesn't need this silly thing,' Sharni says condescendingly. 'It's dirty and full of germs. What's wrong with you, letting him put this filthy thing into his mouth? The bunny rabbit is far better. What a fuss you made over this stupid thing and he doesn't even want it now.'

She stands up and walks towards Clare who gasps for breath and turns to run downstairs. She trips over her towelling robe in her haste. She puts out her hands to soften her fall. Sharni watches as Clare's body bounces down the stairs, her hips jarring against the steps. Clare cries out as she lands with a thump on to her knees.

'You must be careful,' says Sharni, moving slowly down the stairs.

'Sharni please, you don't know what you're doing,' Clare begs.

'I know exactly what I'm doing.'

Clare scrambles to her feet and tries to limp to the kitchen but Sharni gets there before her and slices through the phone cord with the scissors.

'What are you doing Clare?' she asks.

She pushes Clare roughly and she falls against the cooker.

'Oh God,' Clare groans.

She can't see Sharni for the tears blurring her eyes.

'I don't think he can help you either,' says Sharni pulling out a kitchen chair. 'I really don't want the police to come just yet. You and I need to talk Clare.'

Chapter Forty Nine

Sharni

Once the memories started to flow I felt they would never stop. They would come at odd times, taking me by surprise.

'Are you okay?'

I looked up. My hand felt hot and I realised I was gripping the mug of coffee. I'd forgotten where I was and looked around. Then I remembered the café at Silecroft Beach. I'd gone with my camera.

'I'm fine,' I said softly, 'I just felt a bit faint but I'm fine now. Thank you.'

I rubbed my eyes and the action triggered another memory. I gripped the table with my other hand. I pulled my phone out of my handbag and checked the time. I had fifteen more minutes. I'd expected Tom to believe me. I never for one moment doubted he wouldn't.

. . .

'Sharni, I think you need therapy. The doctor warned you something like this might happen. The mind plays tricks in grief. You have to face the truth and move on.'

'Are you saying I'm making this up?'

'It's sounds too crazy to be true.'

'I don't believe I'm hearing this.'

'All I'm saying is that your mind is making it up. It's easier than accepting Nathan has gone.'

'What?'

He took my hand.

'Sharni, you have to accept that Nathan has gone and that we can never replace him ...'

'I don't want to replace him,' I shouted. 'You don't have to remind me that I can't have any more children.'

'You need the counselling, Sharn. You should have had it. Women who lose babies like this sometimes lose their minds.'

I'd stared at him. Is that what he thought? That I was losing my mind?

'I'm not losing my mind. I'm remembering things and the police will believe me.'

But they didn't. Oh, they acted as if they did and they did all the right things. Conducted all the right investigations but all the time I knew they agreed with Tom. It was a figment of my imagination. A way to justify things and after a while I began to wonder if they were right. Maybe I should make a bigger effort to move on. Tom said I should look at the last photos I'd taken. It will give you closure, he'd said. But what if it hadn't been a figment of my imagination? What if it had all been real? How would I know?

I sat in the café and sipped the coffee. It was now cold. I looked at the clock. It was almost time for my counselling session.

Chapter Fifty

Clare watches in horror as Sharni fills the kettle. She's totally insane and frighteningly calm.

'Do you want a cup of tea?' she asks in a matter of fact tone.

Clare shakes her head. She wishes she could stop her knees from trembling. Her body is damp from sweat and her eyes are sore from staring at the scissors in Sharni's hand. She pulls open the towelling robe and checks her hip. It's grazed and bruised but thankfully there is no swelling.

'I'm having one,' Sharni says casually. 'By the way, have you heard from Chris? Is everything going well? You do have the perfect life you two don't you?'

Clare's throat is so dry she feels she will choke.

'I ...'

'Don't you think it's perfect?' says Sharni, her voice now hard.

'It's not perfect. No one's life is perfect. You have a much more perfect life,' Clare stammers.

Sharni seems to ignore her and pours water into a mug.

'Tom will be looking for you,' Clare says.

'I doubt it. He's gone to a dinner. Both our husbands have deserted us tonight.'

Clare lets out a small sigh as Sharni places the scissors on the table. Sharni looks at her and smiles.

'I'm not going to do anything silly with these,' she says, pointing to the scissors. 'I'm not an idiot.'

'Sharni please, If you leave right now I promise I won't tell anyone that you came here. We can just pretend this never happened.'

Clare's voice is high and shaky and she hates herself for it.

Sharni laughs.

'Yes, you'd like me to pretend none of this ever happened, wouldn't you?'

'Sharni, we ...'

'Do you want a diazepam?' she asks. 'Do you have any left? I've got loads.'

She pushes her hand into her handbag and produces a bottle.

'I've been stealing yours. Very bad of me wasn't it?'

Clare stares in disbelief at the tablets.

'No one believed you, did they? You told Chris that you hadn't been taking more but he didn't believe you, did he? It's horrible when no one believes you, isn't it? You feel so alone and isolated don't you? I know exactly how you've been feeling because that's how you made me feel. I wanted you to know what you put me through. You took my life away from me Clare and you think you can just run away from me and move house.'

Clare widens her eyes.

'I saw the estate agent come here. I saw him taking photos of the house. I see everything.'

'It was just a valuation. Chris wanted to know how much the house was worth,' Clare lies, clenching her fists.

'You're such a liar,' laughs Sharni.

'Why would you do this to us?' Clare sobs. 'We've done nothing to you.'

Her eyes are transfixed on the chain around Sharni's neck. She's wearing a pink dress that sparkles at the collar. Her hair is blonde and shimmers against the deep pink of her dress. That sense of familiarity about her nags at Clare again and she tries to remember where she'd seen her before.

The sound of Clare's mobile comes from the baby monitor and Sharni shakes her head in annoyance.

'Why did you leave your phone in Nathan's room? It is bound to disturb him.'

She gets up and walks to the stairs. Clare sees her opportunity. If she can just get to the front door and shout for help someone will hear her. If she could only catch the eye of Mrs Riley, surely she would help her. She stumbles to the lounge and waves her arms at the window. The sound of footsteps on the stair sends her hurrying back to the kitchen.

'Going somewhere?' Sharni asks, pushing her back into the chair. 'He's still asleep fortunately. It was a call from your friend Helen. I think Helen likes me, what do you think? Oh, and you've had a text from your loving husband, Chris. I've texted him back for you, saying you'll call him later. You're having a well-earned bath. It's not a complete lie is it?'

She places the phone on to the table next to the scissors. As she sits back the light catches the chain around her neck and Clare gasps. It's her Celtic harp necklace, except it can't be, because she's wearing it. Her hand instinctively goes to the chain around her own neck.

'I had a copy made. It's good isn't it?' says Sharni fingering it. 'It wasn't easy but you can get anything as long as you have the money to pay for it.'

She holds out the pendant for Clare to see.

'I don't like it much myself. Too tacky, but Nathan's

attached to it isn't he? So, until I wean him off it, I don't have much choice.'

Clare swallows before saying, 'It's Ben, his name is Ben. I'm really sorry about Nathan ...'

'How dare you,' snarls Sharni. 'You of all people, you're not sorry not in the least. How fucking dare you.'

Clare reels back.

'I'm sorry I didn't mean ...'

'Are you really sorry, are you really really sorry?' demands Sharni.

Clare's nails dig into her palms. Her eyes land on the diazepam and a stupid sense of relief washes over her. She hadn't taken that many after all.

'I don't know what we're talking about Sharni, but you must understand you can't have Ben. I know how awful it is to lose a child and if I can help ...'

Sharni laughs mirthlessly.

'A cot death wasn't it? Were you a good mother?'

Clare's mouth won't seem to open and all she can do is nod.

'And you want to help me?' Sharni smirks.

Clare nods again.

Sharni fiddles absently with Clare's phone.

'Do you like my hair this colour?'

'Yes, it suits you and ...'

She breaks off and stares at Sharni as she removes her black-rimmed glasses.

'Oh my God ...' Clare mutters.

'Remember me?' Sharni says dryly.

Chapter Fifty One

Sharni

It was Leah, the therapist, who suggested I look at my photographs of Nathan. She said it would help me come to terms with things and that I may find some closure in looking at them. It took me several days to do it and each time I went to look my heart raced so much that I could barely breathe. Tom suggested that we go through them together, especially the ones taken more recently. It wasn't as painful as I'd feared. It was a pleasure. I'd made memories, good memories. I printed the best ones and Mum helped me make a memory scrapbook.

'He should believe you,' she said as she pasted photographs into the scrapbook. She wrote *Baby Nathan* in bold letters on the front of the book. I hugged her in gratitude.

'Do you believe me?' I asked. 'No one else does.'

'Yes, I do believe you. Why shouldn't I?'

I squeezed her hand. Her wedding ring was loose. She wasn't well. I knew that but didn't want to face it. I couldn't bear the thought of losing her. I spent a lot of time with her and tried to fight the hysteria that was building up within me. My mind fought for answers. Every night I struggled to remember but the more I tried the more things eluded me.

Apart from Mum, no one believed me. I started to find it hard to be at the cottage. Everywhere I looked there were memories of Nathan. Tom suggested moving to London and then Dad phoned.

'It's not good,' was all he said. 'But we're going to be okay.'

'How long?' I asked.

The question hung in the air between us.

'Three months. Six months at the most.'

'But how?'

'These things move quickly Sharni. One minute it didn't seem so bad and then the next ...'

'Why didn't you tell me?'

'She made me promise. It's been hard, nightmarish, in fact. She didn't want you to be upset.'

'She's my mother,' I said, holding back my tears. 'Why didn't she tell us?'

'She didn't want to unsettle everyone, you in particular, especially with the baby due and then when Nathan arrived, it got harder to tell you.'

'I'd rather have known,' I said flatly.

I felt guilty at ignoring my mother's pale face, the dark circles under her eyes. I hadn't asked because I hadn't wanted my own happiness to be overshadowed by sadness. How could I have been so selfish?

'Make the most of the time,' Dad said softly.

I moved in with her and Dad and took care of her. It was the most natural thing in the world and Tom understood that I needed to do it. The night she died the memories flooded back and I thought I would drown in them. I'd lain alone in my old bedroom, the dark closing in on me. The memories had come naturally, just like my mum had said they would. Everything was suddenly crystal clear. The accident played in my head like it had only happened yesterday.

. . .

I opened my eyes and felt the throbbing in my head. It took time for my eyes to focus and for a long time I couldn't understand where I was or what had happened. I then heard Nathan whimper and went to turn my head. A sharp pain shot through it and I groaned. The car was moving slightly and I gasped as I remembered. Oh God, we're on the edge of the bridge. The car had broken through the wooden side of the old bridge and I could see the water of the lake ahead of me shimmering in the moonlight. The seat belt was cutting into my chest and the air bag was preventing me from moving. I struggled to reach Nathan.

'It's okay,' someone said.

'Oh thank God,' I mumbled. I could taste blood in my mouth.

'The baby is okay, you just relax and I'll get him out,' she said.

I felt movement and then she was leaning over me

'Come on little one,' she said kindly and I saw the small bundle in her arms. My baby was going to be okay.

'Thank you,' I said, gratefully.

'You were driving very dangerously,' she said.

I remembered the deer and the blinding headlights but my head was fuzzy and her face kept fading.

'You should drive carefully when you have the baby.'

'No,' I said weakly. 'I wasn't driving fast.'

She leaned down and looked me in the face. My eyes were sore and gritty. I couldn't see her very well. I heard the click of the seat belt and felt the pressure released from around my chest. Something dangled close to my face and I stared mesmerised at the charm that hung from a chain around her neck. Her hands grabbed me roughly under the arms and pulled me from the car.

She laid me on the road. I could feel the cold wetness on my back. I could hear her straining and the creaking of the bridge, I heard the crash as my car hit the water.

'I saw you. I know how fast you were going,' she said. She stopped to get her breath and I listened to her panting. 'You should be grateful I was here. God knows what would have happened to your baby otherwise. You're so careless. You're always leaving him alone in the pram in the garden. There are nutcases about, you know.'

I tried to lift my head to see Nathan but the pain knocked me back down.

'You were going too fast,' she repeated.

I struggled to keep my eyes open. The darkness seemed to penetrate my very soul.

'It's alright darling,' she murmured and I heard Nathan's whimpering. I could hear her steps moving away from me and Nathan's cries becoming more distant. I tried to yell but nothing came out. My body wouldn't move, and my lips wouldn't open. I pushed my hands against the ground to lift myself up but it was futile. My eyes were heavy and it was an effort to keep them open. I turned my head and watched as she laid my baby on to the seat of her car. I heard the door close and then her footsteps as she walked back to me.

'He'll be well looked after,' she said quietly. 'You need to sleep. It'll be over soon.'

I heard the door close and then the sound of her car driving away. I felt tears run down my cheeks. I was helpless to save my baby. I closed my eyes and allowed death to take me.

Chapter Fifty-Two

I insisted over and over again that I saw her. The police officer asked me to describe her, but of course I couldn't. I couldn't even describe the pendant around her neck and even if I could what help would that be? I couldn't describe the car or give them the registration number.

'I couldn't see her. It was dark,' I said, but it all sounded so ridiculous when I said it out loud.

'Can you tell us what kind of car she was driving?'

'I was on the ground, I couldn't see the car.'

'We'll need more information,' the officer said, but I didn't know any more. I only knew she had taken my baby.

'She took Nathan,' I kept saying. 'She kidnapped my baby.' But no one believed me. The officer said the car had gone over the bridge and that Nathan must have still been in it. They were very sorry. The water was deep under the bridge and the currents could have swept him anywhere in the lake. They had divers in the water for a week but found nothing.

'I saw her, she took my baby. She must have been watching me. She knew I'd put Nathan out into the garden in his pram. She told me I was a bad mother.'

They all gave me pitying looks.

'You were in a terrible state when they found you,' said Tom. 'You weren't conscious. You couldn't have seen anyone, and besides, what sort of person would take Nathan and leave you to die?'

The police found no evidence in the car. It was five days before they lifted it out of the water and by then any forensic evidence would have been washed away. The only fingerprints they found in the car were mine and Tom's.

'She must have worn gloves,' I said to Tom but it sounded feeble even to my own ears.

'Please stop this, Sharni,' he'd begged. 'You must accept he's gone. God knows I wish he were here too. I just thank God that you are.'

A motorcyclist called Sid had found me. He'd almost hit me as I was lying on the road. The police said I must have climbed from the car before it went over the bridge and that I hadn't managed to get Nathan out. I got tired of telling them that it didn't happen like that. It had been her that had pulled me out, her that had rescued Nathan and her that had left me to die. Rachel came to visit often but I was distant. I couldn't understand why no one believed me.

The photos haunted me. I packed away the scrapbook and albums and refused myself the luxury of looking at them. I tried to work and attended the counselling sessions just as everyone wanted.

Chapter Fifty-Three

'But I thought you were dead,' says Clare.

'I'm sorry to disappoint you,' Sharni says coldly.

'You can't have him. You're a terrible mother, I know, I saw you. You have no right to a child.'

Clare flinches as Sharni's hand comes up and connects with her face, the slap stinging her cheek. She grabs the table to support herself and sobs uncontrollably.

'You bitch, you crazy bitch,' Sharni yells.

'There's something wrong with you,' Clare screams.

Sharni laughs and throws the bottle of pills at her.

'There's something wrong with me? Talk about the pot calling the kettle black.'

Clare lurches for the scissors but Sharni is quicker and gets there before her. She brandishes them in front of Clare's face.

'I should kill you,' she snarls, her eyes sparkling. 'You stole my child and left me to die.'

Clare stares at Sharni. It can't be her. It's not possible that she survived that night. She closes her eyes and feels her body sway. If only she could get to a phone. But who would she call? Chris is in Amsterdam and there was no one else. She can't let her take Ben. She'd rather die than let her take Ben. Her eyes fall on the scissors and a surge of hope shoots through her.

'How did you ...?' she begins.

'A motorcyclist found me. I expect you hoped I'd be there all night.'

Clare bites her lower lip until she draws blood.

'How did you find me?' she asks.

Sharni sips from the cold mug of tea.

'It was easier than I thought. You were everywhere. I don't know why I didn't see you. You were in every photo, just hovering in the background, stalking me.'

'Someone had to watch over Ben,' Clare says defensively.

'I started thinking how odd it was that you were in every photo, so I decided to zoom in closer on you. I recognised you but I couldn't remember where I'd seen you. I couldn't see the woman who stole my baby that night so I couldn't be sure it was you but then I remembered. You holidayed at the cottage. You and Chris came that summer. You were getting over the cot death weren't you? And then you saw us, me and Nathan.'

'You neglected him all the time,' Clare snarls. 'You left him alone in the garden, alone on the beach while you frolicked with your friends. Once you left him in the garden while you played loud music. God gave him to me so that I could look after him and love him.'

'You don't know what you're talking about. Nathan was loved. He was never left alone. I was always close by. You just needed any excuse to steal my baby. You're mentally unbalanced.'

'It isn't your baby it is ours. His name is Ben, not Nathan.'

'You're so deluded. Did you really believe you could just steal someone's baby and never be found again? Did it never occur to you that I would come looking for you?'

Sharni leans towards her and Clare shrinks back.

'This was your downfall,' she says, pulling at the chain around Clare's neck. 'It was in every photo. You were wearing it the night you stole my baby, I remember seeing it dangling in front of my face.'

Clare fiddles with the necklace nervously and says, 'No one will believe you.'

Clare was right, nobody had believed her. Memories flash unbidden into Sharni's head.

'Can't you see it?' I demanded. 'Can't you see it's the same necklace as the one I saw?'

Rachel bit her lip.

'Sharni, I ...'

'What?' I questioned.

'Loads of women could have that necklace?' she said nervously.

'No, I've looked into it. It's made by a craftsman in East London. Every piece he makes is unique and ...'

'Have you told Tom this?'

I'd shrugged.

'He thinks everything is in my mind.'

'This is crazy Sharn.'

'Why is it crazy?'

'You can't accuse some woman of taking your baby because she wears a necklace.'

'I just told you that ...'

'The police found no evidence in the car, apart from you and Nathan ...'

'She was wearing it. I saw her. I didn't imagine it.'

'I'm not saying you imagined it but ... it was a big shock and ...'

'So, you are saying I imagined it?'

'No, I'm ...'

'Oh, for Christ's sake Rachel.'

'I can't do this Sharni.'

'Fine, then don't do it.'

I'd listened to her car pull away and then went back to the photographs.

Everyone had said looking at photos would be healing for me. It had been difficult looking at them all over again, especially with Mum gone. But no one could have known how healing it would be. Nothing mattered to me except getting my baby back. I'd phoned the agency who rented out the holiday cottage but they wouldn't give out the names of their customers. My neck ached from studying the photos. The weather was cooler now and I strolled around the garden. I'd looked at the holiday cottage. The cleaner had waved and my heart had jumped into my mouth. I took a bracelet from my jewellery box and hurried over.

'Hi, it's a lovely day isn't it?' I said tapping on the door.

She turned and smiled.

'Yes, sunny.'

'I wonder if you can help me,' I said venturing into the cottage. It was different to how I imagined. It smelt musty and the furniture was outdated and tatty. It was smaller than I had envisioned, but cosy and perfect for a holiday.

'I try,' she smiled.

'Where are you from?' I asked, hearing her accent.

'Romania,' she said.

'I have heard it is beautiful there,' I enthused. 'But I don't want to take up your time. I found this in the lane and I am sure it belonged to the guests from last week.' I show her the bracelet. 'I will post it to her if you have the address.'

'Oh, I don't ...' she had begun.

'I was wondering, would they have written in a visitor's book?'

'Ah yes,' she said, beckoning me into the living room.

I fought back my eagerness to grab the book out of her hands.

'Oh, these are lovely,' I said as I flicked back through the pages. 'Such nice things everyone has written.'

I stopped on the entry for June 24th:

Clare and Chris Ryan. Lovely holiday thank you,
Hammersmith, London

My baby was in Hammersmith. I would find him and I would make Clare Ryan regret the day she ever came near me.

Chapter Fifty-Four

Sharni

'You're right. Even my husband didn't believe me.'

I empty the mug down the sink and then put the baby monitor to my ear. Nathan will sleep through the night now. In a few hours he will be home with me.

'It was easy to find you,' I say clicking on the kettle. 'As chance would have it Tom got an appointment in London. He thought looking at houses would take my mind off my baby. Everyone had different ideas on what would take my mind off my child.'

Clare is still, her eyes glancing at the scissors on the table.

'Who'd have believed the house right next door to you would be up for sale? It was like God sent you to me. Do you believe in karma, Clare?'

She opens her mouth and then closes it again. I whip the scissors from the table and smile.

'I wouldn't get any ideas,' I say.

I make another mug of tea and help myself to the biscuits in her biscuit tin.

'So, there's one thing that really bothers me. Didn't Chris

ever tell you to take the baby back? Don't tell me, he was too afraid of what you might do?'

Clare closes her eyes and I wait.

Clare

'The mother was dead,' I said, laying Ben on the couch in the holiday home.

Chris turned white and stared at Ben.

'Clare, what ... where ...?'

His hands began to shake.

'I'll get that wine,' I said, walking into the kitchen.

When I returned he was leaning over Ben.

'What are you doing?' I said sharply.

He turned his ashen face towards me.

'Clare, where did you get the baby?'

'It's our baby.'

'Where did you find our baby?' he asked.

He was struggling not to raise his voice.

'I need to feed him,' I said.

'Clare, we can't feed him.'

'I've got bottles and formula,' I said. 'I bought them the other day.'

'Clare, listen to me ...'

'She had him. She was driving like a lunatic. I've been following her trying to think of a way to get our baby back. She wouldn't have handed him over and there was no point in calling the police.'

He fell into a chair and dropped his head into his hands.

'The car is in the lake,' I explained. 'There was an accident. The car crashed into the bridge. She was driving too fast.'

'Oh Christ,' he muttered. 'Did you leave the mother to die?'

'She's not his mother. I'm his mother,' I cried.

He jumped up, his hands grabbing my shoulders so roughly that I began to cry.

'Do you have any idea what you've done?' he yelled.

I sobbed into his shoulder.

'But I got him back. She was neglecting him and ...'

'It's not our child. Our child is dead Clare.'

He looked into my eyes.

'Have you been taking your pills?'

'I don't need to take the pills.'

'Answer me. Have you been taking your medication?'

'Yes,' I shouted. 'I've only missed a few.'

Chris picked up the baby.

'Where are you going with him?' I screamed, grabbing his arm roughly. 'Where are you going with Ben?'

He stopped abruptly.

'Ben?' he repeated. 'Ben is dead Clare, he is not Ben. I'm taking him back to his mother. I thought a two week break would help you come to terms with things but clearly it hasn't.'

'She's dead,' I said flatly. 'She died in the accident.'

He flopped on to the couch.

'He needs a mother,' I said. 'Please I beg you Chris. I'll kill myself if you take him.'

Before he could stop me I'd grabbed a knife from the kitchen and slashed it against my wrist.

'God, no, Clare.'

I watched the blood drip on to the carpet before Chris had wrapped a towel around my hand.

'Jesus, Clare,' he wept.

'Don't take him from me. Please, Chris. He's got no one.'

'Clare, we can't just ...'

I struggled against his arms.

'Tomorrow then, I promise, tomorrow I'll take him back.'

But of course, tomorrow never came.

It had been easier than I could ever have imagined. I didn't plan it. Fate sent me to him, sent me to the holiday cottage so I could rescue him from his evil mother. It had been Chris's idea to take me away. He thought it would be good for me. 'To help you get over the cot death', he'd said. How could he ever believe that I would get over it?

Dr Marks had suggested it. I'd admitted that I hadn't continued my medication. I felt fine. I coped throughout my pregnancy. I didn't need them. He'd phoned Chris, said I was a danger if I wasn't on my medication. What a lot of nonsense. I was perfectly fine.

'Grief could exacerbate things,' Chris had said.

'I'm fine,' I argued.

'You must go back on them Clare. How about if we have a little holiday and go to the Lakes.'

And so I'd pretended to take them again. I didn't really need them. I wasn't like my mother. How could I be a mummy again when the time was right if I was taking that stupid medication? I kept telling Chris everything would be okay but he insisted I take the stupid pills.

'You do strange things when you're off them,' he'd said.

I'd seen them in the garden the day we arrived. She and her husband were sitting out there listening to the radio. The baby was lying on a blanket beside them. I craved to see him. I watched from the window or strained to see them when we walked past. Sometimes Ben would be there all alone. I could see them through the window, sipping wine or preparing food. The whole time their baby alone in the garden. I followed her when

Chris played golf. It broke my heart how she neglected Ben. She was always more interested in her photography than she was in her baby.

I waited for her to return that night. I couldn't understand why they were so late getting back. Didn't she realise the weather was terrible? That there were floods? Then of course there was that awful bridge. Fear seared through my body like fire. Ben would be hungry. How could she neglect him like this?

I prowled around the holiday home like a lion, waiting for her to come home. Chris watched a stupid comedy film on the television. I pretended to watch it with him but the silliness of it annoyed me. I couldn't stop thinking about Ben. Was he all right? I told Chris I fancied some popcorn. I said I felt sure I'd seen some in the little shop in the village. I wanted to see her come home. I needed to know that Ben was okay. What if she didn't see the flood by the bridge? I should warn them.

'Be careful,' Chris had warned. 'It's heavy rain out there.'

'I'll only go to the shop,' I said.

I didn't get to the shop. Her car got to the bridge shortly after me. I'd flashed my headlights to get her to slow down but the stupid woman had just ignored them. I was grateful to be there and to be able to rescue Ben at last from her incapable hands. Women like that should not be allowed to have children.

Chapter Fifty Five

Sharni

I found them on the electoral role, them and several other Ryans, although Clare didn't live at the Hammersmith house any more. I'd sat outside in my car for hours, just waiting. I prepared myself for the sight of her. I'd rehearsed what I would say if she saw me but the young girl pushing twins in a buggy couldn't possibly be her. But I needed to be sure. I'd climbed from the car and called out.

'Excuse me. I'm looking for Clare Ryan? Are you Clare?'

She turned her innocent face my way and I knew immediately this wasn't the woman who had taken Nathan from my car.

'Who?' she asked.

'Clare Ryan, she used to live here?'

'Oh yeah, I dunno where they went. Sorry.'

'Right, thanks anyway.'

I experienced a sense of relief and disappointment. I should have known it wouldn't be that easy. Perhaps she saw the disappointment on my face because just as I climbed back into my car she called out to me.

'She worked at the school though. Why don't you ask them?'

But the school was reluctant to give out information. I had only one option. I phoned a private investigator.

It took a while but I eventually tracked them down. They had a three-bedroomed terrace house in a quiet street in Kensington.

I'd sat in my car staring at the house for almost an hour, praying she would come out with Nathan. But she hadn't. I'd thrown up at one point. What if she didn't have Nathan? What if I had everything all wrong? My eyes had strayed to the 'For Sale' sign that wavered in the front garden of the house next door.

I went back to the flat we were renting and told Tom about the house for sale in Kensington. He was distracted. The new firm had just given him a big case. He was excited and nervous. He'd leave the house search to me, he said. It would give me something to do.

I drove back to the house the next day and met the estate agent. I had to force my eyes away from the house next door.

'It's a nice little property,' Brian the estate agent said. 'Good price. It's in a popular area and will be snapped up in no time and ...'

'What are the neighbours like?' I asked nonchalantly, looking out of the kitchen window.

'A young couple that side,' he said pointing to Clare's garden. 'They have a toddler but you won't hear much through these walls and the other side ...'

My head spun and I held on to the back door.

'Sorry, I missed what you said.'

'A young couple that side ...'

'I didn't hear about the other neighbours.'

'You're end of terrace so you've just got a little park that side.'

I followed him upstairs, straining to hear Nathan.

'Do you know how old the child is?' I asked.

He shook his head.

'I wouldn't know,' he said shrugging. 'I've seen her with a stroller, but you shouldn't get any noise through these walls. You got a place to sell?'

'No we're renting at the moment.'

'Great. No chain for you then.'

'I'll come back with my husband,' I said.

I checked out the nursery. They didn't have any spaces until the following year. I said that was fine. I was happy with it. They showed me around. It was good enough for Nathan; at least for now.

While the sale was going through I asked the private investigator to check out Kathryn and to look into Clare's background. Tom was happy. He thought I was busying myself getting the new house ready. I couldn't really give a fuck about the new house. I just wanted to be near my baby.

'The mother's in a mental home,' he stated bluntly.

He pushed the folder across the table to me.

I stared at it. I couldn't touch it. Information about the woman who was claiming to be my child's mother was encased inside.

'A mental home,' I repeated.

'Yeah, schizophrenic, been there for years. The daughter never visits.'

'Is Clare Ryan also insane?' I asked softly, not wanting to hear his reply.

'Say again?'

'Is her daughter, Clare, also insane?' I say loudly.

'We're all insane,' he laughed.

I stared stonily at him.

'I ... well, I'm no expert. I'm just a private investigator. She's been under psychiatric care in the past. She's on medication. It's all in there.' He nodded towards the folder.

'Can't you tell me?' I asked.

He pulled the folder back and opened it.

'Her medical records state she was on anti-psychotics. She has a history of schizophrenia ...'

'But, she had a baby,' I said.

'Yeah, she has a son, Benjamin, two years old. I've got a copy of the birth certificate here,' he said, handing me the paper. 'It seems the condition is well controlled on medication. Although it looks like she hasn't been filling her prescriptions for some time. Her new doctor has her on anti-anxiety drugs.'

'So, she's been looking after a child without medication?' I said, my heart thumping in my chest.

'Yep, looks like it.'

'How did you get that information?'

He coughed.

'Well ... erm ... we don't divulge our sources I'm afraid.'

'Thank you,' I said standing up and grabbing the folder.

The ticking of the clock on the wall was driving me crazy. The door to Dr Grant's office opened and he beckoned me in. I looked at the folder on his desk and felt my breath catch in my throat.

'We've done the DNA tests, Sharni.'

I looked at him hopefully. The muscles in my chest tightened with tension.

'They were conclusive.'

I exhaled and relaxed in the chair.

'Oh God.'

'Ben is your child. I'm presuming you will contact the social services.'

'Nathan,' I corrected.

I began to shake.

'Let me get you some water,' he said kindly.

I took the glass with shaking hands.

'This is the documentation that you need. It's something that needs to be handled delicately, Sharni, you realise that?'

I nodded.

'You've got to contact the social services.'

'Yes,' I said taking the paperwork. 'I will'.

'Would you like to come back with Tom?'

'I'll tell Tom,' I interrupted.

'You must think of what's best for the child.'

I stared at him. How dare he? I'm the one who has thought about Nathan. Not one person believed me. Not even my husband. Tears rolled down my cheeks when I thought of my mother. I couldn't even phone her to say Nathan had been found. Nathan was okay and I was going to get him back.

'Thank you,' I said, tucking the envelope into my handbag.

'If there is anything ...'

'Yes, thank you,' I repeated and walked to the door.

I walked past the receptionist and into the cold outside. I lifted my face to the wind. He was my child. I hadn't been wrong. My baby had been stolen from me and I was going to get him back. I didn't need the social services to help me and I didn't need Tom. They didn't help me when I needed them most. I'll be damned if I'll let them do this.

Chapter Fifty-Six

Helen stumbled down the steps of the restaurant and giggled.

'I can't believe I'm pissed on cider,' she laughed.

'Plus those beers,' laughed Julia.

'Oh yeah,' giggles Helen.

'How many bottles are you taking to Clare's?' asked Julia.

'Well, I'll drink them even if she doesn't.'

Julia lurched down the steps behind her.

'I don't know why you bother with her. She's totally nuts if you ask me. Have you got the school photos to show her?'

'She's alright and she is all by herself tonight,' Helen hiccupped.

'Maybe we'll come with you then?' said Julia.

Helen shook her head.

'No way, she'll bloody kill me. It's enough I'm going round there half pissed.'

She kissed Julia on the cheek and hailed a cab.

'Thanks for a great night.'

. . .

Helen was worried about Clare. She'd been funny with her ever since the school photo session with Sharni. She'd ignored her calls and only responded to the drinks invitation when Julia had texted her. It concerned Helen that maybe she hadn't come because she'd been there. She didn't want to fall out with Clare but lately she had been behaving a bit oddly, especially about Sharni. It was a bit extreme all the things she had been saying. Everyone at school thought she was a bit odd. Helen burped and ignored the cab driver's look of disgust.

'You're not going to throw up are you?' he asked.

'I've not drunk that much,' she lied.

Hopefully she'd be able to get a cup of coffee at Clare's and sober up a bit. Surely the teacher Christmas photos would cheer Clare up. Then again she thought, maybe not, especially as Sharni was the one who took them.

'Here please,' she said as they pulled up to Clare's house.

The lights were on and she sighed with relief.

Chapter Fifty-Seven

Sharni pulls a letter from her handbag and places it on the kitchen table. It sits between them. She nods at it.

'That states that I am Nathan's birth mother. I took him to be tested when I was looking after him one day. It's a DNA test. It proves without doubt that I am his real mother.'

Clare stares at the sheet of paper.

'It's all lies,' she says.

'You know you took him. You deliberately flashed your lights at me on the bridge. You could have killed him too.'

'You were driving too fast.'

'Look at it,' Sharni screams.

Clare throws the letter angrily on to the floor. 'You're threatening me in my own home. You're the one holding the scissors,' she says boldly.

Sharni picks up the paper from the floor and looks at Clare, her eyes menacing. She suddenly lunges at Clare grabbing her hair and pulling her head down forcing her to look at the paper. Clare's eyes smart and she struggles to focus on the writing in front of her.

'Read it,' Sharni yells.

The doorbell sounds but Sharni doesn't hear it. She is too intent on pushing the letter into Clare's face.

'Read it,' she repeats.

Clare closes her eyes against the words. Sharni finally releases her and Clare looks up into her angry face.

'What does it matter,' Sharni says, folding the paper. 'You know the truth.'

Clare looks past her to the kitchen window and sees Helen watching them. She gives her a pleading look. Helen shakes her head, her eyes full of horror.

'I'm going to take Nathan now, and then I'm going to call the police to tell them who took my baby and where they can find you,' Sharni says.

Clare watches in horror as Sharni gets up and walks out of the kitchen.

'You can't take him,' she screams. 'I won't let you.'

'Do something,' screams a voice in Clare's head. *'Don't let her take your child. Stop her, stop her now!'*

She hurries to the cutlery drawer and grabs the carving knife, cutting her hand on another as she does so. She can't be without him. She'd kill her before she lets Sharni take him from her. She should be dead anyway, she should have died that night on the bridge.

'Christ, what's going on?' Helen mutters as she stares through the window. A wave of nausea overtakes her and she throws up the cider she had consumed earlier. When she looks back through the window Sharni has gone. She twists the handle of the back door and it swings open.

'Are you all right?' she shouts from the doorway. 'What in God's name is going on?'

'Helen,' Clare shouts. 'You have to help me. She's got a knife and she's trying to take Ben from me. Please help us.'

'Oh my God, I'll call the police,' Helen says fumbling around in her bag for her phone.

'I've called the police. I need you to help me.'

Sharni

I'd underestimated her. I was so intent on getting my child back that I hadn't planned things properly.

Her eyes are wild and her features contorted as she leaps forward, swinging the carving knife in her hand. She swings it viciously from side to side and I feel a sharp pain as the blade strikes my hand. I manage to grab the scissors but not before she aims the knife at me again and I grimace as it catches me in the thigh.

'You're not having him, you fucking bitch. He's my baby and I'll do anything to keep him,' she screams.

My foot gives way beneath me and I fall against the kitchen door, the scissors dropping from my hand. I back away as she runs towards me with the knife. Her screams rip through the air and I shudder at the sound. I scramble back and squeeze through the gap to the hallway, kicking the door shut behind me. I look frantically around for something to block it, but there's nothing.

I need to get Nathan. He's all that matters. I curse myself for being so stupid.

'Are you all right?' Helen shouts. 'What in God's name is going on?'

'Helen,' Clare yells hysterically. 'You have to help me. She's got a knife and she's trying to take Ben from me. Please help us.'

I trip on the stairs in my haste to get to Nathan. I'm almost there when her hand grips my calf and I'm pulled down, my elbows banging roughly on the stairs.

'You should have died, bitch,' she hisses into my ear.

I look up at the glittering blade and watch as it comes down towards me. I turn and knee her in the stomach. She doubles over and I scramble up, taking the stairs on my hands and knees. The carpet is stained with my blood. I limp towards the bedroom, but she's quicker than me.

'I don't think so,' she says calmly, standing in my way.

She smiles.

'You didn't think I'd let you take him. When the police come I'll tell them how you tried to steal my baby and how you tried to drive me mad. I've got proof you had the comfort blanket and my pills. A desperate mother, totally out of her mind, and after all, grief does terrible things doesn't it? I'll explain I had to defend myself and protect my child, otherwise who knows what might have happened.'

I try to grab the bannister but she rips my hands away.

'Goodbye Sharni.'

'Christ Clare, what are you doing?' Helen's terrified voice stills the air.

'She's trying to steal Ben,' Clare cries. 'She attacked me with a pair of scissors.'

I grab the bannister to stop myself falling.

Helen's eyes are wide and her mouth open in surprise.

'Why have you got a knife Clare?' Helen asks.

'I had to protect myself,' Clare says angrily. 'I couldn't let her take Ben.'

'You need to call the police, Helen,' I say weakly. 'I'm not stealing anyone's baby.'

'Shut up,' snarls Clare, stamping her feet and waving the knife around. 'Just shut up.'

'But I thought you already called the police?' Helen says, looking nervously up at Clare.

'She hasn't,' I shout.

'Don't listen to her, she's completely insane. She's ripped Ben's comfort blanket to shreds. It's in the kitchen, go and have a look, and she slashed the phone line. Don't listen to her Helen.'

'I ...' begins Helen.

'Look in the kitchen if you don't believe me,' Clare shouts.

'Helen ...' I begin.

'Shut up,' growls Clare, brandishing the knife. 'She's here to steal my baby, Helen, and she's been doing things to make me look mad just like I told you. I need you to get something for me to tie her up. There's some tape in the drawer in the kitchen.'

Helen shakes her head nervously.

'I think we should wait for the police.'

'She's dangerous Helen,' Clare shouts.

Helen looks at me and then hurries to the kitchen.

Clare turns to me and sneers, 'It's a shame she came. Makes things a bit more complicated.'

'I don't understand, what is this?' Helen asks, holding the letter from Dr Grant.

'Get out,' I scream to Helen as Clare rushes down the stairs. 'She is going to hurt you.'

'Give that to me, you nosy bitch,' snarls Clare, saliva running down her chin.

Helen turns horrified eyes on to Clare charging towards her with the knife raised high. She gives a piercing howl. I want to block my ears and close my eyes but I can do neither. I watch as she brings the knife down on to Helen. The knife stabs deep into Helen's left shoulder, sending Helen crumpling to the floor.

My legs give way from the shock and I tumble down the stairs. I land heavily and groan. The hall light flickers above me. For a moment I'm disoriented and then I hear Helen's moans. I'm lying on the floor at the foot of the stairs, looking up at the ceiling. An excruciating pain shoots through my leg. I look down to see it is bleeding profusely. I can't move it without pain shooting through my body. I prop myself up against the wall to look at Clare. My body feels heavy. I try to work out if I could make a lunge for her, wrestle her to the ground. Am I strong enough to overpower her? Helen is gasping for breath and for a moment she looks up at me imploring me to help her. I need to get Clare's attention away from her. Clare looks at me and I gasp at the hate written across her face. Her eyes are wild, her hair tangled and her hands are covered in blood. The knife hangs loosely at her side.

'What have you done?' I say.

'It's not fucking fair,' cries Clare. 'You're all against me.'

'Helen isn't against you,' I say, trying to calm her. 'She's on your side. She told me that.'

Helen is slumped against the front door, a crimson pool of blood surrounding her. The wound in her shoulder is seeping blood at an alarming rate. I feel angry with myself. I'd handled it all wrong. I wanted Clare to feel what I had felt, an eye for an eye, a tooth for a tooth, but I had misjudged her. She is totally insane. I'd got Helen involved and I was afraid for her. She'll die if her bleeding isn't stopped soon.

'Fucking whore,' Clare roars. 'If you had died on the bridge none of this would have happened. Why did you have to turn up? Why didn't you die on the bridge? Now I have to kill you to make you go away.'

She kneels beside me and presses the carving knife against my throat. Her stale breath suffocates me. From the corner of my eye I can see Helen struggling to stand. Her eyes meet mine. I watch mesmerised as she picks up the vase from the hall table.

'You can have Ben,' I say, in an attempt to stall Clare.

'Do you think I believe you?' she snaps. 'You have lied to me from the first day I saw you.'

'We can work something out, for Ben, he could still see you.'

Helen struggles with the vase. I have to keep Clare's eyes on me.

'I'm not making fucking deals with you,' Clare scoffs.

I watch Helen lift the vase with her right hand. Her left arm, red with blood, hangs limp at her side.

'You're nothing but a liar,' Clare spits, pressing the knife into my throat.

At that moment Helen releases a piercing scream and brings the vase down on to Clare's head. The vase smashes, showering splinters of ceramic over me. Clare falls limp into my lap. I feel the blood seep through my dress and on to my legs.

Helen falls to the floor beside me with a grunt. I turn to look at Clare's face. Her eyes are wide and accusing. Even in death she is angry. I push her off my lap and turn to Helen.

'Helen, stay with me,' I beg.

I rip the sleeve of Clare's bathrobe and press it against Helen's wound to stop the bleeding. She is pale and her eyes heavy.

'Talk to me Helen,' I say. 'Don't close your eyes.'

Helen mumbles something and I feel her pockets for her phone. With trembling hands I call 999 while pressing against the stab wound. It seems like an eternity before I hear screaming of sirens and I cry with relief.

Chapter Fifty Eight

When Tom arrives the street is cluttered with police cars and ambulances. I sit in a wheelchair cradling Nathan in my arms and watch without emotion as they bring out Clare's lifeless body on a stretcher. The blow from the vase had cracked her skull.

'I believed you,' Helen had whispered before losing consciousness.

'Will she be okay?' I ask.

'She will be fine,' the paramedic smiles. 'She's lost a lot of blood but that's all.'

I watch Tom walk towards us, his face is haggard and his eyes are soft and wet.

'Christ Sharn, I knew she was unbalanced but I never for one minute ...'

I look down at my clothes. I'm covered with blood and my hand and leg are bandaged. He sits beside me on the doorstep and I hand him Nathan.

'I'm not looking my best,' I say, making a feeble attempt at a joke.

'You've looked better,' he agrees, taking Nathan.

'Say hello to your son,' I say simply.

A small tear drops on to his hand as he takes him.

'My son,' he says quietly.

Nathan wraps his hand around Tom's little finger.

'Why didn't you tell me?' he asks, his eyes meeting mine.

'Because you wouldn't have believed me, just like you never believed me before,' I say, trying to hide the bitterness from my voice.

'You could have tried.'

'I was afraid you'd stop me. That you'd stop me seeing him and I couldn't bear that.'

He cradles Nathan, stroking his tiny fingers.

'Sharni, I'm ...'

'She lost her mind after her baby died. You remember, you said that to me, you said, "Women who lose babies like this sometimes lose their minds."'

'I'm so sorry Sharn, can you ever forgive me?'

He lays his other hand in mine.

'It's just I don't know that I can forgive,' I say, wiping the tears from my eyes. 'It's been very hard Tom, finding Nathan all on my own. Fighting against all the people that didn't believe me, and lying to you because I didn't want you to treat me like a mental case.'

He winces.

'Sharni, I'm so sorry. Perhaps it was easier for me to deal with the fact that he'd gone rather than having to think someone had taken him ...'

'But someone did take him and I nearly died getting him back.'

He wipes tears from his cheeks.

'I just don't understand how you could have given up on him like you did,' I say.

'I'm sorry.'

'I'm going home to the cottage. That's where I belong. I belong by the Lakes. You belong here in London.'

I can return to the cottage now I have Nathan. Everything is complete again. Finally I can go home. He doesn't attempt to argue.

'Will I see you?' he asks.

'I hope so. We'll want to see you. I'll stay a bit longer. I want to make sure Helen is okay.'

'I want to make this up to you. I know it's a huge thing to ask but will you let me try?'

I nod.

'I can't stay in London,' I say.

He holds out his hand and I take it gratefully.

'You need to get checked over at the hospital. Come on.'

'I wonder if Chris knows,' I say with a shiver.

'Let's go,' says a paramedic. He pushes me on to the ambulance tail lift. I look back at the house one last time before closing my eyes.

Chapter Fifty-Nine

I take the lemonade into the garden. The sun is hot and I lift my face to it. Nathan toddles towards me, clapping his hands with pleasure.

'This is your favourite isn't it?' I laugh.

He'd forgotten the pendant and the comfort blanket. I like to think he's forgotten Clare but I don't suppose he has. I tell myself it is just time before I get my child back completely. I still have nightmares about that night. Clare's wide, mad eyes haunting me.

I place the tray on to the patio table and pour the lemonade into glasses.

'Here,' I say.

Helen takes a glass. 'It's heaven here,' she says, stretching out on a sunlounger.

'It certainly is.'

'I love that dress,' she says nodding.

'Oh this, it was just a cheapie.'

I pull the lemon-coloured cardigan around the flowery chiffon dress and smile.

'You must take me shopping sometime. You've got great taste.'

A sense of déjà vu washes over me.

'Sure,' I say.

'Thanks so much for inviting me. It's the perfect place to chill in the summer break.'

I nod.

'How's the arm?'

'It's still weak, but, you know, it will get better.'

'How are things at school?'

'Oh fine, you know, still the same little monsters,' she smiles.

Her face clouds over.

'It was weird those first few weeks. You know, when we looked back we could see the signs were all there. We just weren't aware of them at the time. I wish you'd said something.'

'Would you have believed me?'

'I guess not.'

She turns at the faint sound of music.

'Are they your neighbours?' she asks.

I glance at the holiday cottage where a young couple are sitting in the garden.

'No,' I say softly. 'They're holidaymakers. I never know who they are.'

'I guess you're very wary since ...'

I smile.

'Still,' she says innocently, 'holidaymakers can't do much harm can they?'

THE END

A note from the publisher

Thank you for reading this book. If you enjoyed it please do consider leaving a review on Amazon to help others find it too.

We hate typos. All of our books have been rigorously edited and proofread, but sometimes mistakes do slip through. If you have spotted a typo, please do let us know and we can get it amended within hours.

info@bloodhoundbooks.com

About the Author

Lynda Renham's novels are popular, fast paced and with a strong theme. She lives in Oxford UK and when not writing Lynda can usually be found wasting her time on Facebook.

Lynda is author of the best-selling thriller novels including *Watching You, Secrets and Lies, The Lies She Told, The Day Henry Died, and She Saw What She Did.*

Also by Lynda Renham:

Not published by Bloodhound Books

The shocking psychological thriller you can't put down ...

"What a thriller! Loved this book kept me guessing all the way through, Brilliantly written with a good twist. I couldn't stop reading."

"Totally gripping, I couldn't put it down. Full of twists and turns."

"A chilling read that will keep you turning the pages. It had me gasping as I read on. I have rated it five but this book deserves a ten."

Printed in Great Britain
by Amazon

18371045R10181